PROMISES
PROMISES

PROMISES PROMISES

BUCK TURNER

PAGE
&
VINE

Page & Vine
An Imprint of Meredith Wild LLC

Paperback ISBN: 978-1-964264-06-6

*This book is dedicated to those who
keep their promises.*

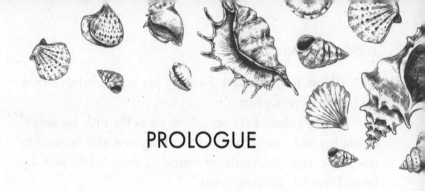

PROLOGUE

People with good intentions make promises.
People with good character keep them.
—Unknown

He stands in the doorway to his daughter's room, watching as she meticulously places her toys—Barbie dolls, blocks, and her Disney princess tea set—into their designated places in the toy box. She handles them with such care and consideration, as if they are precious treasures instead of mere playthings. As he observes her, memories flood his mind; she is the spitting image of her mother. From the curve of her dark, almond-shaped eyes to the curls in her brown hair, and even down to the way she scrunches up her nose when she laughs—so much of her is a mirror image of the woman who orchestrated the most significant moment of his life.

Lost in thought, the sound of her voice pulls him back to reality.

"Ready for bed?" he asks, stepping into the room.

She looks up at him with those same familiar eyes and nods, then climbs into bed alongside Fuzzy—her trusty stuffed teddy bear.

"I'm tired," she says with a small yawn, snuggling deeper under the covers.

"Too tired for a bedtime story?"

"Uh-uh. See," she says, blinking her heavy eyelids, doing her best to convince him.

"All right then. Let's see ..." He scans the little bookshelf beside her bed, searching for something new and exciting to read. "We have Cinderella, of course ... Snow White and the Seven Dwarfs ... Sleeping Beauty ..."

"I want a new one."

"A new one, huh?" He ponders before a lightbulb goes off in his head. "I think I have just the story."

She beams a smile at him. "Does it have a princess?"

"Yes."

"And a handsome prince?"

"Of course," he answers in an over-dramatic voice as he runs a hand through his hair. "What kind of story would it be without a handsome prince?"

"What about monsters?" she asks in her scariest voice.

Monsters? He pauses, unsure if she's ready to hear the full extent of this story. "Not in this one," he says, deciding to save the unabridged version for another night.

Satisfied, the girl pulls the covers up around her chin, clutches Fuzzy tightly, and waits for the story to unfold ...

PART 1

CHAPTER 1

2017

Harper Emery's designer heels clicked against the marble floor as she strode purposefully through the atrium of her East Side high-rise. The thirty-year-old fashion executive wore a flawless navy-blue pinstripe suit that hugged her curves, accentuated by a dazzling smile, and chestnut hair that cascaded in perfect waves down her back. With each step she exuded confidence and poise, as if she was ready to take on the world.

"Morning, Ms. Emery!" the doorman called out, tipping his hat to her as she breezed past him.

"Good morning, David." Her voice was smooth and velvety.

As she exited the building, Harper was greeted by the sounds of honking car horns and the chatter of New York's busy streets. For a moment, she paused to take it all in, feeling invigorated by the crispness of the spring air and the energy of the city around her. At seven-thirty sharp, Harper's assistant, Kim Galloway, pulled up and opened the door of her SUV. "Good morning," she said, greeting Harper with a smile.

"Good morning to you, too." Harper slid into the back seat and glanced at her iPhone. "You're on time again. Congratulations, I think you've finally mastered the midtown traffic. So what's on the agenda today?"

"You have a meeting with Madeline from Vogue at nine, followed by a call with the design team at Elle at ten, and lunch with Bella from Gucci at eleven thirty."

"Excellent. How's the afternoon looking?"

"Jam-packed, as usual. But don't worry—you should be finished in plenty of time to see Dr. Andrews. I had to pull a few strings, but I got you on his calendar at six, just as you requested. Oh, and one other thing," Kim added as she merged into traffic, "Sidney called. She wants you to meet her for dinner at Gramercy Tavern at seven thirty."

Harper stopped scrolling through her phone and looked up in surprise. "Sidney? I didn't know she was in town." She checked her unread texts and missed calls, but there was nothing from Sidney. "Did she happen to tell you what this is about?"

Kim shook her head, focusing on the cars in front of her. "Only that it was of the *utmost importance*—her words, not mine."

In all the years Harper and Sidney had been friends—twenty-two to be exact—only twice had Sidney used the words *utmost importance*. Once, when she had been accepted into the University of Pennsylvania's Wharton School, and more recently when she announced her engagement to Jason. Which meant that whatever she wanted to talk about was monumental. Huge. Life-changing.

On the bustling corner of 7th Avenue and 38th Street, Kim brought the car to a smooth stop. Harper gracefully exited from the backseat and disappeared into the towering skyscraper, its shimmering glass mirroring the busy city. In the lobby, she stepped into the elevator and rode it up to her office on one of the top floors. After saying good morning to the receptionist, she settled into her plush leather chair and opened her laptop. But before she could even open her first email, her phone began buzzing with an incoming call.

"It's me," said Kim in a panic. "There's been a change of plans. Madeline just messaged me and said she needs to reschedule for next week. But," she went on, "I just got off the phone with your old pal, Eleanor Le Roux. She wants to see you right away."

Harper's heart stuttered. "Eleanor? Did she say what she wanted?"

"Only that it was urgent."

"Oh." Harper took a deep breath to calm herself. "Thanks for letting me know. Where are you now?"

"I'm turning around. I'll meet you out front in two minutes."

***

Harper's skin prickled with apprehension as she stepped into Chanel's sleek Manhattan headquarters. She had spent five years as a designer under the notorious Eleanor Le Roux before starting her own company, so she was familiar with every inch of the building. However, their split had been anything but amicable. Some even called it cataclysmic. The fashion industry thrived on drama, but this was a fiery spectacle that few could forget. Despite the hurtful words, betrayal, and reckless accusations, this place still felt like home to Harper.

"Hello, Harper." Eleanor's presence was impossible to miss as she made her way across the lobby, dressed impeccably in a designer suit and high heels. The same ruthless aura that matched her cutthroat reputation seemed to radiate from her.

She reached Harper with confident strides and greeted her with a strong handshake and a guarded smile. "It's great to see you again. How have you been?"

Harper scrutinized every detail of Eleanor's demeanor, searching for any signs of treachery in her steely blue eyes. "I've been well, thank you," she replied cautiously. "And yourself?"

"You know me ... busy as always." The wistful smile faded from Eleanor's lips as she ushered Harper toward the elevator. "You're probably wondering why I asked you to meet me here."

"The thought did cross my mind," Harper admitted, recalling the last time they were face to face; it hadn't ended well.

"I suppose I could have called but felt like this conversation needed to be in person. I hope you don't mind."

That depends. "Not at all."

When they reached the 44th floor, Eleanor escorted Harper into the board room, the same one where they had first met all those years ago, and where they had waged war against one another at the end. The room was largely unchanged, still dominated by the imposing mahogany conference table, surrounded by high-backed chairs. On the walls hung photos of the latest Chanel collections and fragrances.

"I'd almost forgotten how incredible this view is," said Harper, taking in the stunning sight of Central Park below and the majestic buildings surrounding it.

"Yes, it's something, isn't it?" Eleanor took a seat at the head of the table and offered Harper the seat adjacent to her. "I apologize for the last-minute summons," said Eleanor, watching Harper with an appraising eye as she settled into the chair. "But I had a cancellation this morning, and I thought, *what the hell,* why not see if you were available."

"It must be fate," Harper remarked with a smile. "I too had a cancellation."

"Oh?"

"Apparently, there was a mix-up with Madeline Marceau's schedule, so she moved our meeting to next week."

Eleanor let out a soft chuckle and said, "That sounds like Madeline, all right. But perhaps you're right; maybe this was meant to be." She paused and stared at Harper. "I'm sorry, it's just ... It seems like only yesterday that you were here, working for me. And now look at you, a star in your own right. It's amazing how quickly life can change, isn't it?"

"Yes, it is," Harper answered cautiously, knowing Eleanor was aware of her recent personal and financial struggles. "I'm sorry, was there something specific you wanted to talk to me about?"

"Yes," Eleanor replied, her tone shifting from lighthearted to serious. "When we last spoke, I said some things that I'm not particularly proud of. I'll admit, I handled your departure poorly, and for that, I'm truly sorry. The truth is, you're the most talented designer I know, and on top of that, you're a genuinely good person. That's why it hurt me so much when you told me you were leaving to start your own company. That, and I saw you as my protégé, someone who would take over for me when I decided to ride off into the sunset."

Harper was speechless. She had never heard Eleanor apologize for anything, ever.

"Your departure felt like ... like a betrayal," Eleanor finally confessed.

Betrayal? Harper knew the feeling of being stabbed in the back all too well.

"But I see now how selfish that was," Eleanor added.

Harper felt a pang of guilt at Eleanor's confession. "I'm sorry too," she replied, feeling the resentment she'd been holding onto instantly melt away. "You took a chance on me when no one else would, and that's something I've never forgotten."

Eleanor glanced at Harper, her blue eyes softening beneath the lines of age. "I suppose we both could have handled things better," she conceded. "But what matters now is reconciling and moving forward. Don't you agree?"

Harper nodded, knowing this was a significant moment. "Yes. I couldn't agree more."

Eleanor let out a sigh of relief as a small smile made its way onto her face. "Wonderful. Now that we've got that settled, I want to talk about a potential collaboration between us. You're aware that Chanel has always been known for its elegance, sophistication, and timeless beauty. However, we want to expand our target audience to include a younger, trendier crowd. That's where you come in."

Intrigued, Harper leaned forward. "What do you have in mind?"

"I'd like us to work together on a limited-edition collection. I want your fresh perspective on fashion to merge with the classic Chanel style. The best of both worlds, if you will. With your attention to detail and unique vision, I believe we can attract a new generation of fashion-lovers while still staying true to our brand."

Harper's mind raced. "Wow! I don't know what to say."

"I hope you'll say yes," said Eleanor as she reclined back in her chair.

"Yes! I'd be thrilled to work with you again." Harper took out her phone and glanced at the calendar. "Is there a specific timeline you had in mind? Fall? Winter?"

"Fall. Which means time is of the essence. I know it's short notice, but with the combined efforts of our teams, I'm confident we can make it happen. But we need to get started right away. And just to clarify, this will require your full dedication and presence over the next few months, so I hope you weren't planning any time off."

"No," Harper responded, having already cleared her schedule to focus on her fledgling business. "You know my work is my life."

Eleanor nodded approvingly. "Excellent," she said as her lips curled into a smile. "In that case, I'll have my legal team draft up a contract right away."

Before Harper left, Eleanor walked her to the door and added, "I also want you to know how truly sorry I am for what Grant did to you. It was a terrible betrayal, and I can only imagine how much it must have hurt you personally and professionally."

Harper nodded in understanding. "Thank you. And thanks also for the flowers and card you sent. They meant a lot to me."

"It's the least I could do. Besides, we women have to stick together, right?"

"I suppose you're right," said Harper, offering her a thin smile. "Well, thanks again, and I look forward to hearing from you."

On her way out, Harper stopped by her old friend Georgina Wright's office. They had both joined Chanel at the same time, determined to make their mark in the fashion world. But unlike Harper, Georgina had found her calling on the financial side of things, rising through the ranks to become vice president of finance, controlling the purse strings of the global empire.

She found Georgina hunched over her desk, reviewing what appeared to be profit and loss statements.

"Georgie," Harper said softly, not wanting to startle her. "How are you?"

The young woman looked up from behind her trendy glasses. "Harper Emery! It's so good to see you," she exclaimed, pulling her old friend in for a hug. "How have you been?"

"Good, Georgie. You?"

She shrugged her shoulders while Harper sat down across from her. "You know me, same old, same old. So what brings you by?"

"I'm here on business, actually. Eleanor invited me."

Georgina raised an eyebrow. "Really?"

"I was as shocked as you," said Harper. "But our conversation was surprisingly pleasant. In fact, she wanted to discuss a partnership for the fall clothing line."

Georgina leaned back in her chair, her initial shock replaced with a thoughtful expression. "A partnership? That doesn't sound like Eleanor. Maybe the Iron Lady is mellowing in her old age. Although, now that I think of it, she always did have a soft spot for you."

Harper laughed. "Hardly. Regardless, it couldn't come at a better time for me or my company. After the money Grant stole from me, I really need this."

Georgina nodded knowingly. "Well, it couldn't happen to a better person."

"Thanks, Georgie." Harper stood to leave. "I know you're busy, so I won't take up any more of your time ... just wanted to drop by and say hello."

"I'm glad you did. It's been far too long. And the next time you're this way, let me know and we'll do lunch."

"Yes, I'd like that."

As Harper moved toward the door, Georgina called after her. "Harper, wait. Just be careful with Eleanor, all right? I'm not saying her intentions are anything less than pure, but with her, there's usually an ulterior motive."

***

Harper took a deep breath as she settled into the backseat of Kim's car, still trying to process her conversation with Eleanor.

"So, what did she want?" Kim asked anxiously.

"She wants to work together," Harper replied, still in disbelief. "She needs our help to generate fresh ideas for her brand."

"What!? Eleanor La Roux asking for help? From you? That's ... that's ... incredible! And unbelievable. Wait, you don't think this is some kind of cruel joke, do you? A way for her to get back at you for leaving?"

Harper leaned back, considering the possibility. It was true—Eleanor had a reputation for being ruthless, but to kick Harper when she was down would be low, even for her. "I don't know," she said. "Eleanor seemed ... genuine."

"Let's hope so," said Kim. "Because if it's true, this could really turn things around for you."

Harper nodded as a smile tugged at the corners of her lips. "I know. This is a game-changer, and not just for me. For all of us."

"Wait until the team hears about this. They're going to freak!"

"Actually ..." Harper raised a hand. "You can't breathe a word of this to anyone until I see the contract. Not even Marco.

I don't want everyone running around like chickens with their heads cut off before I know what we're getting ourselves into. And if I know Eleanor," she said, tilting her head and looking up at the towering building as they drove away, "there's always a catch."

***

Harper's hands shook slightly as she held the delicate porcelain teacup to her lips, the fragrant jasmine tea doing little to calm her nerves. Dr. Allen Andrews—an expert in dealing with broken hearts—had a reputation for direct yet gentle consultations. He was known to slice through the veils of denial and self-pity with surgical precision, exposing the raw wounds beneath.

To make his patients feel more at ease, he filled his office with comfortable armchairs and shelves of leather-bound books. It was calm, an oasis of sorts, and a stark contrast to the chaos inside her head.

"Harper," Dr. Andrews said gently, snapping her back to reality. "The last time we spoke, you mentioned that your breakup with Grant has been quite difficult for you. Can you tell me more about that?"

Harper inhaled sharply, steadying herself as she recounted the painful experience. "It wasn't just the end of our relationship," she said, twisting the teacup on her knee. "It felt more like the end of the world. I had invested so much time and energy into us, only to find out he was someone else entirely."

Dr. Andrews nodded thoughtfully, his pen hovering over the notepad in his lap. "It's natural to feel betrayed and hurt when someone we love turns out to be different than who we thought they were. But remember, this is not a reflection on you or your worthiness of love."

Tears clouded Harper's vision. Her lip quivered. "I know that," she said, blinking the tears away. "But it's still hard to accept. Despite my professional successes, I've been somewhat unlucky when it comes to love. I just thought that this time was different, that I'd finally found my someone." She hung her head, embarrassed by her vulnerability.

"What about your financial difficulties? Have you been able to navigate through those as well?" Dr. Andrews asked, shifting the topic subtly.

Harper's gaze drifted to the window, where rain was beginning to patter against the glass. "Yes," she murmured. "I mean, it hasn't been easy, but I believe the worst is behind me." She drew a breath and exhaled. "I'll likely never see a penny of the money Grant took from me, but at least I still have my company. I'm just glad Sidney was there to lend a helping hand. Otherwise ..."

Dr. Andrews seemed to sense her discomfort and offered an encouraging smile. "You're fortunate enough to have such an understanding and supportive friend, Harper. But don't forget, it's you who had the courage to ask for help and take control of the situation. That's commendable."

Harper offered a small smile in return. "I don't feel courageous. I feel like I'm running on a treadmill, and at any moment now, I'm going to trip and fall flat on my face." She paused, the knot in her stomach tightening. "But more than that, I feel ... broken."

"Sometimes, courage doesn't feel like a heroic act or a grand gesture. It feels like getting up in the morning when you'd rather stay in bed. It feels like taking one step after another, even when you're not sure where the road, or the treadmill, is leading," Dr. Andrews said. "And that brokenness you feel? Don't worry. It too will heal. But you have to be patient and be willing to open your heart to love again."

The room fell into a comfortable silence. The only sound came from the ticking of the clock on Dr. Andrews' desk and the persisting throbbing of rain against the window.

Harper looked at him, her eyes welling up again. "I want to believe you, but I just keep circling back to the thought that maybe I'm not meant for love—that I'm somehow unlovable?"

"No." Dr. Andrews shook his head slowly. "No one is unlovable, you included. You deserve the same happiness as everyone else, and it's crucial for you to understand that your past relationships, however unsuccessful they've been, do not define your future potential for love."

Harper sniffed and wiped away a tear that had escaped before taking another sip of her tea. Then, forcing a small smile, she said, "Thank you, Dr. Andrews. You don't know how much I needed to hear that."

"Of course," he replied with a gentle smile of his own. "Was there anything else you wanted to discuss?"

Harper hesitated, biting her bottom lip. "There is something else ... someone else ... It's about Cameron."

"The man you used to love before Grant?"

"Yes. I had thought I was over him, but recently ... he's been on my mind a lot."

Dr. Andrews leaned back in his chair, studying Harper keenly. "Have you been in contact with Cameron? Or seen him lately?"

Harper shook her head. "No. I haven't seen him in a long time. But these thoughts ... these feelings ... they just rushed back all of a sudden, and I don't know why."

Dr. Andrews folded his hands across his chest, looking thoughtful. "Dreams? Memories? What triggers these thoughts?"

"I'm not sure ... Just little things, like the smell of toasted marshmallows or the sound of waves crashing."

Dr. Andrews nodded, pulling gently at his lower lip in thought. "Sometimes when we face difficulties in our current relationships, our minds may drift to past ones where we felt loved or comfortable. It's a form of escapism."

Harper looked up at him then. "But what if it's more than that? What if I never truly moved on from him?"

Dr. Andrews steepled his fingers together. "Harper, the human heart is complex," he began slowly. "And it's very possible that you may still be holding onto a piece of Cameron. But remember, just because you're experiencing these feelings doesn't mean you should act on them. Especially without clear understanding or perspective," he added. "Rushing into decisions often leads to more harm than good."

Harper nodded slightly. "I understand that, but if these feelings for Cameron never go away? What if I'm meant to be with him?"

Dr. Andrews leaned in, his expression serious. "Harper," he said gently, "It is important to understand that the intensity of emotions can often trick us into thinking that they hold some greater truth or destiny. While it's crucial to acknowledge what you're feeling, it's equally important not to let those feelings drive impulsive decisions. If you truly believe there's a chance for something meaningful with Cameron, it warrants further introspection before any action."

***

An hour and a half later, Harper stepped through the door of Gramercy Tavern. The scent of fresh herbs and garlic wafted to her nose, and as she took a deep breath, her stomach rumbled with anticipation.

Harper found Sidney sitting at a table in the back, wearing a chocolate brown cardigan that matched her eyes.

"Harper," said Sidney, standing and pulling her into a hug. "It's so nice to see you."

"It's good to see you too, Sid," Harper said as they parted.

"I was starting to think you weren't going to make it. It's not like you to be late."

"Sorry." Harper shrugged out of her coat and settled into her seat. "I got here as soon as I could. Traffic is a... nightmare."

"Tell me about it. The drive into the city seemed to take forever."

"So," Harper began, taking note of Sidney's appearance, "it looks like you finally decided to take my advice and go with a new hairstyle."

Sidney laughed, running her fingers through her short, honey-colored waves. "Yes, I needed a change. And you know what? I think you were right. It suits me better."

When the waitress appeared, Harper ordered wine and a brussels sprout salad while Sidney chose a chilled tomato soup.

As they waited for their food to arrive, Harper filled Sidney in on her recent meeting with Eleanor. "She actually apologized for the way she treated me when I left. Can you believe it?" Harper shook her head in amazement.

"That's ... great!" Sidney replied. "Maybe things are finally turning around for you."

"I hope so." Harper sighed, her smile fading to a frown. "If only my love life would follow suit."

"Speaking of that, the last time we spoke, you mentioned Dr. Andrews. Have you been to see him yet?"

"Yes," Harper answered brightly. "As a matter of fact, I just came from his office. That's the reason I was almost late—our session ran long."

"What did he say?"

"The usual—stay strong ... keep your head up ... don't lose hope ..." After a sip of wine, she added, "But he also said that the love of my life is waiting for me out there somewhere and that when I least expected it, things will fall into place for me."

"He's absolutely right, you know. I've been saying the same thing for years. Maybe in the future, you should save yourself the hassle and expense and come to me instead. I'll even give you the best friend discount," she added with a playful wink.

Harper rolled her eyes. "I'll keep that in mind."

When the appetizers arrived, they devoured them before the conversation turned to Grant.

"So you haven't heard from him?" Sidney asked as she dabbed the corners of her mouth with the napkin.

The question was unsettling. "No, and I don't expect to either. He's probably in Mexico or Greece, searching for his next unsuspecting victim. I just can't believe I allowed myself to be taken by a con man."

"Don't be too hard on yourself. Grant had everyone fooled, me included. At least he's gone now, and you won't ever have to worry about him again."

"I'll drink to that." Harper finished her wine and asked the waitress for another. "You know, I'm not asking for the world, Sid, just for someone to love me for who I am, not who I am in the fashion world."

Sidney shifted her gaze to the side and whispered, "I do

know of one man."

"No." Harper shook her head again and wagged a finger at Sidney. "Don't even go there. Cameron and I are just ... friends, I think. Besides, last I heard he was still on the other side of the world, saving the day. And anyway, we hardly talk anymore. I mean, we haven't spoken since ..." She paused, counting the months in her head. "Well, not in a long time."

When the main course arrived, they ate while discussing Sidney's flourishing real estate empire.

"Business is booming," she said in between bites of duck meatloaf. "Last quarter was my most profitable, which means I'm on track to retire by the time I'm forty."

"That's great," said Harper, and beamed a genuine smile at her. "You've always wanted to retire young and travel the world. And don't worry, as soon as my company is back on its feet, I'll repay you every penny ... with interest."

"Take your time," she replied with a gentle wave of her hand. "I'm just happy to have been able to help, especially after all the times you've saved my ass over the years."

Harper laughed as she recalled the drunken calls in the middle of the night, the emotional breakdowns after failed relationships, and the time she'd bailed Sidney out of jail for public indecency. Yes, over the years, Harper has played many roles: friend, therapist, rescuer. But their bond was not forged in these moments of desperation alone. Rather, it was the steady undercurrent of shared laughter, secrets, and dreams that truly held them together. Their friendship was a tapestry woven with threads of shared experiences and dyed in the colors of trust and intimacy. And this latest act of Sidney's generosity was yet another strand added to their rich history.

Sidney gave a lopsided grin and raised her glass. "Here's to us. To a friendship that may bend but never breaks, no matter what life throws at us."

"To us," said Harper, and clinked glasses. She took a sip of wine, then speared an asparagus shoot with the end of her fork and held it in front of her. "So, how's Jason?" she asked, changing the subject. "Last time we talked, you said he was working on a new book."

"Jason is great," Sidney replied. "His book's almost finished, and he thinks this is the one that will take him to the next level. Honestly, I've never seen him happier."

"Really? That's pretty exciting." Harper paused, tucking a loose strand of hair behind her ear. "And what about you, Sid? Are you happy ... with Jason, I mean?"

"Absolutely. Why wouldn't I be?"

Harper shrugged, setting the fork down on her plate. "It's just ... Are you sure he's the one? I mean, don't get me wrong, I adore him and think he's the perfect guy for you, but—"

"But what?"

"Well, after everything that happened with Steven, I just want to make sure you've put those issues behind you and that you're ready for a committed relationship."

Sidney glanced down at her half-empty wine glass, swirling the dark liquid around slowly. "I appreciate your concern, Harper," she said carefully. "But like I've told you, that's all behind me now. Besides, Steven was as much to blame as me. But with Jason, it's different. I'm different, and I don't ever want to go back to being that person again."

"Good," said Harper. Hearing the sincerity in Sidney's voice gave Harper hope that this time would be different. But as life had taught her, change was not easy. Pushing aside her doubts, she took a bite of asparagus, chewed, and swallowed before adding, "Because I want you to be happy, Sid. I truly do."

"I know," Sidney replied, reaching for Harper's hand. "And that means everything to me."

"So," Harper began, trying to lighten the mood, "have you and Jason set a date for the wedding or are you still mulling it over?"

"Actually ..." Sidney placed her knife and fork on the table and cleared her throat. "That's the main reason I asked you here tonight. I have a little surprise for you."

Harper let out an exasperated sigh. "Sid, you know how I feel about surprises."

"I know, but just hear me out. Jason and I have agreed to a summer wedding, which means there isn't a lot of time for planning or dillydallying."

"Why the rush? Wait," she said, raising a hand in the air as if physically holding off Sidney's response. "You're not pregnant, are you?"

"No, of course not," Sidney replied. "We want to do this before Jason's book is released so he can focus on the promotional tour without any distractions. And the best part—it's going to be a destination wedding!"

Harper's left eyebrow lifted up. "Let me guess: Jamaica? Mexico? Hawaii? I've always wanted to see Maui."

"Florida," said Sidney, and it took a few seconds for Harper to register. "Destin, to be exact. I know it isn't Mexico or Hawaii, but it's where my parents had their beach house and where I spent summers growing up. Call me old-fashioned, but it holds sentimental value for me." She took another drink of wine and added, "For you too, I imagine."

"Yes," said Harper, fondly recalling summers spent with Sidney's family at their beach house—the feel of the wind in her hair, the sound of the waves crashing against the shore, the turquoise waters of the gulf. But those weren't the only memories that came to mind. Close to her heart, Harper kept safe another set of memories—memories of Cameron, the boy with deep blue eyes, sun-kissed skin, and a charming smile. Memories of long walks on the beach, of endless conversations and stolen kisses. Memories of a love that had shaped the course of her life in ways that she was only beginning to understand.

The clink of wine glasses nearby snapped Harper out of her reverie. "I'm sorry, you were saying?"

Ignoring Harper's flightiness, Sidney continued telling her about the wedding. "And the reason I asked you here tonight is because I want you to be my maid of honor."

Harper was simultaneously shocked and unsurprised by Sidney's request. "Me? Really?"

"Yes, you. Who else would I ask? You're my best friend ... the one who has been by my side through all the ups and downs of the last twenty-two years. There isn't a single person alive who knows me better."

Tears threatened to spill from Harper's eyes as a wave of joy washed over her. "Thank you, Sid. That means the world to me."

"So you'll do it?"

"Yes," she answered through blurry eyes. "I'd love to be your maid of honor. And I promise I'll do whatever it takes to make sure your day is perfect."

CHAPTER 2

When the elevator reached the top floor of Harper's apartment building, Harper led Sidney down a wide hallway and into an open kitchen with an oversized island. "Here we are—home sweet home."

While Sidney marveled at the opulence of her surroundings—Carrara marble countertops, high-end stainless appliances, and custom cabinetry—Harper flicked on the lights and shrugged out of her coat.

"Damn, Harp, you didn't tell me you bought a penthouse." She paused to take it all in.

"I didn't," Harper quickly clarified. "This belongs to a friend of Marco's who is out of the country for a year. She offered to let me stay here while I search for a place of my own."

"Regardless, this place is incredible! And look at that view." Sidney stood at the window and looked out over the twinkling city below.

"I still can't believe it myself," said Harper. "Even if it's temporary, it's definitely a step up from my last place, don't you think?"

Sidney turned back to look at Harper. "I'll say! You know, despite everything you've been through recently, you've managed to do remarkably well. And I couldn't be prouder. You've come a long way, Harp."

"We both have," said Harper, acutely aware of Sidney's professional successes. Harper opened the refrigerator and took inventory of her beverages—neatly stacked bottles of Fiji water lined the top shelf, beneath which sat a San Pellegrino and two bottles of wine–one white, the other red. "Can I get you something to drink? Mineral water? More wine?"

Sidney turned down the wine and opted for water instead.

"Suit yourself." Harper grabbed two bottled waters and handed one to Sidney before flicking on the fireplace and settling into the oversized chair in the living room. "So tell me more about the wedding. Will it be an intimate gathering or are you inviting everyone you know?"

Sidney twisted off the top of her water and took a drink before answering. "Jason and I have agreed to keep the guest list to family and close friends," she said.

"And you said it's close to the beach club where we used to hang out when we were teenagers?"

"Actually, it's in the exact same spot!" Sidney replied. "The old place was destroyed in a hurricane several years ago, so they leveled it and built a new resort in its place. I can't wait for you to see it. There are pools, a rooftop bar, fantastic restaurants, and, of course, amazing views of the Gulf."

"It sounds wonderful," said Harper, recalling warm summer days, the smell of suntan oil as they lay by the pool, and the sound of the surf in the distance. "And it'll give me something to look forward to. Which is exactly what I need right now." Then, she remembered something. "Oh, no! I'll have to run this past Eleanor. I already told her I wasn't planning any time away."

"That won't be a problem, will it?" Sidney asked.

"It shouldn't be," Harper responded slowly, trying to assure not just Sidney but herself as well. "But I'll run this by her, just in case."

They talked well into the night, catching up on each other's lives. This was the first time they had seen each other since Grant had taken off with Harper's money, so Harper soaked up every ounce of her time with Sidney.

"I can't wait to move back to Kentucky," Sidney said as she warmed her hands by the fire. "After Jason and I are married."

"Move back? I thought you were happy in Danbury?"

"We are. But the real estate market is shifting. I don't know if you've heard, but interest rates are expected to climb soon, and there's talk of a recession. Plus, the cost of living is so much cheaper in Kentucky, and ever since Dad had his health scare earlier this year, it's made me realize life is short, and I want to be around my parents more."

"That's understandable," said Harper, thinking of her own parents and the fact that they too weren't getting any younger. "What does Jason think of your plan?"

"Honestly, I think Jason would be happy anywhere. He spends most of his time writing, so he's less concerned with where we are so long as he's comfortable and has access to his laptop. His parents on the other hand ..." She rolled her eyes. "Let's just say they're not thrilled about the prospect of us moving."

"I'm sorry to hear that," said Harper. "But give it time. I'm sure they'll come around. Besides, it's not like you're moving tomorrow."

"True. But we've already started the process." Sidney returned to the sofa and pulled the cover over her legs. "I reached out to Chelsea last week and told her what we were looking for."

"Chelsea McRae? She's a realtor now?"

Sidney nodded. "She just got her license." While Harper

digested that, Sidney continued. "What about you—have you thought any more about moving back home?"

Harper gave a one-shoulder shrug. "I've thought about it, but"—she shook her head—"with all I have going on here, I don't see myself moving anytime soon."

Sidney smiled. "Things sure have changed, haven't they?" She let out an easy laugh, then added, "It wasn't that long ago when you were terrified of the city, and I was the one desperate to leave our small town. Now look at us, trading places." Harper looked on as Sidney's expression turned thoughtful. "Not only that, but I'm engaged and talking about giving up my real estate empire. Meanwhile, here you are, living in a penthouse on the Upper East Side and CEO of your own design firm." Sidney shook her head in disbelief. "See ... what did I tell you, Harp? It's amazing what you can accomplish when you step outside your comfort zone."

"You were right," Harper agreed with a chuckle. "And I couldn't have done it without you. If you hadn't challenged me when we were younger—forced me out of my shell—I'd probably still be in Nicholasville, working at JCPenney or Macy's. Having you nearby while I built my career has been a real blessing."

Sidney smiled and said, "As much as I'd like to, I can't take all the credit. You were always destined for bigger things. I just helped nudge you in the right direction."

Harper smiled back, grateful for her best friend's support over the years.

"I just hope I can live up to the hype on this collaboration," she said, circling back to their earlier conversation. "Given my history with Eleanor and my recent financial woes, I don't have to tell you how important this is to me or to my career."

"Don't sweat it." Sidney waved a hand in the air. "Knowing you, you're already creating epic designs in that head of yours."

Sidney was right. Ever since the meeting that morning, Harper's mind had been on overdrive, racing with ideas. "I'm still trying to wrap my mind around this whole thing," she said, pulling one leg up and tucking it under the other. "It came completely out of the blue."

"Speaking of *out of the blue* ..." Sidney paused, set the water bottle on the coffee table, and steadied her gaze on Harper. "Guess who called me the other day?"

Harper didn't need to ask who it was; she already knew, and a chill ran down her spine. "What did he want?" she asked, playing nervously with her earring.

"To check in ... and to see how you were doing."

"I didn't know you two still kept in touch."

"We don't, for the most part. But every once in a while, I'll get a call or text from him."

Harper looked away, a frown creasing her forehead as she absorbed the news. "Does this mean he knows about the wedding?"

Sidney nodded, her lips straightening into a tight line. "But I doubt he'll show."

Harper swallowed hard, the image of his face looming in her mind's eye. She hadn't seen Cameron in eighteen months, yet the memory of him was as vivid as ever. The piercing eyes, the crooked grin that always hinted at some unsaid joke, the way his hair seemed to fall effortlessly into place. She half hoped he would be there, just to give her the chance to tell him how she truly felt, that she was still in love with him. But she knew better than to hope for things like that.

Sidney peered at Harper, a hint of curiosity appearing in

her brown eyes. "I still can't believe you haven't told him about what happened with Grant. I figured he would have been the first one you called."

"Yeah, well ..." Harper thought back on the dozens of text messages she'd typed, only to erase them, or the times she'd pulled up his number but never found the courage to call. She'd even checked his social media accounts, wondering if he'd moved on. There were pictures of him surfing in Cyprus, hanging out at a bar with friends, even attending his cousin's wedding without a guest on his arm. But, surprisingly, there was no evidence of another woman. "I was going to. It's just ..." She cleared her throat. "So what did you tell him?"

"I gave him the thirty-thousand-foot view—told him that things didn't work out. Of course, I left out the part about Grant swindling you out of your money for fear he might hunt him down and kill him."

"I wish someone would," Harper said, recalling the embarrassment she felt when she had to remove all traces of her engagement and wedding from Instagram. "And what did he say?"

"Not much. He seemed more shocked than anything else but also concerned for you. Mostly, I think he wanted to make sure you were okay. I take it he hasn't reached out? He said he might."

"No." Harper looked downward, her head shaking from side to side. "No, he hasn't. In fact, I haven't heard from him since the engagement."

Sidney's brows shot up. "Has it been that long?"

Harper nodded slowly. "Which officially makes this the longest we've gone without speaking since we met." There was an unmistakable sadness in Harper's voice, one she could not mask, no matter how hard she tried.

"So call him. You still have his number, don't you?"

Harper glanced reflexively at her iPhone. "Yes, but—"

"What?"

"I don't think he wants to talk to me, not after—"

Sidney leaned forward, her brows furrowed with concern. "Not after *what*?"

CHAPTER 3

18 months earlier

The night of the fashion show, Harper's stomach was in knots. She'd experienced butterflies before, but nothing like this. Backstage, while everyone hurried about to get ready for the runway, Harper did her best to steady her nerves. All the hard work—the blood, sweat, and tears—had brought her to this moment. As she took a deep breath, she recalled the last nine years of her life—four years at Parsons School of Design, four years rising through the ranks at Chanel, then choosing to start her own company. Now, here she was, on the cusp of fashion immortality, and all at the tender age of twenty-eight.

"Nervous?" asked Marco Migliozzi, her lead designer, slipping in through the open door.

"That's an understatement. I don't think I've ever been this nervous in my entire life. Look at me," she said, holding out her trembling hands. "I'm shaking."

He handed her a glass of champagne. "Something to take the edge off."

Harper upended her glass, emptying it in just a few gulps. "Thanks. I needed that."

"Don't be nervous," said Marco. "This is your night, the culmination of everything you've worked so hard to achieve. Look." He parted the curtain just enough for Harper to have a look out into the growing throng of people. "Marc Jacobs, Tom Ford, Alessandro Michele, Stella McCartney—they're all here for you."

Seeing the biggest names in the industry seated around the runway, anxiously awaiting the start of the show, Harper gulped. "But what if they hate my designs? What if this goes poorly and ruins my career? What if—"

"Relax." Marco took her by the shoulder and looked her in the eye. "You're the most brilliant designer in all of New York. You have style, flair, confidence, and most importantly"—he tugged at the velvet lapel of his tuxedo—"you have me."

"Thanks, Marco," she said as the pressure subsided. "What would I ever do without you?"

***

The first wave of models sporting Harper's designs were met with thunderous applause. The echo of clapping hands and whistling lips filled the lavishly decorated room, bouncing off the crystal chandeliers and white marble floor. Backstage, Harper peered through the thin gap in the curtain, watching anxiously as her designs, weeks upon weeks of hard work, sweat, and endless nights were finally out there, alive on the runway.

When the show concluded, Harper took to the stage and received a standing ovation, officially bringing fashion week to a close. Despite her anxiety, the show had been a smashing success. Her dream had finally come true.

At the after-party, Harper was met with more adulation, bolstering her confidence and solidifying the success of her first collection. Finally able to breathe a sigh of relief, she wandered around the room, thanking everyone for coming out. And as she did, a familiar face appeared among the crowd.

"Cam!" She was momentarily frozen, unsure of what to do. It had been nine long and agonizing months since they last spoke. It was a conversation that still haunted her. But despite it all, she couldn't resist running over to him and wrapping her arms around his neck.

"Hey there," he whispered, holding her. "Congratulations. The show was amazing. Your designs were so ... you."

They parted, and she blushed. "Thank you," she said, her gaze fixed on his blue eyes. "You're the last person I expected to see tonight."

"Yeah, well ... I wanted to be here for your big day," he said thoughtfully.

"Thank you," she replied. "That means a lot. But how did you even know about it?"

"Sidney told me."

Harper laughed under her breath. "I should have known. Wait a minute! How did you get the time off? I thought you were flying missions in Afghanistan?"

"I was, but I'm on leave for a few days," he said. "So I figured I'd start my vacation here in New York."

Despite the war raging inside her, Cameron's gesture overwhelmed Harper, and she had to bite back tears. "I'm glad you did. Truly, I am. Having you here is the icing on the cake."

"I'm glad you think so," he said, looking relieved. "I was worried." There was a pause, the kind that's dense enough to drown in. "Listen, I was wondering,"— he took a step toward her—"when you get a minute, there's something I'd like to talk to you about. Something important."

She tipped her head to the side and studied his face, wondering what he could possibly want to say to her that hadn't already been said. "Okay. But it may be a little while. I need to finish saying goodbye to some people first."

"Take your time," he said. "I'm not going anywhere."

Just then, Grant Thornton appeared in a perfectly tailored tuxedo, grinning from ear to ear. "I hope I'm not interrupting anything," he said, his eyes drifting from Harper to Cameron.

"No. Not at all," Harper reassured him. "Your timing is actually perfect. There's someone I want you to meet." She gestured toward Cameron. "Grant, this is Cameron Spears, my ..." Harper stopped, struggling to find the words.

"Friend," Cameron interjected, perhaps sensing her hesitancy. "An old friend."

"Pleasure to meet you, Cameron," Grant said, flashing a perfect smile.

"Likewise." Cameron gave him a firm handshake.

"How exactly do you two know each other?" Grant inquired as he put his arm around Harper's waist and drew her to him.

"Cameron's the guy I was telling you about—the one who saved me from drowning when I was a teenager."

It took a few seconds, but Grant finally made the connection. "Ah, yes, now I remember. In that case, I owe you a debt of gratitude, sir." He shook Cameron's hand again. "So what do you think of our girl—amazing, isn't she?"

"Yes," Cameron replied as his gaze steadied on her. "She certainly is."

There was a moment of awkward silence before Grant turned to Harper and said, "I hate to interrupt but we should probably finish making our rounds before people start leaving."

"Of course. I'll be right there," Harper replied.

"It was nice to meet you, Cameron," Grant said as he shook his hand once more before leaving.

When they were alone, Cameron asked, "So Grant is your ...?"

"Boyfriend," Harper responded without hesitation, twirling her earring between her fingers. "He's my boyfriend."

Cameron recoiled at this revelation. "Really? How long have you two been together?"

"Since the spring."

"I see. Is it serious?"

Harper nodded, her eyes following Grant as he walked away. "Yes, it is. He's been a tremendous help with getting my brand off the ground, managing shows and appearances, which has allowed me to focus all of my time and energy on designing."

Cameron produced a smile that didn't quite reach his eyes and said, "I'm glad to hear it. I know how important all of this is to you."

Harper turned her focus back to Cameron. "I should really go and say goodbye to everyone. Why don't you grab something from the bar, and I'll catch up with you in a bit."

While Cameron eased over to the bar, Grant took to the stage and made an announcement. "If I could have your attention, please! I wanted to take this opportunity to publicly congratulate Harper on a successful show. Tonight, she showcased her remarkable talent and proved that she is a force to be reckoned with. Harper, my love, I am so proud of you."

Applause erupted throughout the room, causing Harper to blush. As the applause died down, Grant looked at Harper with a mischievous gleam in his eyes. "And now, if you'll all bear with me, I have a little surprise. Harper, would you join me?"

With her heart beating wildly, Harper made her way through the crowd toward the stage. She smoothed out her dress before stepping up onto the platform, joining Grant at his side.

"Harper," he began, his voice full of sentiment, "from the moment I met you, my life has changed in ways I never thought possible. You have brought so much joy, love, and inspiration into my life, and I cannot imagine a future without you by my side." Grant reached into his pocket and pulled out a small velvet box, a smile playing on his lips. The room buzzed with anticipation as he dropped down to one knee. "Harper, will you do me the incredible honor of becoming my wife?"

The crowd held its breath, waiting for Harper's response. A flood of joy, love, and an overwhelming sense of disbelief swept over her. This was the moment she had longed for ever since she heard tales of princes on white horses, but now that it was actually happening, it felt more like a dream.

Harper's eyes flickered from Grant's hopeful eyes to the sea of expectant faces surrounding them. Uncertainty and fear coursed through her veins. This was the man she loved, the man who had six months earlier appeared seemingly out of the blue and swept her off her feet. But was she ready for this? Doubts and fears crept into her mind, gathering like dark clouds on the horizon. Then, she locked eyes with Cameron, who appeared to have a mix of shock and disappointment etched on his face. Cameron, her first love, the man with whom she had been through so much, the man who had always supported her dreams and encouraged her to chase after what she wanted. Her heart wrenched at the sight of him, torn between the man who had just asked for her hand in marriage and the man she had once loved so fiercely.

Amidst the soft murmur of the crowd, love, uncertainty, regret, and fear warred within her, all competing for dominance in her heart. She knew that whatever decision she made would change everything, and once she'd made it, there would be no going back. Once upon a time, she had wanted this moment with Cameron, certain that he was the one who would make all her dreams come true. However, commitment to the service of his country and frequent absences during crucial moments in their relationship had eroded her trust in their ability to stay together through the myriad of twists and turns life offered. But with Grant it was different. He wasn't away for long periods of time, and she didn't have to worry about his safety. He was present, dedicated to Harper and her career.

Finally, Harper silenced the storm within her. Turning to Grant, she gave a single, decisive nod before saying, "Yes, I'll marry you."

Grant's face broke into a wide grin, relief and elation radiating from every pore. The room exploded into cheers and applause as Grant opened the velvet box to reveal a shimmering diamond ring. He gently took Harper's trembling hand and slid the ring onto her finger, sealing their commitment to each other.

For the next few minutes, Harper's world was a blur of laughter and tears, of congratulations and toasts. Every now and then, she would glance at the ring on her finger, the diamond glinting with a thousand prisms, proof that this momentous evening was not a dream but beautifully real.

Yet in the midst of the celebration, a strange unease tugged at Harper. A whisper of doubt, perhaps, or just the lingering nerves she'd felt when Grant had first gone down on one knee. She shook it off, laughing at her own silliness.

In the chaos of all the excitement and confusion, Harper had lost track of Cameron. As the guests began filing out, she was reminded of the fact that he had wanted to talk to her. *Something* important, he had said. But what? She chewed on her lip as she navigated the maze of bodies, her eyes darting around in a desperate search for his familiar face. She made her way over to the bar where she had last seen him, wondering about his true motives. He was never one to act impulsively; everything he did was planned, intentional, and meaningful. So why had he really come here? Finding the bar empty, she sighed, her heart sinking further.

"Excuse me," she said to the bartender. "There was a man here earlier, dressed in a Navy uniform. Have you seen him?"

The bartender nodded toward the open door. "He left through there," he said in a deep voice.

A sharp pang of disappointment hit her. She moved toward the open door, pushing past clusters of guests who were still lingering.

"There you are," she said, finding Cameron sitting on a bench outside. "I thought you might have left without saying goodbye."

He looked up, and there was a mix of sadness and resignation in his eyes. "I figured it was best to give you some space. I didn't want to intrude on your big moment."

Harper glanced at the ring on her finger, still in disbelief that she was now engaged. "Never in my wildest dreams did I expect this," she whispered. "I mean, we haven't dated for that long ..."

"Sometimes, love doesn't adhere to timelines or expectations, does it? It simply sweeps us off our feet when we least expect it."

Harper sat down on the bench beside Cameron. "I guess you're right." In the silence that followed, she could feel the weight of his unspoken feelings hanging heavily in the air between them.

Finally, after what felt like an eternity, Cameron took a deep breath and looked into Harper's eyes. "Can I ask you something?"

"Anything."

"Are you happy ... with Grant? I mean, truly happy?"

Harper hesitated before answering, her mind conflicted. She looked at Cameron, searching for the right words to convey the complexity of her feelings.

"Yes," she finally said, her voice barely above a whisper. "He's kind and caring, and ... It's just different, you know?"

"Different? How?"

Her heart thumped against her chest like a drum. How could she explain this to Cameron, the man who had once held her heart and still claimed a piece of it? "It's ... it's stable, predictable. With Grant, we don't have to deal with deployments or long periods of time apart. Plus, he's invested in my success." She paused, letting her words sink in. "But mostly, with him, there's no fear of the unknown. No constant wondering if I'll receive a phone call in the middle of the night telling me he's died in some firefight halfway across the world. His devotion is to me and my career."

Cameron was silent, the ghost of a smile tracing his lips. "I see." His voice was steady, but something in his eyes flickered, a shadow of longing that disappeared as quickly as it had come. "Then that's all that matters," he said, forcing a smile. "If you're happy, then I'm happy too."

Silence filled the air before Harper spoke up again. "Earlier ... there was something you wanted to talk about. What was it?"

Cameron looked at Harper, studied her face. "It doesn't

matter now," he finally said, shrugging it off. "It's not important anymore."

"Promise?" Harper asked, looking at him intently.

"Yeah," he said, spearing her with his gaze. "I promise."

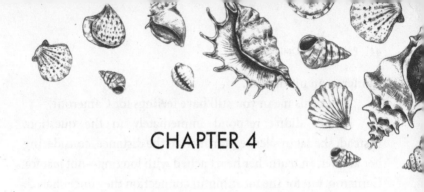

CHAPTER 4

"I knew that Cameron was there that night, of course," said Sidney, bringing Harper back to the present. "But I didn't know any of that happened. Why didn't you tell me?"

Harper hesitated, her eyes fixed on the flicker of flames in the fireplace. "Because it didn't seem important at the time. But now ..." She played nervously with her pinky. "I can't help feeling that there was something else he wanted to tell me that night ... something important."

"Like what?"

A light shrug was the only response Harper could muster. "That he still loved me, that he had changed his mind about staying in the Navy. I don't know. I mean, we hadn't been together in almost a year, but ... you should have seen him, Sid—the deep sadness in his eyes when I said yes to Grant." She shook her head as if trying to scatter the image that had been seared into her memory. "It was as if his heart had been ripped out. I've seen devastation before, but nothing like that."

Sidney leaned in, her eyes narrowing with curiosity. "So what are you saying?"

Harper sighed. "I don't know. I can't help but wonder if things would have turned out differently had I not rushed into a relationship with Grant, or if I hadn't lost my temper and given

Cameron an ultimatum."

"Does this mean you still have feelings for Cameron?"

Harper didn't respond immediately to the question. Instead, she sat in silence, staring into the distance, considering her answer. In truth, her heart ached with longing—not just for Cameron, but for the meaningful connection they once shared. She yearned for someone to understand her deepest fears and desires, to share in her triumphs, and soothe her sorrows. She yearned for a partner. "No matter how hard I try to deny it, there's a part of me that still holds on to him, a stubborn flame that refuses to be extinguished. Despite everything that has happened, the love that we once shared still lingers."

***

It wasn't until Sidney left around two that Harper finally kicked off her heels and changed into comfortable silk pajamas. She stood by the window, admiring the view. Reflecting on her conversation with Sidney, Harper again wondered what might have been if she'd only waited to talk to Cameron. Perhaps none of this would have happened; perhaps she wouldn't be alone, silently suffering in her little corner of the world. She sighed, her breath fogging up a small patch on the glass before dissipating again into the night.

Finally, she turned away from the window and took a seat at the bar. She opened her laptop and scrolled through the flood of emails, stopping when she located the one with the contract Eleanor had promised.

Anxious to review the terms and conditions of the agreement, Harper scanned the document. It was all pretty standard fare; the legalese wasn't cumbersome, the terms manageable. As for the compensation—*Holy shit!* It wouldn't make up for all the money Grant had embezzled, but it was an excellent start. The only issue was the deadline—the end of July—which meant Harper would be forced to juggle work and Sidney's wedding. When she was satisfied that everything was in order, Harper signed her name electronically and pressed send, then reached for her sketchbook and began to draw.

Harper woke to the first rays of light seeping in through the sheer curtains. Her eyes fluttered open as her internal clock reminded her of the ambitions that drove her every day. The scent of lavender from the diffuser on her bedside table filled her nostrils, and she inhaled deeply before pushing back the covers and sliding out of bed.

"Another day, another opportunity," she whispered to herself as she put on her running gear. With the press of a button, the treadmill hummed to life, its digital display blinking expectantly. Harper stepped onto the machine with practiced ease, adding her Air Pods as she began her morning run.

"It's a new day," she said as the sun radiated in the eastern sky. As her feet pounded rhythmically on the belt of the treadmill, her thoughts began to wander. The conversation with Sidney the night before was still fresh in her mind. The fact that Cameron had reached out to her after all this time was both unsettling and exhilarating. As she was discovering, the past had an uncanny way of making its presence known at the most unexpected moments.

What could Cameron possibly want after so long? Sidney had been vague about the details, but there was no hiding the excitement in her voice when she told Harper that Cameron was worried about her. Still, Harper was grounded in her reluctance to dig up old bones. She had moved on, built a life in the city, and was content with her routine.

When her workout was complete, Harper padded into the kitchen, her damp hair clinging to her forehead. She pulled out a blender, meticulously measuring out spinach, mixed berries, almond milk, and a scoop of protein powder. With a flick of a switch, the blender roared to life, transforming the ingredients into a thick, nutritious smoothie. Harper poured the concoction into a tall glass, sipping it thoughtfully as she scanned her phone for any urgent messages.

"Today is the day," she murmured, her thoughts drifting to the project. Her passion for her career and dedication to her work fueled her, driving her to create designs that shaped the world of fashion. But this project was her magnum opus, the culmination of all her hard work and creativity.

Harper, I'd like you to start sketching some ideas. A text message from Eleanor flashed across her screen.

Already on it. I'm meeting with my team first thing this morning. We'll get started right away, she quickly typed back, her fingers flying over the touchscreen. Harper finished her smoothie and set the glass down with resolve. There was no time to waste; the Chanel project demanded her full attention, and she would give it nothing less.

"Let's make magic happen," she whispered to herself as she turned on the shower, already envisioning how her designs would come to life on the runway.

***

By the time Harper got to the office, her mind was filled with ideas. After settling into her comfortable, high-backed chair, she rolled up her sleeves and prepared to dive headfirst into her work.

"Morning, Harper!" Tiffany, one of her designers, called out cheerfully from across the room. "Are we continuing work on the new fall line?"

Harper shook her head. "There's been a change of plans." She told Tiffany about her meeting the day before. "And Eleanor wants us to get started right away."

Tiffany's eyes popped wide. "Whoa! Is this for real?"

"I signed the contract early this morning."

"Does this mean you and Eleanor patched things up?"

"Yes, as a matter of fact, we did. By the way, where's Marco? He needs to hear this too."

"He just got here. Do you want me to get him?"

"Yes, and grab the others while you're at it," said Harper, rising from her chair. "Let's all meet in the conference room in five."

As Tiffany went to round up the team, Harper made her way down the hall to the renowned war room. It was a large room dominated by a sprawling glass table, skirted with sleek, modern chairs. On the walls hung magazine covers showcasing their designs, a reminder of their recent success, and a motivation to continue striving for more.

"All right, everyone," Harper announced when her staff was gathered around her. "I have some exciting news. We've been tasked with a special project, which will require our collective best. Until now, we've been highly successful because of our creativity and dedication—to the brand and to each other. Each of you is like family to me, and as a family, I want us to succeed." She drew a breath before going on. "Yesterday, I had a meeting with my former boss, Eleanor Le Roux. And before you ask," she could sense their collective curiosity, "we reconciled our differences. What's more, Eleanor would like us to partner with her on a new fall collection."

A collective gasp went up.

"She's trying to reach a younger audience," Harper continued. "And she thinks this firm is the right one for the job. I don't have to tell you how important this is, not only to this company but to me personally, so I want everyone sharp and focused on this. This is the kind of deal we've been waiting for, one that could solidify our futures and get us out of the red."

When the excitement died down, Harper spread her drawings across the table, revealing a series of elegant, timeless designs that captured the essence of Chanel's iconic style.

"These are just a few concepts I've been working on since last night. Nothing super detailed, just ideas at this point. Go ahead, take a look." She backed away, allowing everyone to get a glimpse of her vision.

"Wow, these are stunning, Harper," Marco marveled, his eyes drinking in every detail. "I absolutely adore this neckline."

"Yes, I knew you would."

"Stunning, as usual," said Tiffany.

"I'm glad you like them." Harper allowed herself a brief smile before continuing. "Now, let's discuss fabrics. I was thinking a mix of silk, tweed, and some delicate lace accents. Thoughts?"

"Love it!" Tiffany exclaimed, already rifling through fabric swatches to find the perfect matches for Harper's vision. "The mix of textures will really make the designs pop."

"And I want to incorporate some metallic strands throughout the collection to give it that extra sparkle," Harper added.

"Brilliant choice." Marco held up a shimmering gold

thread that caught the light just right. "This will look amazing under the runway lights."

It didn't take long until Harper's designs began to take shape. The room buzzed with creative energy, and she could feel the excitement of her staff as they collaborated on what was sure to be the most memorable collection of their careers.

***

After a long but productive day at the office, Harper arrived home, changed out of her work clothes, and settled into an oversized chair. Too tired to endure the hustle and bustle of the city, she dined in, heating up leftovers from the lasagna she'd made two nights ago.

Once she had finished eating, Harper rinsed the dishes in the sink and retired to her room with her sketches. Since going into business for herself, she'd taken on more strategic responsibilities, but this partnership with Chanel had ignited her passion for design again, which is the reason she'd chosen fashion in the first place.

After narrowing down the designs to only a handful, Harper worked herself into a semi-comfortable position and reached for her phone. Checking her text messages, she found the usual: one from her mom, telling her she missed her, and another from Sidney letting Harper know she'd arrived home safely. But it's what she didn't find that alarmed her. To ensure Cameron was still in her phone, she checked her contacts. Sure enough, there he was, in between Sax Fifth Avenue and Aubrey Stewart, an old friend from college. Just seeing his name sent chills all over her body. She clicked on his picture, revealing his number and the various ways to make contact. Should I?

Her thumb hovered above the call button as she contemplated calling the man who had once stolen her heart. She checked the time. He'd be up by now, likely eating breakfast or going through pre-flight checks.

Despite the urge to call, Harper resisted and put her phone away. "Chicken," she muttered as she rested her head against the pile of goose-down pillows. *You've always been chicken when it comes to him.* It had irked her when she was younger, the way she felt utterly inferior in his presence. After all, she was the smart one, the brilliant one, the one with all the talent. But he had talent too, not to mention good looks and intelligence. He'd finished at the top of his class at Annapolis—no small feat—and had achieved his goal of becoming a naval aviator.

But Harper had successes of her own. At thirty, she was one of the youngest fashion executives in New York—also no small feat, had launched two successful clothing lines and was the envy of friends and colleagues alike.

But that was before she'd been swindled out of millions by the man who had promised to love her and left her with nothing but shame and scandal for the whole world to see. Now, she was left picking up the pieces of her once lavish life, struggling to rebuild her empire and her image, from the ground up.

***

Harper was back at it again the next morning, pouring over sketches and discussing color palettes. For hours, she and her team worked meticulously to refine her designs, choosing just the right fabrics and narrowing down color selections. But as the hours stretched into the afternoon, Harper's mind began to wander. And it wasn't until Marco knocked on the table a few times that Harper snapped back to the present.

"What's with you this afternoon?" he asked, giving her a curious look. "Ever since lunch, it's like you're off in another world."

"Sorry," she said. "Just ... thinking."

"About the project ... or something else?" He eyed her carefully. When she didn't respond, he asked, "This isn't about *him* again, is it?"

"Who?"

"You know who—that backstabbing bastard Grant."

"Oh, him. No." She shook her head. "I refuse to give him another thought."

"Good. I'm glad to hear it," he said, looking relieved. "He was a low-down, good-for-nothing thief who didn't realize what he had, and you deserve so much better."

"That's exactly what I told Sidney," Harper murmured as she absentmindedly traced the outline of a lace pattern with the end of her finger. "But ..." Her voice trailed off as doubt crept back in.

Marco placed a supportive hand on her shoulder and said, "Keep your head up, Harper. Things are going to turn around. I mean, I think this project with Chanel is an omen. Maybe the stars are finally aligning for you."

Harper gave a small smile, wanting to believe what Marco was telling her. But if experience had taught her anything, it was to be cautiously optimistic.

"And if not," Marco continued, "don't worry. You're doing amazing things here. Everyone thinks so. Focus on that for now."

"You're right. I need to focus." She took a deep breath to clear her mind. "I blame Sidney, by the way. All this talk of destination weddings and maids of honor has my head spinning."

CHAPTER 5

In the weeks that followed, Harper spent every waking moment balancing her responsibilities as lead on the Chanel project with her duties as maid of honor. By day, she met with her designers, fine-tuning each intricate detail. And by night, she found herself knee-deep in color swatches, guest lists, and bachelorette party planning, each detail seemingly more important than the last.

But as time went on, the demands of her high-profile job seemed to multiply each day, leaving her with little time to focus on the upcoming wedding. And despite her best efforts to prioritize, by May, the stress had begun to take its toll on her.

"I need a break," she confided to her mom during a phone call one evening. "A chance to clear my head. Even if it's for just a day or two."

"You could always come home," Brenda suggested. "I could make that lasagna you like so much, let you sleep in, and I won't tell anyone you're here."

Harper sighed, imagining the cozy embrace of her childhood home—the smell of her mother's delicious cooking wafting from the kitchen, the sound of her father's voice reading out loud from the newspaper. How she yearned to be in that safe haven once again, if only for a few days. "Actually, that sounds like a perfect idea. Are you sure it's no trouble? I could always get a room at the Griffin Gate."

"Nonsense," said Brenda. "Besides, it's been ages since you stayed here. And it will be nice to catch up."

***

The following Friday, Harper found herself driving down the familiar streets of her hometown, the cool breeze in her hair. As she approached her parent's home, the sight of it brought a comforting smile to her face. The two-story farmhouse stood tall and proud, exuding a sense of warmth and familiarity that instantly eased the tension in her body.

Brenda Emery stood on the weathered porch, her arms open wide to welcome her daughter back home. She was wearing her usual attire of a flowery home dress with a well-worn apron tied around her waist. Her curly hair, now streaked with gray, was tied back in a bun as she beamed at Harper.

Harper parked her car in the gravel driveway and practically ran up the steps, embracing her mother with a sense of relief she hadn't felt in months.

"Welcome home," said Brenda, showing her into the house.

"Thanks, Mom," Harper replied. "It's good to be home."

Inside, the house was just as Harper remembered, each room a treasure trove of memories. The cozy living room with its worn-out armchair where she used to curl up with her favorite books. The kitchen, always filled with the savory aroma of her mother's cooking. And upstairs, the hallway leading to Harper's bedroom, adorned with family photographs and certificates of achievement.

Harper dropped her bags on the floor and wandered around the room, her fingertips grazing the familiar textures of her childhood. She paused in front of each photograph, a mosaic of smiles frozen in time. Her parents, beaming with pride on their wedding day. Harper as a freckle-faced teenager, awkwardly posing with her braces at a school dance.

"Everything's just how you left it," said Brenda, appearing in the doorway. "You'll be comfortable here, won't you?"

Harper turned to face her mother, a genuine smile gracing her lips. "Yes, I will," she said. "Thank you."

"You're welcome." Brenda smiled warmly.

"Where's Dad?"

"He went to the store to get some groceries, but he'll be back shortly. Why don't I give you some time to get settled? I'll holler when supper's ready."

After emptying her suitcase, Harper sat down on the end of her bed, admiring the photographs that lined the bookshelf where she used to keep her favorite books. There was a picture of her family visiting the arch in St. Louis and another from when Harper went to Washington, D.C., as part of the safety patrol. The rest were of her and Sidney, bringing back memories of long ago.

She riffled through the writing desk, where she'd once scribbled down her dreams and aspirations, the uneven lines telling stories of a young girl who believed anything was possible. It was a trip down memory lane that led to a stack of papers filled with words of encouragement penned by her younger self. Harper's heart ached as she read through them. *Dream big*, one note read. *Never stop chasing your dreams*, said another. And there was one that contained a quote from her favorite book: *I want to do something splendid ... something heroic or wonderful that won't be forgotten after I'm dead. I don't know what, but I'm on the watch for it and mean to astonish you all someday.*

But before she got completely swept up in the moment, the sound of the front door opening interrupted her thoughts.

"I'm home," her dad's voice rang out, making her smile.

"Hi, Daddy!" She greeted him on her way down the stairs.

"Sweet pea!" Rob Emery gave her a tight hug. He had on his usual work uniform from the lumber mill, smelling strongly of pine and motor oil.

It broke Harper's heart to see him still working after all these years. Before her fall from grace, Harper had attempted to give him money that would have allowed him to retire, but he was a proud man and had always turned down her offers.

His grizzled beard scratched her face in a comforting familiarity. "Sorry I wasn't here when you got home," he said, pulling back to look at her. "Your mother sent me on a grocery run."

"I forgive you," said Harper. "As long as you got cookies."

Rob laughed heartily, patting her on the back before reaching into one of the brown paper bags he was carrying. "Way ahead of you, kiddo," he said, producing a box of Oreos.

"Supper!" Brenda called from the kitchen, and they all sat down to dinner.

"This is nice, isn't it?" Rob asked as he spooned out mashed potatoes, green beans and added a hamburger steak. "All of us around the same table again." He let out a sigh, his deep brown eyes gleaming with fond memories. "It reminds me of the good old days."

"Yes, it does," Brenda replied with a wistful smile. "We need more days like this."

Harper smiled back at her parents, the warmth of the moment enveloping her.

"This food is delicious," she said, hoping to lighten the mood. "I haven't had a home-cooked meal in ages."

"You don't cook anymore?" Brenda inquired.

"I do, but ... you know what I mean."

They ate in silence for a few minutes until Brenda asked about the wedding preparations. "So how are all the preparations going?"

Harper took a drink of her iced tea before answering. "Good. In fact, the invitations went out earlier this week."

"That reminds me." Brenda reached behind her into the mail basket and pulled out an envelope with their names written in calligraphy on the front. "We received ours yesterday," she said, showing it to Harper. "I was just telling your father this morning how beautiful it was." She ran her fingers over the intricate gold design, admiring the craftsmanship. "Did you help Sidney pick these out?"

"Yes, I did," Harper confirmed.

"I can tell," said Brenda with a genuine smile.

"So are you thinking of attending?" Harper asked.

Brenda gave a noncommittal shrug. "We're thinking about it. It's been years since we've been to the beach. Besides, as much time as you girls spent together growing up, Sidney practically feels like family. Speaking of Sidney, a little birdie told me that she and Jason are considering moving back to Kentucky after the wedding. Is there any truth to that?"

Reaching for the saltshaker, Harper nodded in confirmation. "They've already started looking for property."

Brenda raised an eyebrow. "What do you think about that?"

"I think it's great," Harper replied. "She's been talking about moving back home for years."

"Maybe you'll consider moving back too, someday."

Rob chimed in then. "Come now, dear. At least let her get through supper before you start twisting her arm."

Harper gave him a grateful smile. "Just so you know, I have

considered it. I mean, no matter how much time I spend in New York, this will always be home. But even if I do decide to come back—and I'm not saying I will—it won't be anytime soon. I've got too many irons in the fire right now to think about moving."

"I understand," said Brenda, thinly disguising her disappointment. "But what will you do when you meet a nice man and settle down? Surely, you're not still thinking of raising a family in the city, are you?"

Harper considered that. She used to think that the city, with its opportunities for growth and exposure to culture, was the best environment for raising a family. But after her tumultuous relationship with Grant and subsequent media frenzy, her priorities were starting to shift. Being home again, she found herself drawn to the comfort of small-town life—the close-knit community, the quiet simplicity. It gave her a sense of calm that had eluded her in all the years she'd spent chasing her dreams. "I don't know, but I'll cross that bridge when I get to it. Besides, I have to meet a man first," she said, making light of the situation. "And at the rate I'm going, it isn't a problem I'll have to contend with anytime soon."

"Speaking of men," said Brenda, without skipping a beat, "there's a nice young man named Kevin who just moved to town. I think he's in sales ... or is it insurance?" She looked at Rob, who seemed uninterested, but Brenda persisted anyway. "Regardless, he's very polite and single, and I hear he attends the Baptist church on Sycamore. Maybe I could give him your number?"

Harper shot her mother a look of warning. "Thanks, but the last thing I need is you playing matchmaker." She got up and rinsed her plate in the sink. "Plus, I'm way too busy to be thinking about a relationship. Between work and this wedding,"—she collapsed into the chair and sighed—"I've got enough on my plate for the foreseeable future."

***

After supper, Harper sat on the front porch swing, listening to the birds chirping in the trees. The sun had begun its descent, painting the picturesque countryside in hues of purple and orange.

"Mind if I join you?" Brenda asked as she stepped out onto the front porch.

"Not at all." Harper scooted over to make room for her mother.

Brenda let out a contented sigh as she settled into the swing. "I come out here every evening at this time," she said. "It's so peaceful listening to the birds and crickets."

Harper nodded, her eyes fixated on the distant horizon. "It really is," she replied absently. The evening air was cool against her skin, a gentle breeze playing with strands of her hair. She welcomed the tranquility that enveloped them as they swung back and forth.

"Sweetheart," Brenda began, her voice soft and gentle, "I don't mean to pry, but are you happy?"

"Of course, I'm happy," Harper answered involuntarily. "Why do you ask?"

Brenda shrugged and looked out into the distance. "I know how heartbroken you were after the whole situation with Grant." She turned to face her daughter, concern showing on her face. "I just want to make sure you're okay."

Harper tried to fake a smile, but it felt foreign on her face. The truth was that she was still hurting, not only because of what Grant had done but because she had truly loved him once, and she wasn't sure if she'd ever fully recover. "You're right," she admitted. "Grant's betrayal left scars, not just financially but emotionally, but I'm trying to move on."

Brenda acknowledged Harper's words with a quiet nod, her eyes glinting with a mix of admiration and worry. With a sigh, she reached out to tuck a loose strand of Harper's hair behind her ear, the way she had done when Harper was a child.

"I'm glad, darling," she said, her voice shaking slightly. "Just remember it's okay to ask for help if you need it. You don't always have to go it alone."

Harper nodded, swallowing the lump in her throat. "Actually, I've been seeing Dr. Andrews, and he's been helping me navigate this situation. I was skeptical at first, but the work we're doing is making a difference. He even referred me to a lawyer who is helping me sue Grant. Though I have little hope of ever recovering the money he took from me. Despite that, I finally feel like I'm starting to heal."

"That's wonderful. And what about work—are you still burning the candle at both ends?"

"Yeah, but that's nothing new. Plus, it won't last forever—just until this project is completed. And the best part,"—Harper turned to face her mother—"with the money I'll earn, I can finally pay Sidney back and send you and Dad on that trip to Italy you've always dreamed of."

"That's nice, dear." Brenda was quiet before asking, "But do you ever wonder if you take your career too seriously? That if you spent a little less time working and a little more time enjoying the simple pleasures in life, you might be happier?"

Harper's brow furrowed as she considered her mother's words. It wasn't the first time Brenda had voiced her concerns about Harper's single-minded dedication to her work.

"I appreciate your concern, mother," she said with an edge. "But I'm perfectly content doing what I'm doing. Besides, my career is important to me."

"I know, and I'm not trying to downplay the wonderful work you're doing, it's just ... As your mother, I want what's best for you. And whether you want to admit it or not, life is so much better when we have someone to share it with."

Harper sighed, her frustration momentarily overcoming her. "Look, I know you mean well, but you're wrong. I don't need someone else to make me happy. Not only am I a strong, independent woman, but I'm perfectly capable of finding fulfillment on my own."

Brenda reached out and gently squeezed Harper's hand. "I know you're strong, Harper. Strong as steel. And I'm proud of the independent woman you've become. But strength doesn't mean you have to face everything alone. It's okay to let someone in again, to share your life with someone who loves and supports you. Not everyone is like Grant."

Harper looked into her mother's eyes, seeing the genuine love and concern reflected in them. Over the years, they'd had their disagreements, but they were finally in a good spot—a spot where they could have these conversations without Harper losing her cool.

"Maybe you're right," Harper said, taking the high road. "Not that I need someone, mind you, but I do miss having someone to talk to, someone to share my hopes and dreams with. But it can't be just anyone. It needs to be the right one."

"Exactly." Brenda was silent a moment before going on. "What about that pilot you used to be crazy about ... Cameron ... Whatever happened to him?"

Cameron—the one person Harper couldn't quite let go of. The mention of his name brought back memories she had buried deep within her heart. Memories she had tried to forget, to move on from. But now, sitting there on the swing with her mother, they resurfaced like ripples on a pond.

"Honestly, I don't know," Harper said. "He's not a part of my life anymore."

"I'm sorry, sweetheart," Brenda sympathized. "I didn't mean to bring up painful memories."

Harper forced a smile. "It's okay. It's just one more thing I'm learning to live with."

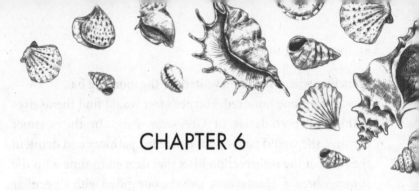

CHAPTER 6

The next morning, Harper woke early and got dressed for her morning walk. Stepping out into the brisk morning air, she inhaled deeply, the cool chill filling her lungs. The neighborhood was still asleep, the sun barely peeking over the horizon. Closing the door behind her, she glimpsed the dew on the grass, glistening in the morning sunlight. It reminded her of all the times she'd ventured out early as a child. Her mother used to scold her for those early morning escapades, worried she might wander off and get lost. But Harper had always relished the tranquility the morning had to offer, more concerned with reaching her destination than any potential risks. And where was she headed on these early morning adventures? Sidney's house, of course.

16 years earlier

It was exactly two hundred steps from Harper Emery's front door to the house at the head of the road, and she had taken the path so many times that she knew each one by heart. Like step ten—marked by a weathered stepping stone, cracked and slightly upturned at one corner. Or step twenty-three, where her yard, a narrow strip of land worn down and rutted from years of use, met a whitewashed gate that welcomed her in and out. At step seventy-two stood the ancient oak tree with its soaring branches, where she often waited for the morning bus.

By step one hundred, Harper's feet would find themselves within the boundaries of Greenway Park. In the warmer months, she would pause on the pebbled pathway and drink in the scent of the resurrection lilies that danced in time with the summer breeze. Her favorite was the one gifted with a peculiar twist, the petals swirling into an odd concoction of nature and art, its blush hues contrasting with the earthy green of its leafy surround. It was named Sidney, after her best friend.

Every day, Harper would whisper a greeting to the lily on route—"Morning, Sid," or "Afternoon, Sid," depending on the time of the day. Even in winter, when frost crystallized the edges of the petals, she would murmur gentle encouragements to the shivering lily.

Ninety-nine steps further, Harper reached the friendly confines of a familiar porch. It was a spot where she and Sidney had sought refuge from the sweltering heat, shared their deepest secrets and dreams under the twinkling stars, and sipped on hot cocoa during the dead of winter. Harper felt as welcome here as she did in her own home.

The last of the two hundred steps always brought Harper to the old wooden door with its peeling blue paint and shiny brass knob. She would rap on it three times, a secret rhythm that only Sidney knew. And then she would wait. On certain days, the wait was short, and Sidney would appear in a flurry of excitement. On others, Harper would stand there for what seemed like an eternity, her fingers tracing over the spots where the paint had peeled. But regardless of how long it took, Sidney appeared without fail. This has been their routine since they became friends at eight years old. Even at fourteen, Harper found herself hoping it would never change.

But lately, changes had begun to creep in. First came Sidney's delayed response to Harper's knock, then followed days when Sidney's mom would answer, only to inform Harper that Sidney was at the mall or at another friend's house. Harper noticed these shifts but dismissed them as temporary aberrations.

Then, a few weeks ago, Harper had stood at Sidney's door and knocked until her knuckles hurt. Only this time, no one answered. She had waited on the porch until twilight painted the sky in shades of dimming hope before finally leaving with a heavy heart.

But today everything seemed to be in its right place as Sidney opened the door and greeted her.

"Oh, hey, Harp," said Sidney, looking surprised to see her. "I was just about to call you. What's up?"

"Nothing much. I just came by to make sure we're still on for tonight ... sleepover at my house, remember?"

"About that." Guilt flickered in Sidney's brown eyes. "Do you mind if we postpone it?"

Harper's heart sank at Sidney's request. The Friday night ritual had been their constant for years, a special time they set aside just for each other. But ever since high school started, everything had begun to change. And now, Sidney was asking to temporarily put it on pause. Sensing this was only the beginning of many more missed sleepovers, the words rang out like a siren in Harper's head. She felt like she was standing on shaky ground, unsure of what to say or do. After all, Sidney was her only real friend. She'd tried to make others in the past, but her introverted nature always left her on the outskirts, observing rather than participating. Sidney was different. Despite her outgoing personality, she shared Harper's love for the quiet, the odd, and the in-between moments. Their friendship wasn't flashy or even particularly exciting, but it was safe. And Harper cherished that safety.

"What do you mean—postpone?" Harper asked, trying to keep her voice steady.

"I promise it won't happen again," said Sidney. "It's just that I was sorta invited to a party tonight at Macy's, and I already said I'd go. But maybe I could stay over tomorrow night," she said, offering a compromise.

Harper took a step back, the sting of betrayal and hurt sinking in. All those Fridays spent with Sidney, just the two of them, sharing stories and laughs, promising each other that they'd be best friends forever, seemed insignificant now. "I see," she said, bracing herself for the disappointment and loneliness that would come with a Friday night alone. "If that's what you want." Harper forced a smile that didn't quite reach her eyes.

Sidney seemed relieved, a faint blush spreading on her cheeks. "Cool. I knew you'd understand. So, I'll see you tomorrow night?"

"Yeah," said Harper as she backed off the porch. "See ya."

She made her way back to her house, her hand tightly gripping the infinity symbol pendant hanging from her neck. Sidney had given it to her when they were eleven, a symbol of their unbreakable friendship. Now, as she felt the cool metal against her skin, Harper had to question just how unbreakable that friendship really was.

That night, Harper cried more than she had in a long time, her sobs muffled by the worn cotton of her pillow. Her thoughts churned, battered by the fierce waves of hurt and disappointment, as she tried to reconcile with this new reality. Sidney was growing, changing, and pulling away from her.

Harper clutched her chest, feeling the dull throb of loneliness pound against her ribcage. She had always known they would eventually grow up, but she had also naively believed that nothing, not even the inexorable march of time, would alter their Friday night ritual. This was their sacred time, an unbreakable bond forged between childhood friends and strengthened through adolescence. It was as essential to her as air and now it felt as if she was gasping for breath.

Harper woke the next morning, her eyes red and swollen. She dragged herself out of bed, her limbs heavy with exhaustion. Her reflection in the mirror was a reminder of last night's anguish and the cruel reality of what lay ahead. For as long as she could remember, Sidney had been her guiding light, her support system in the tumultuous journey of life. And now Harper was all alone, drowning in the frigid reality of her existence.

"Morning." Harper's mother, Brenda, greeted her, looking up from where she sat at the kitchen table, a cup of coffee in her hands. Her brown eyes narrowed, taking in Harper's pathetic state. "Rough night?"

Harper nodded, avoiding her mother's too-perceptive gaze. She slumped down onto the chair opposite Brenda and stared at the plate of bacon and eggs. The mere thought of food churned her stomach.

"What happened with Sidney last night? I've never known you girls to miss a sleepover. Did she get that stomach bug that's been going around?"

"She was ... busy," Harper replied, still trying to make sense of the situation.

"Busy?" Brenda offered a sympathetic smile. "Do you want to talk about it?"

"Talk about what?" Harper replied defensively.

"About whatever happened between you two."

"I told you already, she was busy!"

Brenda flinched at her daughter's outburst, raising her hands peacefully. "Okay, sweetie. I was just asking."

Harper instantly felt a pang of guilt. It wasn't her mother's fault that Sidney had decided to ditch their Friday night sleepovers for ... for whatever it was she was doing now. "Sorry," Harper muttered. "It's just ... yesterday, everything was normal, and now ..." She dropped her head. "Everything feels different."

"Different, how?"

"Just ... different," Harper said, searching for the right words. She couldn't shake the feeling of unfamiliarity that had started to permeate her relationship with Sidney. It was as if the Sidney she had come to know—the one who preferred sweatpants to skirts, who would rather spend Friday nights with her best friend than be seen at a party—was slowly being replaced by a stranger.

"Listen, if it makes you feel any better, the same thing happened to Beth and me when we started high school," said Brenda.

"You mean Beth Ridenour—the lady you only talk to when you run into each other at the grocery store?"

Brenda winced but nodded. "Yes, that's the one. Believe it or not, we were once as inseparable as you and Sidney. But," she sighed, "eventually, we grew apart."

Harper frowned, toying with the mug of hot chocolate she had yet to touch. "But what if I don't want Sidney and I to end up like you and Beth? What if I want us to stay best friends forever, just like we promised?"

Brenda sighed, scooting closer to Harper. "Look, I know

you want things to stay the same, but change is inevitable, sweetheart. Sometimes, people, even best friends, just … grow apart."

Harper remained silent, her thoughts stirring like a hornet's nest.

Brenda, appearing to sense her daughter's turmoil, softened the blow. "Look, I'm not saying this is the end of your friendship with Sidney. Just give her some time to figure things out, that's all. You're both changing, growing into the people you will become. It's a scary time, but it can also be exciting."

Harper didn't want it to be exciting. She wanted it to be familiar, comfortable, predictable, the way it had always been. But she also knew her mother was right. Whether she liked it or not, change was inevitable.

***

The next evening, Harper sat in her upstairs loft, engrossed in her drawings. For hours, she'd been sketching ideas for pieces of clothing that she hoped would someday turn the fashion world on its head.

"Harp! Hey, Harp—you home!?" The sound of Sidney's voice echoed all the way upstairs.

Harper glanced briefly at the clock on her wall, a smile playing at the corners of her lips. Sidney had delivered on her promise. She quickly descended the stairs, two at a time, and opened the door. Just as she imagined, there stood Sidney, hair tousled from the wind, rosy cheeks glowing underneath the porch light.

"Did you get lost?" Harper teased, a hint of relief in her voice.

Sidney rolled her eyes and mimed an overly dramatic shiver. "It's freezing out here! Are you going to let me in or what?"

With a soft chuckle, Harper stepped aside, allowing Sidney to enter. The warmth inside the house seemed to embrace Sidney; Harper could see her muscles relax almost immediately upon crossing the threshold.

She watched as Sidney kicked off her boots and shrugged off her coat, revealing a sweater that Harper herself had knitted for her last birthday. It was a cozy piece woven in various shades of brown to match the color of Sidney's eyes. Harper took it as Sidney's way of apologizing for breaking their routine.

Once they were settled in with sodas and snacks, the girls talked late into the night. They discussed school, Sidney complaining about math, and Harper venting about her art teacher's inexplicable aversion to modern styles. They talked about family, fashion and even touched upon their current crushes, causing an outbreak of giggles that earned them a mild reprimand from Brenda downstairs.

As the night deepened, their conversation turned quieter, more serious. They spoke of dreams and aspirations, fears and failures. Outside, the wind howled, bringing with it a chill in the air that pervaded the drafty old house.

"Listen," said Sidney, "I'm sorry about last night ... for changing plans on you at the last minute."

"Don't worry about it," Harper replied, shrugging her thin shoulders. "Besides, it gave me a chance to finish a few sketches—something I've been putting off." Harper nodded toward the wall, where several new pieces were proudly displayed. Harper watched Sidney's face as her eyes darted from one sketch to the other, a flicker of amazement passing through them.

"You really are talented, Harper," she said, admiring them. "Don't let anyone ever tell you otherwise, you hear?"

Harper looked down at her hands, trying to conceal the satisfaction that crept over her face. "Thanks. So, how was the party? Since I wasn't invited, I'll have to live vicariously through you," Harper said, only half-joking.

Sidney sighed, still transfixed on Harper's sketches. "It was all right," she said at last. "Typical high school party, you know? Loud music, too many people, too much alcohol ..." She paused then, turning her brown eyes back to Harper. "The only reason I went was because Macy told me that Bradley Stevens wanted to talk to me."

"Bradley Stevens?" Harper asked, her eyebrows lifting in surprise. "You've had a crush on him since middle school."

Sidney nodded in agreement, curling her legs under her as she settled deeper into the sofa. She tasted her Coke and then started to twirl a lock of her hair nervously. "I never thought he even knew I existed until Macy mentioned it at lunch."

Sidney had always been open about her attractions. Harper, on the other hand, preferred to maintain a veneer of indifference. It was one of the lessons her mother had ingrained in her: never let anyone see your weaknesses.

"But," Sidney continued, averting her eyes. "It turns out he's more into Macy than me."

"Macy? But she's ..." Harper trailed off as she struggled to find an appropriate descriptor that wouldn't offend Sidney. Macy was a notorious flirt, at least in their circle, known for her ability to easily ensnare the boys with her vivacious charm and promises of advancing beyond first base.

"Yeah, I know," Sidney cut in, her voice bleak. Harper noticed a hint of vulnerability creeping into her friend's tone for the first time. "He barely even spoke to me."

"I'm sorry, Sid," Harper said softly, her amusement slowly ebbing away.

Sidney merely shrugged, her last traces of a good mood dissipating. She picked at the label on her Coke bottle, her eyes distant. "I thought things would be different this year," she murmured. "I thought ..."

Harper reached out, placing a comforting hand on Sidney's knee. "Hey, you're worth more than Bradley Stevens or Macy Reynolds or anyone else at that dumb old party."

The corner of Sidney's mouth quirked up in a smile. "You really think so?"

"I know so," Harper assured her, her voice steady and firm. She gave Sidney's knee a reassuring squeeze, hoping to drive the point home.

"You're right," Sidney admitted. She drew in a shaky breath and then let it out. "I just ... I guess I hoped he'd be different."

That was what it always came down to, wasn't it? Hope. Harper knew that feeling all too well. The endless cycle of hope and disappointment, building up and crashing down. She thought back to the time she'd got up the nerve to call the most popular kid in school and ask him to the movies or the time she'd auditioned for the lead role in her middle school's production of "Romeo and Juliet". Each time, it ended in rejection. Each time, she had picked herself up, dusted herself off, and tried again. Hope shimmered like a mirage—always present, always just out of reach.

It was a cruel game of the heart, one that everyone seemed forced to play at some point. And it seemed that Sidney, despite her usual confidence, was not immune to its bittersweet pull.

They sat in silence for a while, the only sound the soft

crackling of the radio stuck between two stations. The room was dim, lit only by the lamp on the nightstand and the faint glow of the streetlight seeping through the thin curtains. Sidney's face was painted in soft contrasts, her high cheekbones catching the light while shadows pooled under her eyes.

"What about you?" Sidney suddenly asked, breaking the silence. She turned to face Harper. "When are you going to start looking for a guy?"

Almost instantly, heat flooded Harper's face. "Me?" Harper stammered, taken aback by the sudden change of topic. The corners of her eyes crinkled as she uncomfortably shifted under the penetrating gaze of her friend. "I ... I don't know. Boys are the last thing on my mind."

Sidney smirked, a knowing glint in her eyes as she leaned back into the worn-out cushions of the couch. "Is that so?" she challenged, her eyebrows rising slightly in a teasing gesture.

"Yes," Harper insisted, crossing her arms defensively over her chest, hoping to conceal her lie. "I have enough on my plate without throwing boys into the mix."

Sidney's smirk grew into a full-blown smile, playful and mischievous. "You just wait. One of these days, a guy will come along and make you forget all about your books and sketches."

Harper rolled her eyes, a wry smile tugging at the corners of her lips. "We'll see about that." Despite the awkwardness earlier, Harper felt relieved seeing this brighter side of Sidney again.

The night wore on, but neither girl noticed the passing hours as they delved deeper into stories and confessions, some shared for the first time. They laughed, they cried, they argued—they lived.

As the minutes ticked away, Sidney sank deeper into the

cushions of the worn-out couch, while Harper reclined against the pile of pillows on her bed.

"Is something on your mind?" Sidney asked as the clock struck three.

"I was just thinking about ... never mind," Harper said, dismissing her concerns with a wave of her hand.

"Are you sure?"

"It's fine, really," Harper insisted, her motion becoming more animated with her discomfort.

Sidney set her coke on the nightstand. "It's clearly not fine, Harp," she said. "You've been acting weird lately. Is this about the party again?"

Harper shook her head, avoiding Sidney's probing gaze. "It's not just the party." She picked at the frayed edge of the duvet cover, a nervous tick she'd had since childhood.

Sidney leaned back against the couch, crossing her arms over her chest. Her lips pressed into a thin line as she studied Harper's profile. "Then what is it?" she asked, her voice softer now, concern lacing her words.

Harper looked up, summoning the courage to broach the subject that had been on her mind since the previous evening. "I was just thinking about something Mom said to me this morning—that you and I are growing apart."

Sidney stilled, her playful eyes clouding over, the light of the couch-side lamp dimming slightly in their reflective surfaces. Silence hung heavy in the air like woven drapery. Harper watched as the corners of Sidney's mouth fell and her eyebrows furrowed, the usually vibrant features on her face twisting with an unfamiliar seriousness.

"You think we're growing apart?" Sidney questioned.

"Not me," said Harper. "I mean, I hope not. I told her that

we'd never grow apart, that we'd always be best friends, but ..." The words lodged in her throat, refusing to come out. "It's just ... lately, it seems like you're trying to be someone else, someone I don't recognize. I don't know if it's just my imagination or if it's because of your new group of friends, but ... you seem different. You've changed."

Sidney was quiet, her mind seemingly wracked with thoughts. The typical vibrancy she radiated seemed to have been replaced with an unsettling stillness. "You've always been so good at reading people," she finally said. "And you're right, things feel different now. But that's normal, isn't it? I mean, we're not kids anymore."

Harper nodded, her eyes focused on the worn rug beneath her feet. "Sure." She pulled her knees up to her chest, looping her arms around them. "I know things change, people grow up, but I just don't want to lose you, Sid. You're my best friend ... my only friend, and I can't imagine my life without you."

Sidney moved to the edge of the bed and wrapped an arm around Harper's shoulders. "You're not going to lose me, Harp," she affirmed, a soft determination lingering in her voice. "We're like ... like peanut butter and jelly. Different, but better together."

Sidney's words hung in the air, a fresh lifeline thrown to Harper in a sea of worries. Harper leaned into Sidney, resting her head against her friend's shoulder, silent tears dampening the fabric of Sidney's shirt.

"Hey, none of that," Sidney said gently. She brushed away a stray tear from Harper's cheek with her thumb before patting the spot lightly as if sealing a promise.

"But what if we end up ..." Harper's voice wavered as she tried to voice her fears.

"We won't," Sidney cut her off firmly, a resolute look on her face. "This isn't some cheesy young adult novel where best friends turn into enemies." After a pause, she added more softly, "We grow, Harp. We change. But that doesn't mean we grow apart. Not us. Not ever."

Sidney's reassuring words echoed in the small room, bouncing off the walls and seeping into Harper's consciousness.

"Really?"

"Cross my heart and hope to die."

Peering into Sidney's eyes, Harper finally felt her heart unclench. She let out a shaky breath she didn't realize she had been holding. "Thank you, Sid," she managed to mumble around the lump in her throat.

Sidney gave her hand a squeeze before letting go to wrap both arms around her friend in a comforting embrace, "Anytime, Harp. Anytime."

***

Sidney finally fell asleep sometime after six, sprawled out on the couch with a half-eaten bag of potato chips still clutched in her hand. Harper watched as her friend's chest rose and fell rhythmically with each breath, a gentle snore escaping from her slightly parted lips. She carefully took the chip bag from Sidney's hand and set it aside, then draped a blanket over her, tucking it gently around her.

Harper glanced at the clock on the wall, its hands nearing seven in the morning. Her eyelids were heavy, but she found herself unable to sleep. Tonight had been a roller coaster that left her feeling drained yet somehow more connected to Sidney than ever before. Her mother's words rang true—they had both changed, yet their connection remained strong and unbreakable.

With a sigh, Harper pushed herself up from the couch and walked over to the window. Pulling back the curtain slightly, she peered out as the first light of dawn appeared on the horizon. The night had passed in a blur, leaving behind the remnants of confessions and dreams. They were no longer just two eight-year-olds sharing an innocent friendship; they were now young women, standing on the precipice of adulthood.

Present day

Harper's daydream was interrupted by the cheerful melody of a nearby cardinal. She paused in front of Sidney's old house, taking in the fading paint and the overgrown garden. It had been years since she'd been there, but the sight of it brought back a flood of memories. Suddenly, the door opened, and an elderly woman appeared, squinting at Harper. She smiled and waved, beckoning Harper to come closer.

"I'm sorry for staring," said Harper, stopping at the edge of the yard. "My best friend used to live in this house."

The woman's smile softened, her eyes carrying a glint of understanding. "The Westwoods, am I right?"

Harper nodded, feeling a strange sense of relief wash over her. It was as if she was no longer alone in her memories. "But I was young then." Harper shook her head slightly, her gaze drifting up to the attic, where Sidney's room used to be. "Sidney and I ... We had so many adventures in this old place."

The elderly woman chuckled, pulling her cardigan closer around her shoulders. "I can only imagine. You know, my husband Carl and I were the first owners of this house. He built it with his own two hands, just after we got married. Must have been about 1963."

"Really?"

The woman nodded, a hint of nostalgia in her eyes. "We lived here for thirty-two years. But when Carl got sick, we had to sell. So when I saw it come back on the market last year, I couldn't resist buying it again."

"Wasn't that difficult?" Harper asked.

"It was," she admitted. "But you see, dear," she added, "this house holds more than just memories for me, it holds a piece of my soul."

Harper could relate. She fell into silence, her gaze wandering back to the attic window as if she were waiting for it to whisper stories of years past.

"Well, I should probably be going," Harper said, backing away. "I've taken up enough of your time already. But thank you for talking with me. This has meant more to me than you might realize."

"My pleasure. And you're welcome here anytime."

Harper walked home, retracing her steps. At step one-fifty, she crested the hill, her childhood home coming into view. It was awash in golden sunlight, its whitewashed facade glowing like a beacon. As she approached, the details sharpened. The paint chips in the windowsills, the crooked chimney, the long-neglected rose bushes. It was just as she remembered, yet different at the same time. Time had left its mark on her house, just as it had on her.

She moved closer, her shoes crunching on the gravel as she did. The small gaps in the fence, where she and Sidney would spy on the world, were closed by new fencing. Looking down, she noticed a crack in the pathway, the same one she had tripped over countless times before. Pausing at the porch, she glanced up at her old bedroom window. Memories flooded her mind of all those hours she and Sidney had spent gazing out at the world, dreaming about their future.

CHAPTER 7

"Hey boss, how are those final touches coming along?" Tiffany asked, poking her head into Harper's office one bright June afternoon.

"Almost done," Harper replied, eyes fixed on her sketchbook.

"Great! We'll be waiting for you in the war room when you're ready."

Harper took a deep breath, her focus solidifying as she added the finishing touches to her designs. When she was done, she allowed herself a brief moment of pride, marveling at the work she had accomplished. Before her were three designs, each one a testament to her creativity and painstaking attention to detail. The first was a classic black suit with sharp lines and a sleek silhouette. It exuded a sense of authority and power, of long-lasting tradition, of the confidence to stand tall under scrutiny. The second was a softer ensemble made of flowing white fabric that danced with light and shadow to form an almost ethereal vision, its elegance subtle but undeniable. The third was the most daring. The modern take on the "little black dress" was crimson with intricate patterns and daring cuts. It screamed of passion and defiance, of the audacity to challenge norms and chart one's own path. All three spoke to the modern woman, each one capturing a different facet of her complex persona.

"Harper Emery, you've done it again," she whispered to

herself, standing up from her desk and clutching her sketches close to her chest.

When she entered the war room, everyone looked up from their conversations, their eyes immediately drawn to her commanding presence.

"All right, everyone," she announced, her voice steady and confident. "The final designs are complete, so let's dive right in."

Everyone examined the sketches spread out across the table with a critical eye, but it was Tiffany who spoke up first.

"Harper, you've outdone yourself. Your signature style of balancing function with aesthetics is simply remarkable. And the way you've captured the modern woman's strength and elegance with elements of boldness, it's quintessentially Chanel."

"Thank you, Tiffany," Harper replied, beaming with pride. "But I can't take all the credit. Each and every one of you has your fingerprints all over this project. If you remember, when we started this endeavor, the idea was to capture the essence of Chanel while also incorporating some fresh, modern elements. As you can see"—she gestured to the sketches—"I believe we've done that."

"No doubt," Marco chimed in. "This is, by far, the best work this team has done."

"Let's just hope Eleanor is equally pleased," said Harper. "I'm meeting with her and her team tomorrow morning to get their final feedback before we move on to production."

"In that case," said Marco with a wink and a smile, "knock 'em dead."

***

"Harper, you're early." Eleanor greeted her in the downstairs lobby.

"Yes ma'am. As my dad always says, if you're not ten minutes early, you're five minutes late."

Eleanor smiled warmly. "I'm glad to see that you still live by that motto. Nowadays, most people don't know the value of being punctual." She paused, then added, "I was just about to grab a coffee. Care to join me?"

They grabbed a coffee from Starbucks, then rode the elevator to the top floor. Several of Eleanor's design team were already seated in the conference room, thumbing through the latest fashion magazines when they walked in.

"Good morning, everyone," Eleanor said as she took her seat at the head of the table. "We have with us this morning Harper Emery, a former colleague, dear friend, and CEO of Infinity Designs. As you know, several months ago, I selected her firm to collaborate with us on our new fall line, and after several rounds of back and forth, I'm pleased to say she is here today to present the final renderings. So, without further ado, I give you Harper Emery."

"Thank you, Mrs. Le Roux," said Harper with a smile. She looked to Eleanor's team, who eagerly awaited her proposal. "It is a pleasure to be here today presenting to you all. As Eleanor so graciously stated, my team and I were chosen to develop a fall line that embodies the elegance and grace of Chanel, while modernizing the look for a more youthful buyer. We believe these capture the essence of what you're looking for," she said, revealing her initial sketches, one by one. "By incorporating elements of classic elegance with modern sensibilities, we can create a bold and unique collection that appeals to both new and loyal customers."

Eleanor and her lead designer, Emilio, leaned in, seemingly captivated by Harper's vision and expertise.

"Harper, your designs are simply stunning," Eleanor gushed. "I particularly love the fresh take on the iconic tweed jacket."

"Thank you," Harper replied, a hint of pride coloring her voice. "That's one of my favorites as well. My team has worked tirelessly to ensure that the collection stays true to the brand's essence while pushing creative boundaries."

"I agree," said Emilio, "that your designs have certainly hit the mark. However, I cannot in good conscience ignore the financial liability that your company brings to the table."

His words hit Harper hard. Taking a deep breath and composing herself, she replied, "It's true. As you are all aware, my company has taken a major hit ... but I'm happy to say we are recovering."

"Recovering?" Francine Julian, Eleanor's most trusted advisor, chimed in next. Her tone was skeptical, her accent clipped and precise. "And what assurances do we have that your company won't go under and drag us with it?"

Harper stood tall, her eyes filled with determination. "Mrs. Julian, every business faces its ups and downs," Harper began, her voice steady despite the knots in her stomach. "While it's true that my company has suffered a setback, I believe it is in these moments that our true character and resilience are revealed." She paused, surveying the room to gauge the reactions of her audience. "In fact, it is this recent challenge that has inspired my latest designs." Flipping the page, she unveiled the centerpiece of her proposal, a flowing gown showcasing bold lines, innovative patterns, and unconventional materials, all bearing the signature marks of a Harper Emery design, while maintaining the Chanel brand identity.

"And what do these designs symbolize, Ms. Emery?" a younger woman at the far end of the table asked.

"They symbolize rebirth, resilience, and a bright future," Harper replied, her fingers tracing the edges of her designs. "They represent the journey my company has been through—that I've been through—from the pinnacle of success to the pit of despair, and now our slow but steady climb back to the top."

The room was quiet. Everyone seemed to be considering Harper's words, her confidence apparently piercing through their doubts.

Francine leaned closer, her eyes scanning the designs. After a moment, she leaned back in her chair and removed her glasses. "You've certainly evolved, Harper," she said, her tone softening ever so slightly. "These designs do have a certain *je ne sais quoi* about them."

Her statement echoed through the room, transforming the tense atmosphere into a curious anticipation. Harper's heart pounded in her chest as she watched each face soften, their eyes flicking over the designs with newfound interest.

"Thank you, Francine," Harper responded earnestly, allowing a sliver of relief to seep through her composure. She took a moment to look directly into the eyes of each of the panel, her gaze steady and resolute. "I assure you that this evolution is not a mere response to adversity, but a testament to our ability to rise above it. My company is more than capable of weathering this storm. We will not only endure, but we will prevail. The only question is, do you want to join us on this journey?"

And with that, Harper concluded her presentation. She closed the portfolio, subtly drawing attention back to herself rather than the designs. The room fell silent once again. Everyone seemed to be absorbing Harper's words, her conviction leaving no room for doubt. After thanking everyone for their time, she left the room and stepped out into the hallway. Taking a deep breath, she allowed herself to lean against the cold marble wall for support. Her knees, hidden underneath the fabric of her designer skirt, were trembling slightly, but she held her head up high. While she caught her breath, she could hear the murmuring from behind the closed door of the conference room. Somehow, this uncertainty seemed worse than an outright rejection. At least then she'd know where she stood.

Just as Harper was about to continue her way down the hallway, the boardroom doors opened. Eleanor stepped out, her stern expression betraying no hint of the outcome. Their eyes locked, and Harper felt a chill run down her spine.

"I won't keep you in suspense, Harper," Eleanor began, her voice icy cool. "The panel has decided ..."

Harper held her breath, her heart pounding louder than ever before. Her mind was a whirlpool of anticipation, fear, and hope, all coming together in an emotional maelstrom.

"... to approve your final designs," Eleanor finally said.

Harper exhaled the breath she didn't know she was holding. A surge of relief washed over her. She tried to maintain her composure, but a smile began to tug at the corner of her lips. She had done it. She had won them over.

"That's ... that's wonderful," Harper stammered.

"This group isn't easily impressed," said Eleanor. "I think I speak for everyone, including Francine, when I say you knocked it out of the park today. I had no idea just how commanding you could be in the boardroom. I've seen plenty of highly talented designers wilt under the pressure."

"Thank you, but it hasn't come easy. In fact, it's taken years for me to feel comfortable in front of crowds, even small ones. When I was younger, I was always the shyest person in the room. I spent most of my formative years in school with my head down, trying not to make eye contact. My greatest fear was being called on by the teacher during class."

Eleanor raised an eyebrow in surprise. "But not anymore. And bravo! It takes a lot of courage to face your fears, and even more to face a room full of critics." She helped Harper gather her things and walked her to the elevator. "So how are the preparations for Sidney's wedding going? The last time we spoke, you mentioned that you were a little overwhelmed."

Harper reached up and brushed a strand of hair away from her face. "Better, now," she said, relieved that the presentation was behind her. "Fortunately, Sidney is more than capable of handling most of the planning on her own. But now that the design phase of this project is behind me, I can focus more of my attention on the wedding and making sure she has a day she'll never forget."

"I hope so, too," said Eleanor. "I know how important this event is to you. But if something should come up, you'll need to make yourself available."

"Understood," said Harper. "And in case anything does come up, I'll have my phone and laptop with me, so please don't hesitate to reach out."

When the elevator doors opened, Eleanor hugged Harper and thanked her again for her time. "In case I don't get to talk to you again before you leave, have a great trip. It isn't every day that we get to be maid of honor in our best friend's wedding."

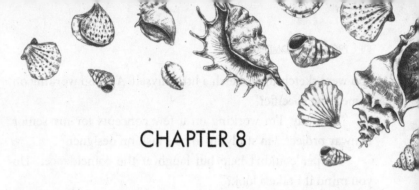

CHAPTER 8

A few days later, Harper stood on the Balcony Bridge in Central Park, basking in the warmth of the afternoon sunlight. Gazing out at the calm lake, she watched as groups of ducks congregated near the far shore, their feathers gleaming under the golden rays.

For the first time since the project began, Harper felt a sense of peace. The last few months had been a chaotic blend of long days and sleepless nights, but now, all of that felt like a distant memory. Here, in the heart of the city, in perhaps the last place she would have expected to find it, Harper found serenity.

She tossed a few breadcrumbs into the pond before slipping off her shoes and wandering barefoot through the grass. The cool blades brought back fond memories of her childhood—cool summer evenings when she and Sidney would wander through the park or venture down to the creek and catch tadpoles and crawdads.

As she reached the far end of the lawn, she noticed a young woman sitting cross-legged on a bench, sketching in a notebook. She looked to be in her early twenties, with long dark hair and porcelain skin. Harper was taken aback by how much the girl resembled her at that age.

Putting on her shoes, Harper approached the young lady, who looked up at her and smiled. "Can I help you?"

"I'm sorry. I didn't mean to startle you; it's just ... I noticed you were sketching. I sketch a little myself. Are you working on something specific?"

"Actually, I'm working on a few concepts for my senior runway project. I'm studying to be a fashion designer."

Harper couldn't help but laugh at the coincidence. "Do you mind if I take a look?"

Without hesitation, she handed over her sketchbook to Harper.

"These are really good," Harper commented as she flipped through the pages. "Very impressive."

"Thank you"

"Where are you studying, if you don't mind me asking.?"

"Not at all. I'm in my final year at Parsons. Have you heard of it?"

"Yes. I went there myself—ages ago."

The young lady's eyes widened with surprise. "So you're in fashion, too?"

"Yes, I am," Harper replied as she handed back the sketchbook.

"What are the odds? Please, join me." The young lady patted the spot on the bench beside her. "I'm Megan, by the way."

"Harper." She shook her outstretched hand and sat down on the bench beside Megan. "So how are things at Parsons these days?"

Megan shrugged a shoulder. "Good, I guess. Except ..." She paused as a frown creased her forehead. "I've got this one instructor, Mr. Gerardo. He's always on my case about something."

Harper felt a smile tug at the corners of her mouth. "Yeah, I remember him. He was just as tough when I was there. But trust me, he only does it because he wants to get the best out of you."

Megan sighed, fingers tracing the edge of her sketchbook. "That's what everyone keeps telling me. It's just ... sometimes it makes me feel like I'm not good enough ... like I don't belong."

Harper studied Megan, taking in the lines of self-doubt carving faint shadows underneath her bright eyes. She was reminded of her own youthful insecurities, of her own time at Parsons when she thought the world was against her.

"Listen, Megan," Harper began, her voice soft yet resolute. "I know we just met, but I can tell just by looking at your sketches that you have talent. More than that, you have something that no teacher can give but all the good ones recognize—the passion. It's evident in every line and curve of your drawings."

Megan looked up at Harper and smiled. "You really think so?"

"Absolutely. But remember, talent and passion are just the start. It takes persistence, hard work, and the ability to take criticism and learn from it to make it in this industry. And there is no shortage of people out there waiting to take away your dreams." She stopped for a second, allowing her words to sink in. "So, have you thought about what you'll do after graduation?"

Megan let out a heavy sigh. "I've been interviewing all over the city, trying to secure an internship for the summer so I can get my foot in the door somewhere. But so far, I haven't had any luck. I think it's because of my accent. I'm a long way from home, if you couldn't tell, and no one seems to want to give me much of a chance."

Harper nodded, understanding the struggle of being an outsider. "Maybe it's that," said Harper. "Or maybe it's just that the right opportunity hasn't come along yet."

Megan shrugged. "I hope you're right. If not, I'll have to move back home and work at the mall selling jumpers and skinny jeans."

"Well, we can't have that, can we?" Harper mused. And then it struck her. "Hey, I have an idea. You could always intern for me. One of my junior designers is leaving for Europe next spring, so I'll have an opening. It's not Gucci or Donna Karan, but I learned from the very best, and I can teach you everything you need to know about this business."

"Really? You'd do that for me?"

"Sure. Believe it or not, I too was an outsider once. But someone gave me a chance, and I'd like to do the same for you."

The smile that bloomed on Megan's face was like a sunrise spreading over the horizon. "Thank you. I can't even begin to tell you how much this means to me."

Harper chuckled lightly, "No thanks needed. Just promise me you'll continue to work hard and never stop believing in yourself."

Megan nodded vigorously, her eyes full of hope. "You have my word."

"In that case,"—Harper glanced at her watch—"I should get going. I have a meeting to get to." Before she left, Harper handed Megan a business card. "I'll be out of town for a wedding in early July, but why don't you give me a call before then and we can set up a time for you to come in and meet the team."

"Yes, I will," said Megan. "And thanks again. I won't let you down."

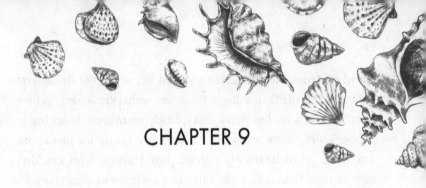

CHAPTER 9

After much discussion, it was decided that the bachelorette party would take place the last weekend in June in New York City, a convenient location for both Sidney and Harper. Despite the hesitation of their small-town friends, they found themselves immersed in the bustling city, surrounded by the towering skyscrapers of Manhattan and flashing billboards of Times Square. They spent the afternoon in Greenwich Village, an area teeming with life and culture. Each street offered a new experience, with everything from vintage boutiques to exotic food markets. As dusk fell, the city transformed into a labyrinth of narrow crowd-filled streets and twinkling lights.

After an exhausting day of shopping and sightseeing, they found themselves in a chic bar, cocktails in hand. The bar itself was a blend of old and new, wood and steel, with exposed brick walls adorned with modern art. The soft jazz music playing in the background added an air of sophistication and gave the bar an intimate atmosphere.

Harper sipped her cocktail, a blend of gin, tonic, and bitters with a dash of grapefruit. The citrusy tang played around on her tongue, leaving her feeling both refreshed and delightfully tipsy. Sidney was nursing a Manhattan, her eyes shining brightly as she swirled the ice around her glass, while Chelsea and Amber both opted for classic Cosmopolitans.

As the night wore on, the girls became increasingly carefree and uninhibited. Amber, the boldest amongst them, suddenly stood up from the table, straightened her sequined dress, and declared, "I think it's high time for some karaoke!" Sidney nearly choked on her drink but quickly recovered, laughing at Amber's audacious proposal. Chelsea, always up for just about anything, wholeheartedly agreed. But Harper, who couldn't carry a tune to save her life, raised an eyebrow in uncertainty.

"Karaoke?" she repeated, the word itself enough to make her cringe a little. "You go ahead. I'm fine where I'm at."

Sidney simply waived her worries away with a casual flick of her wrist and a mischievous grin. "Nonsense. If I'm going to make a fool of myself, so are you."

Harper found herself reluctantly pulled from the safety of her chair and, clutching her cocktail like a lifeline, trailed after her daring companions. As they made their way to the stage, they drew eyes and applause from the other patrons. For a moment, they stood there, basking in the attention and taking in the excited faces that looked up at them. Amber, with a wink and a quick toss of her hair, grabbed the microphone first. The opening notes of "I Will Survive" filled the bar, and Amber began belting out the lyrics with a fierceness only she could manage. Sidney, Chelsea, and even Harper ended up joining in on the chorus, their voices rising and blending together in a harmony that was more laughter than melody. Their shared enthusiasm was infectious, and it wasn't long before the audience joined in.

When the song ended, the girls were met with a round of applause that echoed throughout the bar. Red-faced and breathless, they bowed amidst cheers and whistles. Even Harper found herself laughing, her apprehensions now a distant memory.

A little after two, the bar started to thin out, the high of the night slowly winding down. Gleeful but winded from the night's exploits, Amber suggested they return to the hotel, so they hailed a cab and retreated into the night, arms linked, and heads tilted back in laughter.

Amber and Chelsea excused themselves after a few more drinks in the lobby bar and retired to their respective rooms, leaving Harper and Sidney alone on the cushioned bar stools with their gin and tonics.

"I've been thinking ... about what you said," slurred Harper as she sipped from her highball glass. "That I should contact Cameron."

Sidney shifted on her bar stool, turning her body toward Harper. A hint of weariness clung to her, but her eyes were wide awake, focused solely on Harper. "And?" she prompted, sipping her own drink.

"I think I will," Harper admitted, a weight simultaneously lifting from and settling onto her chest. "But I don't know how to start. What if he doesn't want to talk? What if ..." Her voice trailed off as she stared at her dwindling drink.

Sidney reached over and offered a comforting squeeze on Harper's hand. "You'll never know unless you try," Sidney said softly. "Besides, fear of the unknown is worse than confronting it, Harper. Trust me."

Harper chewed at her lower lip, a habit of hers when she was deep in thought. With a sigh, she nodded slowly. "You're right. Oh," she said, suddenly remembering. Harper reached into her purse and produced a small envelope, a neat Sidney written in her clear handwriting.

"What's this?"

"The money I owe you," said Harper. "Plus interest. I didn't want to give it to you in front of the girls."

Sidney blinked in surprise before looking at Harper with a

warm smile. "You didn't need to do this so soon, you know. You could have waited."

But Harper was insistent. "I always pay my debts," she replied, finishing her drink. "And I never want there to be anything between us, including money, that could complicate our friendship."

Sidney nodded and graciously accepted the envelope. "Thank you, Harper," she said, tucking it into her purse. "But like I told you countless times before, there's nothing that could ever come between us. Not even money."

CHAPTER 10

"I'm glad you decided to see me before you went on your trip," said Dr. Andrews the following week. "We're at a pivotal moment in your healing journey, and I don't want to undo the work we've done."

Harper drew a deep breath and then released it slowly, her shoulders drooping. "I've been thinking a lot about what you said last time, about not letting my past define me. But it's difficult," she began, twirling a strand of hair around her finger. "I feel as if I'm standing at the edge of an abyss, one filled with my past mistakes and regrets. Every time I take a step forward, the abyss grows deeper and darker, threatening to consume me."

Dr. Andrews studied her. "That feeling of being on the edge is very real," he conceded, folding his hands over his notepad. "And I know how frightening it can be to look down into that abyss. But remember, you're not alone in this journey. You have me, and Sidney."

Harper smiled weakly, grateful for the reassurance but still weighed down by her fears. "Now that I'm back on track professionally, I want to move forward in my personal life," she said after a while. "I don't want to be trapped in my past anymore."

"That's a big step," Dr. Andrews praised gently, jotting something down in his notepad. "Which tells me we're making progress. But this trip has me worried." He took off his glasses and set them on the desk. "You're returning to the place where you and Cameron fell in love, surrounded by so many memories ... That can be a lot for anyone, but especially for someone who is healing."

Harper regarded him thoughtfully, biting the inside of her cheek as she considered his words. "I have been dreading it, to be honest," she admitted. "I know there will be a lot of reminders, but I can't avoid my past forever, can I?"

"No," Dr. Andrews agreed, sliding his glasses back on. "You can't. And if Cameron appears at the wedding, you'll have no choice but to confront it directly."

"He won't," Harper said with confidence. "He never RSVP'd, and Sidney hasn't heard from him in months."

"You sound disappointed. I take it you haven't heard from him either?"

"No," Harper said, her eyes downcast. "Not a word."

Dr. Andrews made a thoughtful sound at the back of his throat, scribbling something else in his notepad. "It could be for the best, Harper," he said gently.

"Maybe," she admitted, shifting uncomfortably in her seat. "Part of me is relieved, yes. But another part ... Well, it's complicated."

"It sounds like those feelings you were having for Cameron the last time we spoke have persisted."

"No." Harper sighed. "They haven't. I still love him, Dr. Andrews. Or maybe I'm just in love with the memory of him. I don't know. Either way, I've tried to give it time, gain the perspective we talked about, but it's just so hard. Every time I think about him, it's like a dagger to the heart."

Dr. Andrews watched Harper for a while before finally speaking again. "Harper," he said softly, "it's expected that you would still have feelings for Cameron. You two shared something special, something deep. But I think you're at a crossroads now, and you need to decide which way to go. You can continue to hold onto the past, or you can allow yourself to move forward. It's painful either way, but stagnation can sometimes be more harmful than growth." He paused, allowing his words to sink in before adding, "Either way, I think this trip could be part of your healing process. A chance for you to make amends with the past so you can start looking forward. But I want you to promise me something."

"What's that?"

"I want you to remember that the past is just a story we tell ourselves. It holds no power over you unless you let it."

Harper nodded slowly, absorbing his words. "I understand."

"Good," Dr. Andrews said, leaning back in his chair. "I want you to also remember that if it feels too much, you can always call me. I'll be here for you, anytime you need."

Harper took a deep breath, feeling a small sense of relief wash over her. "Thanks, Dr. Andrews. I'll try to keep that in mind," she promised, wringing her hands together. The clock on the wall chimed, signaling the end of their session.

Dr. Andrews stood and extended a hand to help Harper up from the couch. "We'll continue this conversation when you return. Until then, take care of yourself. Feel the emotions, but don't let them swamp you. And remember, you're stronger than you think."

CHAPTER 11

Harper stared at the stack of clothes on her bed, wondering how she would fit them all into the two pieces of luggage she'd chosen for the trip. Riffling through her designer dresses and vintage tops, she discarded several pieces, consolidating where she could, until she was satisfied with her wardrobe.

"There," she said, taking inventory of the pieces that had made the final cut. "That should do."

When every item of clothing was packed neatly into her suitcases, she turned her attention to the toiletry bag she'd set aside. Deodorant, makeup, lipstick, hairspray, and mascara—they all fit nicely into their assigned compartments. Harper was nothing if not organized. Considering all the trips she'd made overseas for work, she was an old pro at this, and that fact brought a small smile to her face.

With the packing behind her, Harper turned on the TV in the living room and ordered Chinese from the place on the corner. Normally, she would cook, but didn't want the hassle of having to do dishes before she traveled.

When her food arrived, she planned the next twenty-four hours over a box of Kung Pao Shrimp and fried rice. A few hours of work, followed by a drive to the airport, a flight to Destin, an Uber to the resort, unpacking, then finally, relaxing. And there was a dinner reservation at Primrose for her and Sidney at seven.

Harper let out a sigh as she considered all that had to be

done.

Stretching out on the sofa, Harper allowed her mind to wander. She thought about her recent visit with Dr. Andrews, about Grant, and how she was starting to emerge from the devastation of his betrayal. The Chanel project had been a godsend, had come at just the right time, and after receiving the first half of her payment, she felt like her company was finally back on track. But then she thought about the future, *her* future, and whether she would ever find true love again. Or perhaps true love was just an illusion, and she was destined for a life of mediocre, unfulfilling relationships. No amount of money could change that. Then, she recalled that summer—the sand, the surf, and the young man who had first made her believe that true love was possible. She remembered the days when they were inseparable—two young souls full of hope and dreams. But fate had other plans, and distance eventually drove them apart. Harper's eyes misted over as she recalled the bittersweet memories of their time together, and she wondered if it had all been real or just her imagination.

"Get a grip, Harper," she chided herself, shaking her head to dispel the thoughts clouding her mind. She focused on the TV, determined not to allow herself to indulge in what-ifs and reminiscing.

Around midnight, Harper glanced at the time on her phone and realized that she had mere hours before catching her flight for Sidney's wedding. With much still to do, she powered through the remaining tasks, and as she did, her thoughts drifted to the upcoming wedding festivities. The prospect of a brief escape from work and rekindling old friendships tugged at her heartstrings, threatening to unravel the tightly woven fibers of her carefully constructed life. Regardless, Harper remained steadfast in her determination to enjoy herself and to make Sidney's wedding day one she would never forget.

***

Sitting on the tarmac at Newark Airport, Harper hesitated as she took in the city skyline in the distance, her fingers hovering over her phone. Could reaching out to Cameron be the key to finally finding the happiness that had for so long eluded her? She glanced at the carry-on bag by her feet and caught a glimpse of the small golden wings she had received after her first flight. She remembered the exhilaration of taking off, the serenity of soaring above the clouds, and the wonder of seeing the world from a new perspective. The wings, which had once been a symbol of her bravery and newfound freedom, now served as a poignant reminder of the risks she'd taken and the sacrifices she'd made. The choice that lay before her felt reminiscent of that very first flight. If she chose to ignore her feelings, to bury them deep within, would she be forever grounded in her current reality—lonely, unsatisfied, regretful? With a racing heart and trembling fingers, she composed a message.

> Hey, it's me. I realize it's been a while, but I had you on my mind today. I hope you're doing well … wherever you are.

As the plane sped down the runway, Harper took a deep breath and made her decision—it was now or never—pressing send just as the aircraft lifted off.

PART 2

PART 2

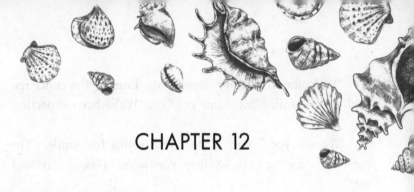

CHAPTER 12

The moment Harper set foot on the sun-kissed shores of Destin, Florida, a warm, salty breeze enveloped her like a long-lost embrace. The familiar sights and sounds of the coastal town that had once been her refuge, pulled at the corners of her mind like the incoming tide, threatening to sweep her away.

Her heart skipped a beat as memories of the summer she and Cameron fell in love came flooding back, each tender recollection more vivid than the last. She could almost taste the kisses they had shared beneath the moonlit sky, feel the thump of their wildly beating hearts, hear their laughter echoing into the night. But those memories were bittersweet, tinged with the knowledge that their love had burned out like a shooting star, leaving behind only ashes of what once was.

"Here we are," said the Uber driver, his Southern drawl pulling her back to the present. "Do you need help with your bags, miss?"

"Thank you, but I can manage."

With a mix of excitement and nostalgia coursing through her veins, Harper grabbed her bags and checked into The Henderson Beach Resort, a sprawling oceanfront oasis situated at the east end of a state park.

As she stepped into the luxurious lobby, Harper was captivated by the elegant decor that exuded both opulence and a sense of tranquility. The hardwood floors gleamed beneath her feet, and the scent of freshly cut flowers filled the air.

"Welcome to The Henderson, Ms. Emery," the concierge said with a smile. "My name is Diana. We've been expecting you."

"Thank you," said Harper, returning the smile. "I'm meeting someone here—Sidney Westwood. Has she arrived yet?"

Diana checked her computer screen. "Not yet, but we're expecting Ms. Westwood any time. Other than taking care of your luggage and getting your room key, is there anything else I can get you?"

Harper shook her head. "No, that will be all for now."

"Excellent." Diana completed Harper's check-in, then handed her the key to her room. "Someone will be along with your luggage shortly. And if there's anything you need during your stay, don't hesitate to ask."

As she made her way to her room, Harper was mesmerized by the stunning view that lay just beyond the hotel's floor-to-ceiling windows. The pristine white sand, the palm trees swaying in the breeze, the gentle ebb and flow of the waves—Destin was just like she remembered.

She opened the door to her room and was immediately greeted by a breathtaking sight. The room was adorned with soft, pastel colors and elegant furnishings, giving it an intimate and cozy ambiance. As she walked further into the room, her eyes were drawn to the large balcony overlooking the pool and the beach in the distance.

"This is more like it," she said to herself as she took in the view.

The bellman arrived, unloaded Harper's bags, and she then tipped him generously. When she had finished unpacking, Harper stepped out onto the balcony and checked her phone.

Hoping to find a response from Cameron, she was disappointed when she saw that he hadn't read her message. She thought about deleting it, erasing any trace of her moment of weakness, but decided against it. If it's meant to be, it'll be, she told herself before putting away her phone.

***

After a dip in the pool, Harper returned to her room and changed out of her bathing suit. No sooner had she finished drying her hair when her cell phone buzzed with a new message. Glancing anxiously at the screen, she felt a tinge of disappointment when she saw it was from Sidney. She had just arrived and requested Harper meet her downstairs.

After slipping into a long, breezy sundress and strappy sandals, Harper made her way to the Grand lawn, where families were engaged in games of cornhole and bocce.

"Harper, you made it!" Sidney exclaimed, her smile as warm as the evening sun. "It's so good to see you!"

"You too, Sid. You were right"—she glanced toward the hotel—"this place is spectacular."

"I knew you'd like it. So are you all settled?"

"Yes, and the room is great. I have the best view of the Gulf. Thank you."

"Anything for my best friend. Sorry I'm late." She sighed. "My flight got held up in Charlotte. I hope you weren't bored out of your mind."

"Me?" Harper chuckled. "Never. I got in a swim and spent some time on the balcony, admiring the view."

"Atta girl," said Sidney, then changed the subject. "So, what do you think of the wedding venue? Too much? Not enough?"

Harper's eyes roamed the enchanting scene before her—a picturesque garden adorned with vibrant white and lilac flowers and delicate lights that sparkled like stars against the darkening sky. It felt like they had stepped into a fairytale.

"It's absolutely stunning, Sid," Harper gushed. "Just like you always wanted."

"I know, right? When the wedding planner shared her vision with me, I couldn't believe it. It's as if she read my mind." Sidney's eyes gleamed with an almost childlike excitement. "I hope you don't mind but I told her you'd meet with her Wednesday to finalize the seating chart."

"You mean you haven't finalized the seating chart?"

"I have, but I wanted another set of eyes on it."

"Oh, well, in that case, I don't mind at all," said Harper. "I'm happy to do it."

"Great. I really think you'll like her. Her name is Rachel and she's fabulous. She reminds me a lot of you."

Harper smiled at the compliment as she took another look around. "She's done an exceptional job so far. This surpasses all of my expectations."

"Just one thing," Sidney said as her expression turned serious. "Make sure there's some space between my parents and Jason's. This whole move to Kentucky has caused quite a bit of tension, and I wouldn't want to add fuel to the fire on my wedding day."

"Of course, Sid," she assured her. "It's your day, and every detail will be exactly as you wish. Speaking of Jason, where is he?"

"He's meeting with his publisher this week to finalize the details of the book. He'll be here Friday."

"I'm sorry," said Harper.

"Don't be. At least now he won't be in the way," Sidney said with a wink.

As afternoon gave way to evening, Sidney and Harper made their way to the atrium, where Sidney thanked Harper again for making the trip.

"My pleasure," said Harper, finding a place on the sofa. "I've been looking forward to this for months."

Sidney plopped down next to Harper, kicking up her feet with an exaggerated sigh of relief. "I don't know what I would have done without you, Harp. You've been my rock through this entire thing, from the invitations to the bachelorette party. And I know it hasn't been easy, given your hectic schedule."

Harper brushed away the compliment with a slight wave of her hand. "Don't thank me yet," she said, grinning wryly. "There's still plenty of work to be done before the big day."

***

That evening, they ate dinner at Primrose, a cozy restaurant overlooking the pool and garden. The air was filled with the intoxicating scent of blooming flowers and the gentle hum of conversation. Soft candlelight flickered on the tables, creating a warm and intimate atmosphere.

As they savored their meals, the stress and worries of Harper's everyday life seemed to melt away in the magical ambiance of the evening.

"I finally took your advice," said Harper, leaning back in her seat when she had finished eating. "I decided to text Cameron."

Sidney's eyes lit up with excitement. "Really? What did you say?"

Harper let out a nervous laugh and swirled the wine in her glass. "Basically, I told him that he's been on my mind a lot lately. I don't know if anything will come of it, but at least I put myself out there. Now," she added, staring into her chardonnay, "the ball's in his court."

"I'm proud of you," said Sidney. "For putting yourself out there. It sounds like the sessions with Dr. Andrews are paying off."

Harper nodded, thinking of the progress she'd made since she started seeing him. "Yes, he's been a lifesaver. Thanks again for recommending him. I only wish I had taken your advice and gone to see him sooner. Maybe then I could have avoided those difficult days in the wake of Grant's betrayal."

"Maybe," Sidney replied sympathetically. "But that's all behind you now. The past is in the past, as they say, and I want this week to be about the future, about fun, and about new adventures."

"You're right," said Harper, raising her glass in a toast. "To new adventures."

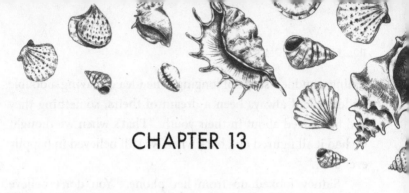

CHAPTER 13

The morning sun peeked through the curtains, stirring Harper from her slumber. As she stretched and yawned, she felt excited for the week ahead. The wedding was four days away, but there was still so much to do—organize the table arrangements, ensure the caterers were well informed about dietary requirements, and, most importantly, finalize the seating plan. But in between all these tasks, there was ample time for Harper and Sidney to relax before the rest of the wedding party arrived.

After a quick check of her email, Harper joined Sidney for a hearty breakfast on the balcony overlooking the beach. Once they were done eating, they took a walk along the shore, then donned their swimsuits and lounged by the pool.

"This brings back memories, doesn't it?" said Sidney, glancing fondly at Harper as they relaxed on the poolside loungers.

Harper smiled, her thoughts traveling back to their teenage years when they would spend countless hours by the pool reading books, ordering strawberry-banana smoothies, and discussing their futures.

"Sure does. Those were good times, weren't they? No worries. Just endless summers and carefree laughter."

Sidney nodded. "Remember when we used to dream about having a double wedding?" She sighed. "I was going to marry Robert Pattinson, and you had your heart set on Zac Efron."

Harper laughed at the idea. "Yeah, I remember," she said,

feeling a sudden surge of longing. The idea of having a double wedding had always been a dream of theirs, something they had fantasized about in their youth. "That's when we thought we had it all figured out, back when we still believed in happily ever after."

Sidney looked up from her phone. "You don't believe anymore?"

Harper shrugged her shoulder. "I used to. But nowadays, it feels like those kinds of stories only happened to our parents, or their parents, back when life was simpler. Now, it just seems like everyone is so self-absorbed, so caught up in their work and trying to make a name for themselves." She thought about her relationship with Grant and the disastrous consequences that had come from her own selfish desires. "Maybe those kinds of love stories don't exist anymore."

"You mean the kind with the prince riding in on a white horse, sword drawn, ready to save the day?"

Harper let out a quiet laugh. "Exactly."

"I don't know," Sidney mused. "They may be less common now, but they still happen. After all, isn't that what keeps us reading romance novels—the hope that the couple will overcome their obstacles and find happiness in the end?"

"I suppose."

"But happy endings require time and patience, and they often happen when we least expect it, and in ways we can't imagine."

"You're starting to sound like Cameron," said Harper as she wiped away a stray hair that had blown in front of her eyes. "He always said that if the bond between two people was strong enough, nothing could break it—not even time nor distance."

"Sounds to me like Cameron is wiser than you give him

credit for." Sidney paused, seemingly lost in contemplation as she sipped from her water bottle. "Whatever happened to those girls—the ones who were obsessed with Robert Pattinson and Zac Efron?"

"They grew up," said Harper, without skipping a beat. "At least you found your Robert Pattinson. I'm still searching for my Zac Efron."

"Don't worry. It'll happen for you. And in the meantime,"— Sidney sat up and smiled—"I want you to enjoy yourself this week. Which is why I have a few little surprises planned for us, starting with one this afternoon, to get us in the right frame of mind." A mischievous grin played about her lips.

Harper groaned. "Seriously? You know I hate surprises."

"Yes, yes," Sidney said with a roll of her eyes. "But something tells me you'll like this one."

***

That afternoon, Sidney and Harper found themselves standing at the entrance of a luxurious spa. The air was thick with the serene scent of lavender and Himalayan Sea salt, and soft music played in the background.

"Welcome to the Henderson spa," said the receptionist, greeting them with a warm smile. "Names, please."

"Sidney Westwood and Harper Emery."

"Yes, Ms. Westwood ... Ms. Emery ... Your relaxation room is ready. Right this way." She waved them forward.

They followed her into a spacious room draped in sheer white curtains and adorned with plush robes and scented candles. The atmosphere was so serene that Harper could feel her tension melt away, replaced by a sense of pure relaxation.

"So," the receptionist began, reading from her clipboard, "it looks like you've chosen the Henderson Dreams package, which means you'll be receiving a mineral salt scrub with eucalyptus, a full body massage with warm mineral stones and an invigorating foot massage." She checked the boxes, one by one. "Denise and Kate will be taking care of you this afternoon and will be in momentarily to show you to your private rooms. In the meantime, take a few minutes to get settled. There are a variety of cold beverages available for you in the refrigerator and snacks on the bar. Is there anything else I can get you?"

Sidney and Harper shook their heads.

"In that case, enjoy."

As the receptionist left the room, Harper turned to Sidney. "Okay, I take back what I said about surprises. This is heavenly."

Sidney chuckled. "I thought you might say that. I wanted to do something for you, as my way of saying thanks for all your help over the past few months. I couldn't have done it without you."

Harper reached for her hand and squeezed it. "You're welcome, and it has been my pleasure. I probably don't say it enough, but you mean so much to me, and I'm blessed to have you in my life."

"Ditto," said Sidney, her eyes misting over. "Best friends forever?"

Harper nodded and said, "Best friends forever."

***

After a relaxing afternoon, they sat down for dinner at the lobby bar, taking in the stunning vistas of Henderson State Park and the Gulf of Mexico. Harper requested a glass of white wine, while

Sidney went for a San Cristobal Manhattan. As they sipped their drinks, Harper commented about the exquisite surroundings.

"This place is stunning, isn't it?"

"Breathtaking," said Sidney before her phone buzzed to life. Glancing at the screen, she said, "I'm sorry, but I need to take this. Be back in a sec."

Harper watched as Sidney eased into the atrium. Alone with her thoughts, she surveyed the lawn below where the wedding would take place in just a few days. The lawn was bathed in the soft evening glow, the emerald grass vibrant against the pastel hue of the sky above.

She imagined the procession—the bridesmaids walking down the aisle, their elegant gowns trailing behind them, the groomsmen in crisp, tailored suits. The guests, an unbroken sea of familiar faces, would turn and watch as Sidney stepped into view. It was a scene she had imagined for herself not long ago, but it was not to be. A knot twisted in her stomach, a reminder of the bitter disappointment of reality.

"Who was that?" Harper inquired when Sidney returned a few minutes later.

Sidney hesitated a second before responding. "That was my, um, realtor. I told him to let me know as soon as anything promising came on the market."

"Him? I thought Chelsea was your realtor?"

"She is," Sidney said around a bite of crab dip. "That was her broker, Todd. He's covering for her this week while she's traveling. Anyway," she said, changing the subject. "Have you ordered yet?"

"No. I haven't," Harper replied. "I'm still torn between the fish tacos and the Cuban sandwich."

"Ooh! Get both. That way we can share."

Harper put down the menu and hailed a waitress. When they'd placed their order, the conversation turned to the wedding.

"And the arbor will be set up on the morning of the ceremony," Sidney said, going over the details once more.

"What about the band?"

"They'll be positioned off to the side, near the front. "Jason was adamant about having live music."

"And you're sure there will be enough room for all the guests?" Harper glanced at the lawn once more.

Sidney nodded, sipping her cocktail. "When Jason and I were here last, we had Rachel arrange the chairs so we could see how much space we would have. Trust me, there will be plenty of room. And once we say our I do's, we'll have dinner on the terrace, with dancing in the ballroom afterward."

"It sounds like you've thought of every detail," said Harper.

"Mostly," said Sidney. "There are still a few loose ends I need to tie up, but other than that we should be ready."

***

After dinner, Harper and Sidney strolled along the beach, savoring the last rays of golden sunlight. The waves crashed against the shore, their rhythmic melody providing a soothing backdrop to their conversation. Harper noticed how Sidney seemed slightly on edge, her demeanor tense despite the idyllic setting.

"Everything all right?" Harper asked.

Sidney nodded as a hint of a smile graced her lips. "I was just thinking ... about Jason. This is the longest we've been apart since we got engaged. I know it sounds crazy, but we rarely leave each other's side."

"You miss him already? You've only been gone a day."

"I always miss him when we're apart," she admitted. "Even if it's only a day. That's how I know he's the one."

Harper felt a pang of longing for that kind of connection as she watched the way Sidney's eyes scparkled when she spoke of Jason.

"I remember what that was like," said Harper as she tiptoed around a sand crab.

"When Cameron and I first started dating, I couldn't stand to be without him." Her smile quickly vanished as she reflected on the challenges of maintaining a long-distance relationship during those early days.

"Was it ever like that with Grant?" Sidney asked.

Harper let out a heavy sigh and stared at the horizon. "With Grant, it was different," she said, her mind drifting back to the winter when they first met. "I never felt the connection I had with Cameron. But that doesn't mean it was lacking," she continued. "With Grant, there was a spark, a certain kind of raw energy. But there was always something missing, something that Cameron had filled without even trying."

Sidney listened intently. The setting sun bathed them in a warm glow, casting long shadows on the sand behind them. "I know I asked you this before, but I get the sense you still have strong feelings for him."

Harper paused, her heart tightening in her chest. "I suppose a part of me will always have feelings for him," she admitted. "Cameron was the first man I ever loved, and you know what they say about first loves ... they leave an indelible mark on your heart." She took a deep breath, gathering her thoughts. "But maybe that's all it was, and all it will ever be."

Sidney reached out and gently touched Harper's arm, her eyes brimming with empathy. "Love is never simple, is it?"

Harper shook her head. "No, it isn't. It's messy, complicated, and it can hurt like hell."

"But it can also be beautiful," Sidney offered. "It can light up your world and make you feel like you're floating on air."

Harper's lips curved upward. "Yes, it can," she agreed, a flicker of hope rising from within her. "And that's what keeps me going—the possibility of finding that kind of love again."

CHAPTER 14

The following morning, while Sidney checked on the floral arrangements, Harper met with Rachel to review the final seating chart. When she was satisfied that all the guests were suitably placed according to Sidney's instructions, Harper returned to her suite where she sat alone, listening to the soothing sound of the rain outside. She checked her phone for the umpteenth time, hoping for a message from him. Yet, the screen remained stubbornly blank. Letting out a sigh, she stared through the deluge at the beach where she first met Cameron twelve years ago, her mind drifting back to a June day when she was eighteen.

***

Golden sand stretched out beneath a sky so blue it made Harper's heart ache. The scent of salt and brine filled her nostrils, mingling with the aroma of suntan lotion and coconut oil that clung to her skin like a lover's embrace. In the distance, the rhythmic lullaby of waves crashing against the shore provided a soundtrack to the laughter of children building sandcastles and seagulls swooping down to steal forgotten snacks.

Harper felt the spray of the ocean on her face, the cool kiss of water as she ventured deeper into the surf.

"Be careful," Sidney called out from the shore, reminding Harper of the single red flag atop the guard tower.

"I'll be fine," said Harper, ignoring the warning. When her feet could no longer touch the bottom, she stretched out on the surface and cut through the water like a fish. With ease, she swam until she reached the edge of the sandbar before turning back toward the beach.

But as she approached the shore, something tugged at her legs, sending a wave of panic through her. She fought against it, struggling to break free of its grasp. Realizing she was caught in a rip current, panic set in. She thrashed violently, her adrenaline-fueled strength pitiful against the ocean's might. She had heard stories of swimmers being dragged out to sea, their screams swallowed by the seething foam, and their bodies never recovered. Harper could not succumb to such a fate; she had too much left unsaid, too many promises to fulfill.

She cried out for help, her voice thin and desperate over the roar of the sea. Her chest tightened as she struggled against the current, her arms and legs growing weaker with each passing moment. Gasping for air, she tried to stay afloat, but the waves crashed over her head and dragged her under. She felt as though she would never reach the surface again, her lungs burning with the need for air.

Just when she thought all was lost, powerful arms encircled her waist and lifted her torso out of the water. She gasped, choking on air as her rescuer swam her to safety.

"Are you okay?" the young man asked when they were safely ashore. Concern had etched itself into the lines on his angelic face.

She peered into his bright blue eyes, wide with worry, taking in the sparkle of his sun-kissed skin. For a moment, she wondered if she was dead, thinking he looked more angelic than human. "I'm ... I'm fine," she finally said, forcing out the words.

Sidney raced to her side. "Harper! Thank goodness you're all *right," she said, hugging her tightly.*

Harper hugged Sidney back, still catching her breath. She focused on the lifeguard again, who had taken a step back to give them some space.

"Thank you," she said breathlessly. "You ... you saved my life."

The young man smiled, his eyes crinkling at the corners. "You're welcome. Are you sure you're okay? I could call an ambulance."

"No!" she said, suddenly aware of the crowd of onlookers that had gathered around her. "I'm fine, really." She got to her feet and dusted the sand from her backside. "See."

"In that case." He backed away. "I should get back to my post."

As he turned to walk away, Harper's eyes lingered on his broad shoulders and muscular arms, and an unfamiliar flutter tickled her stomach.

Sidney patted her on the back. "Come on," she said, "let's get you back to the house. You've had quite a scare."

***

A soft knock on the door made Harper jump, pulling her back to the present.

"Just a second," she called out, rising up from her seat. She opened the door and was surprised to see Sidney holding a bottle of tequila, margarita mix, and a bag filled with limes, salt, and corn chips. "What's all this?"

"I thought since it was raining, I'd bring the party indoors."

Harper smiled at Sidney's spontaneity. "Your timing is impeccable," she said, moving aside to let her in. "I was just sitting here thinking about the day I almost drowned. Do you remember?"

Sidney chuckled as she set the bag of goodies on the table. "How could I forget? That wasn't exactly your finest moment."

"No, it wasn't," Harper agreed. She took the limes from the bag and began cutting them into wedges while Sidney opened the tequila. "But it wasn't all bad, right? I mean, if not for my close call with death, Cameron and I may never have met."

"True." Sidney salted the rims and poured the liquid into two glasses.

"Do you think it was fate that brought us together?" Harper asked.

Sidney looked up. "Fate? I didn't think you believed in things like that?"

"I don't ... normally," said Harper. "But given the randomness of the situation, I can't help but wonder. I mean, aside from that one incident, I've never had any trouble in the water."

Sidney handed Harper a margarita, the liquid sloshing gently over the brim. "Maybe it was *fate*."

Harper took a drink before responding. "But if it was fate that brought us together, why would the universe go to all that trouble just for me to end up here, all these years later, without him?"

Sidney downed the rest of her margarita, then said, "Perhaps the universe isn't finished with you and Cameron?"

Harper considered that. "Are you saying you believe it's in the stars for me and Cameron to get back together?"

Sidney smiled. "All I'm saying is—what if you were destined to be here, right now, at this very moment? And what if all those memories you have of Cameron are just part of chapter one?

Face it, Harp, when it comes to you and Cameron, maybe the best is yet to come."

12 years earlier

"So what's the plan for today?" Harper asked as she spread out her towel on a poolside lounger.

"Well ... I talked my parents into letting us stay here at the beach club instead of going sightseeing with them," Sidney said. "You're welcome, by the way."

"Thanks," said Harper, giving her a small smile. "How'd you manage that?"

"I can be persuasive when I want to be," she answered. "Okay, fine—I told them we'd go to the pier with them tomorrow. Which, if you think about it, is a win for us since it's supposed to rain. So we'll probably end up staying at the house and playing cards all day."

Harper chuckled and shook her head. "You're quite devious when you want to be. One of the many things I love about you." She reached into her bag and pulled out her copy of *Little Women* and turned to the place where she'd left off. "So does that mean we're just going to hang around the pool all day? If so, I may need another bottle of sunscreen."

Sidney shrugged. "We could always give the ocean another try."

Harper shot her a look of mortification. Not that she was suddenly afraid of the water, but her near-drowning had left her shaken. "Maybe we can walk the shoreline and search for shells and shark teeth instead."

"I have a better idea," said Sidney. "Why don't we take a helicopter ride? I've always wanted to see Destin from the air."

"Absolutely not!" Harper exclaimed, her eyes wide as saucers. "There's no way you're getting me into one of those whirling death traps! Besides, you know I hate anything involving heights, especially after what happened last year."

Sidney rolled her eyes. "You'll be fine. Besides, I'm sure you're not the only person who's ever thrown up at the top of the Empire State Building."

After a dip in the pool, Harper returned to her chair and perused the menu. Unable to ignore the rumble in her stomach any longer, she raised the flag, alerting the staff that she was ready to order.

"Hey," said Sidney, tapping Harper on the shoulder. "Isn't that the same guy ... from yesterday?"

Harper's eyes flicked up to the young man, immediately recognizing him as the one who had rescued her from the ocean. He'd traded his lifeguard outfit for a pair of black shorts and a white golf shirt that stretched across his broad chest.

"Uh-huh," she answered, struggling to keep the interest out of her voice.

"I don't know why I didn't notice before, but he's cute," Sidney remarked, pushing up her shades.

"Yeah, not bad," said Harper, downplaying her interest.

"Not bad? Seriously?! Just look at him ... athletic build, broad shoulders, tanned skin. Mmm." She licked her lips. "He's a ten. If I wasn't dating Scott, I'd—"

"But you are," Harper reminded her, feeling a twinge of envy. "So don't go getting any ideas."

"All right, fine. I'll behave myself." Then Sidney got that look in her eye. "But that doesn't mean you have to."

"As if."

"What? You're single."

"Thanks for reminding me. But that doesn't mean he is," Harper fired back. "I mean, a guy like that probably has a girl in every town from here to Gulf Shores."

Sidney gave him another look. "I don't know, Harp. Something tells me you're wrong about him."

Harper rolled her eyes. Sidney had always been the optimistic one when it came to matters of the heart, often seeing the best in people even when it was clear they were nothing but trouble. But Harper knew better.

"Trust me, Sid, I can spot a bad boy from a mile away. And that guy right there has bad boy written all over him."

"So? Every girl needs to experience a bad boy at least once in their life. Trust me," she said, winking at Harper.

"Not me," said Harper defiantly.

Sidney shook her head and dropped the shades over her eyes. "No wonder you're single," she muttered. "You won't give any guy a chance."

"That's not true," Harper responded defensively.

"Yes, it is. Ever since Mark Bradshaw stood you up at homecoming, your standards have gone from unreasonable to impossible."

"Have not!" She slammed down the book. "I just think that when it comes to guys like Mr. Perfect over there"—she nodded at the young man—"they're only after one thing, and I'm not willing or gullible enough to give it to them."

"So you do think he's hot."

Harper's brain fizzled. "Yes," she finally admitted, "he's been blessed with good looks and a million-dollar smile, but—"

"And a six-pack," said Sidney. "Don't forget about his six-pack."

Harper took another look. "Fine ... and a six-pack," she

said, feeling the heat touch her cheeks. "But I'll bet that's the only thing he has going for him."

"Isn't that enough?"

Harper frowned, realizing she was losing the argument. "My point is he's probably not cultured or intelligent, and the only talent he has is his ability to talk girls out of their clothes. Guys like that are a dime a dozen." She turned and looked at Sidney. "And so are the girls that fall for them."

Sidney ignored Harper's jab and laughed at her cynicism. "This coming from the girl who tells me never to judge a book by its cover."

Harper's frown deepened, her arms crossed tightly over her chest. "Let's be real here, Sid. How many times has that actually been true? More often than not, the cover tells you everything you need to know about the book."

Sidney sighed. "Look, I get it. You're afraid of getting hurt. I don't blame you. But you can't let the past dictate your future. Sooner or later, you're going to have to take a chance on someone."

Harper shifted uncomfortably in her chair. Deep down, she knew that Sidney had a point. She couldn't deny that her past experiences had left her guarded and hesitant when it came to relationships. But opening herself up to someone like the young man who had rescued her from the surf felt like willingly stepping onto a minefield without a metal detector.

"Uh-oh," Sidney whispered a moment later. "Don't look now but Mr. Perfect is headed our way."

"Well, well, well, if it isn't the damsel in distress." He beamed his white teeth at Harper. "It looks like you're doing better."

"Yes, thank you," she replied with a smirk.

"Is there anything I can get you ladies to eat or drink? I'm partial to the chicken quesadilla, myself."

"So now you're a waiter?" Harper retorted with a sharp tone while Sidney glanced at a menu.

He chuckled good-naturedly. "Not normally, but when they told me you were hanging out by the pool today, I figured I might be needed, you know, in case you get in over your head."

Sidney joined in on the joke with a laugh, but Harper failed to find the humor.

"Sorry," he said. "Too soon?"

Harper narrowed her eyes at him.

To ease the tension, Sidney ordered two strawberry-banana smoothies while Harper brooded.

"Coming right up."

After he was gone, Sidney said, "Not only is he cute, but he's funny too." When Harper didn't respond, Sidney added, "Wow, Harp, ease up. He was only making a joke."

"Yeah, at my expense."

Sidney dropped the smile and said, "Cut him some slack. He was only trying to lighten the mood. Besides, I'm sure risking his life to save you yesterday was no walk in the park for him either. He could have drowned alongside you."

Harper considered that. "Ugh. I can't believe they fall for that," she said, watching in amazement as he drew smiles from the faces of a table of sorority girls.

"It's called charm," Sidney noted. "And I think it's endearing."

Harper cut her eyes to Sidney. "Like I already told you—it's all an act."

A few minutes later, the young man returned with their drinks and asked if there was anything else he could get for them.

"We're fine, for now," said Sidney, her long eyelashes batting flirtatiously as she flashed him a toothy grin.

He lingered, shifting nervously on his feet before finally working up the courage to say, "Listen, I know we don't know each other, but me and some friends are going to the boardwalk later, and I was wondering if you'd like to go and hang out? I promise it'll be fun."

Harper looked up from her book in bewilderment, certain he wasn't speaking to her. "You're wasting your time," she said with an air of satisfaction. "She's got a boyfriend."

Sidney's face flushed crimson and muttered an apology.

"Oh," he said, rubbing the back of his neck. "I'm sorry. I—"

"Don't feel bad," said Sidney. "It happens all the time."

Harper rolled her eyes in disbelief.

"No—it's not that," he said sheepishly. "I was actually asking out your friend—the damsel in distress."

Harper stared blankly at him for what seemed like an eternity; such an unexpected invitation had left her completely shocked. "Me?" Her reaction was a mix of puzzlement and incredulity.

He smiled at her with his eyes. "But only if you want to. I'm Cameron, by the way. Cameron Spears." He extended his hand. "What's your name?"

Taking a deep breath and shaking herself out of her daze, she slowly reached out and gently grasped his hand while introducing herself. "Harper," she said softly.

Cameron's smile widened, his blue eyes sparkling with genuine interest. "It's nice to meet you, Harper."

Despite the unease of the situation, Harper found herself warming a bit to Cameron's charm. With their hands still entangled, Harper took in the details of him. She noticed his slightly messy hair and the way his smile reached his eyes.

"Likewise," she finally managed to say, pulling her hand back slowly. Something about Cameron's sincerity sucked her in, her initial astonishment gradually transforming into a shy smile.

"So what do you say?"

Harper's heart pounded in her chest as she considered Cameron's proposition. Despite what she'd told Sidney, the thought of going out with him, exploring the boardwalk together, excited her. It was a chance for something new, a departure from her ordinary routine.

"She'd love to," said Sidney, agreeing on Harper's behalf.

When Harper didn't object, Cameron smiled broadly, revealing a perfect set of teeth that only added to his charm. "Great! I get off work at eight. Why don't I pick you up around nine?"

After trading information, Cameron went back to work, leaving Harper to her thoughts.

"Guys like that are all the same, huh?" Sidney teased as she sucked her smoothie through a straw.

Harper sighed, a bemused smile curving her lips. "I guess it's like you said—sometimes they surprise you."

***

When Cameron stopped by the beach house later that evening, Harper was ready and waiting on the front porch, her heart fluttering with nervous anticipation. As he made his way up the sidewalk, she smoothed down her white sundress and felt the ocean breeze sweep through her hair, adding a touch of wildness to her otherwise composed appearance.

"Hey there," said Cameron as he stepped up onto the porch. He drank her in with his eyes before adding, "You look great."

"Thank you," Harper replied, feeling her cheeks flush.

"Are you ready to go?"

After poking her head inside the door and telling Sidney she was leaving, Harper stepped off the porch and joined Cameron. His hand brushed against hers as they walked toward his car, sending a jolt of electricity through her body.

"So where's this boardwalk?" she asked as she settled into the passenger seat.

"Not far."

They drove along the coastal road with the top down and the wind in their hair. Harper stole glances at Cameron, noticing the way he gripped the steering wheel with confidence and how his eyes shone in the twilight.

"Thanks again for agreeing to come with me," he said as they approached a turn that revealed the vast expanse of dark ocean. To their left, houses hung like earthbound stars twinkling in the night.

"No problem," Harper replied, tearing away her gaze from the homes to look back at Cameron. "Thanks for asking me."

Cameron gave her a gentle smile, a smile that made her heart flutter unexpectedly. "You're welcome," he said, then focused back on the road.

The journey continued in comfortable silence, both of them lost in their thoughts. The sea air filled their lungs, clean and free. On occasion, they found themselves stealing glances at each other when they thought the other wasn't looking, and each time, a soft giggle threatened to break the silence.

As they neared the boardwalk, the atmosphere shifted. The air buzzed with the energy of people seeking entertainment and adventure. Neon lights illuminated the night, casting a vibrant glow upon the bustling crowd that lined the wooden planks.

Cameron parked the car, then glanced at Harper. "Ready to have some fun?"

Harper nodded eagerly as they stepped out of the car and joined the throng of people making their way toward the boardwalk.

Near the entrance, Cameron spotted his friends from work, huddled around a palm tree. "Everyone, this is Harper. Harper, this is everyone," he said, introducing them.

Harper smiled and greeted each of Cameron's friends, feeling a little nervous but determined to make a good impression. They were a lively bunch: two guys with bleach blond hair, Randall and Zach, and two girls, Hillary and Liv, one blonde and one brunette, both with dark complexions. They all appeared to be the same age, and full of laughter and inside jokes that made her feel like she was instantly part of their circle.

"And this is my cousin, Trevor," said Cameron, introducing her to a young man with features similar to his own. Only he had brown eyes instead of blue.

"Oh," she said, thinking that explained their similarities. "Nice to meet you, Trevor."

"Likewise," he said, shaking her hand.

With tickets in hand, the group made their way up the bustling boardwalk, taking in the sights and sounds of the carnival. The scent of fried funnel cakes filled the air, mingling with the salty sea breeze that wafted off the water.

"What do you think?" Cameron asked as they strolled

leisurely ahead.

Harper could only nod as she took in the dazzling lights and lively atmosphere. "It's strange to think that I've been coming to Destin for years with Sidney and her family, but never knew this place existed."

"It's kind of a hidden gem," Cameron explained.

"Do you all come here often?" Harper asked as they stopped and leaned against the railing.

"Trevor and I don't. But the others," he gestured toward them as they approached the ring toss, "they're here most nights, especially in the fall when all the tourists go home."

Harper asked, "So what do you do when summer is over?"

"I go home too."

"Oh, so you don't live here?"

He shook his head in response. "I live in Knoxville, Tennessee. I just come here to work while school's out. My grandparents have a place on the beach," he said, perhaps sensing her curiosity. "They're kind enough to let me and Trevor stay with them while we're here."

Harper looked at Cameron with newfound interest. "So besides school, what else do you do back home?"

"I'm a sprinter for the track team," he answered proudly. "And I also play basketball."

His lean, toned physique suddenly made sense to Harper.

"What about you—where do you call home?" Cameron asked.

"Some place you've probably never heard of."

"Oh yeah? Try me."

"I live in a little town called Nicholasville, on the outskirts of Lexington, Kentucky."

Cameron nodded knowingly. "Small world. Trevor lives

in Louisville. It's a nice place, Kentucky. I've been there a few times myself."

The cool ocean breeze tousled Harper's hair as a comfortable silence descended. Finally, she turned to face Cameron. "Can I ask you something?"

"Anything," he said, giving her his undivided attention.

"Why me?"

He tipped his head to the side, a small frown forming on his brow.

"Out of all the girls you could have asked out tonight, why did you choose me?"

Cameron chuckled softly, his dark eyes shining with amusement. "The truth?" he asked, his voice gentle and warm.

"Yes, please. And please tell me it wasn't because you felt sorry for me—for what happened yesterday." She held her breath.

"No." He shook his head. "Aside from being the prettiest girl I've seen all summer, I was fascinated by the book you were reading. Don't tell anyone, but it happens to be one of my favorites."

"*Little Women*?" Harper laughed. "You're joking, right?"

Cameron shook his head, the hint of a smile on his lips. "I know it's not a 'manly' sort of book, but I have my reasons for liking it. And when I saw you reading it this afternoon, I figured you were someone I wanted to get to know better."

Unconvinced, Harper decided to test him. "Okay, if you're such an expert on *Little Women*, what's your favorite line?" She smiled at what she thought would stump him.

Cameron took some time before responding, his eyes scanning the horizon as if searching for the perfect words. "*You are the gull, Jo,*" he quoted. "*Strong and wild, fond of the storm and the wind, flying far out to sea, and happy all alone."*

Harper realized that she had underestimated Cameron; he wasn't just a pretty face. She turned and stared out at the dark water. "I think I owe you an apology," she said, forcing herself to swallow her pride. "I thought you were someone else entirely."

He raised an eyebrow, his expression unreadable. "Oh? And who did you think I was?"

Harper hesitated, unsure of how to explain her initial impression of him. "I guess I just assumed you were like every other guy I've ever met."

"You mean you thought I was arrogant, shallow, and only interested in girls for one thing."

"Well, yeah."

"You know, you're not the first person to think that."

"I'm sorry."

"Don't be." He gave a dismissive wave. "Honestly, I find it rather amusing."

Harper narrowed her eyes in curiosity. "Amusing? How so?"

Cameron leaned against the railing next to her. "People often judge me by my appearance, assuming I'm just another playboy. But that couldn't be further from the truth." He paused briefly before continuing with a hint of vulnerability in his voice. "In fact, I've only ever had one girlfriend."

His looks, that smile, those mesmerizing eyes. He had to be lying through his perfect teeth.

"Come on," said Harper, her voice laced with skepticism. "Just one? No offense, but there isn't enough charm in the world to make me believe that."

"It's true."

Harper searched his eyes for even an ounce of dishonesty

but found none. "Why?"

At this question, Cameron's smile faded slightly, and he looked off into the distance. "I guess ... I guess I didn't want to hurt anyone, or for anyone to hurt me. I've had enough of that in my life."

"So you've just avoided relationships altogether?"

"Not all together. I've had a few dates here and there, but I just never let them turn into a relationship."

"Why not?"

"I don't know. Maybe I've been waiting for the right person. Or maybe..." he paused, glancing back at Harper with an intensity that took her breath away, "maybe I was scared."

Harper stared at him, a mixture of emotions warring inside her. She opened her mouth to say something but then closed it again, seemingly struggling to find the right words. Finally, she spoke up. "I think ...," she started hesitantly, "I think it takes a lot of strength to admit that. Most guys aren't capable of expressing their feelings, let alone admitting they're scared of them."

"Well, I'm not most guys," he said, his voice low and earnest.

"Clearly," she said, puzzled by him.

"And you're not most girls," he said, his tone lighter. "I knew it when I first saw you. You see past the superficial."

Harper fidgeted under his intense gaze, feeling exposed and vulnerable. Eventually, she looked away, unable to hold his penetrating stare any longer. "I've always been good at reading people," she admitted. "Well ... most of the time."

"That's a useful trait," he commented, still studying her in that probing way of his. This time, though, it didn't make her feel uncomfortable. Instead, it made her feel ... seen.

"Yes," Harper hesitated before continuing. "But sometimes it can also be disconcerting—knowing things about people that they haven't told you."

A comfortable silence settled between them as they stared at the ocean. After a minute, Cameron broke it by asking Harper if she wanted to ride the Ferris wheel.

She looked up at the towering structure, its lights twinkling against the night sky. In the darkness, it didn't seem as overwhelming as it did during the day.

"Sure," she replied, feeling a surge of boldness.

They boarded the ride and slowly ascended to the top, where they were greeted with an incredible view of the beach below. The coastline was dotted with glowing lights that stretched for miles like a string of pearls.

As the Ferris wheel reached its peak, a sense of calm washed over Harper. The view from up here was stunning, with the endless ocean in front of them. Suddenly, the night sky erupted into a spectacular display of fireworks, so close that Harper felt like she could reach out and touch them. And somewhere between the playing of the Star-Spangled Banner and the grand finale, Cameron took hold of Harper's hand and held it.

The sudden warmth of his skin against hers startled Harper. She looked up from the exploding sky and met his eyes—those same eyes that had only yesterday held concern for her as he rescued her from the undertow. Beneath his steady gaze, something stirred within her, a feeling so raw and deep she could hardly name it. She felt the heat rising up to her cheeks as the noise of the fireworks grew louder.

And then he did something that caught her off guard. He released her hand, his fingers lingering before slipping away. Harper's heart pounded in her chest as he shifted slightly. A strange silence followed, and Harper found herself lost in the moment, her mind racing to catch up with the sudden emotional onslaught.

"I'm sorry," he said softly, as though he had done something wrong.

"No," she responded. "Don't be. It was nice."

The tension eased around them as the sky lost its vibrant hues, and the last firework fizzled out.

When the ride came to an end, Cameron drove Harper home and walked her to her door. "I had fun tonight," he said with a smile. "I hope you did too."

"Yes, I did," she replied softly as she stepped onto the porch.

Cameron's eyes lingered on her before he backed off the porch. "Goodnight, Harper."

"What, that's it?" she blurted. "No line? No cheap move to get a goodnight kiss?"

Cameron smiled up at her, seemingly amused. "Not tonight," he said. "I usually save that for the second date."

"Second date?" She couldn't hide the smile from her face. "I thought you had a one-date limit?"

He laughed lightly. "I do, usually ... But for you, I'm willing to make an exception."

Harper thought for a minute, perhaps a little too long, just to make him wonder. But she'd made up her mind on the Ferris Wheel that she'd like to see Cameron again. "In that case, I'd like that," she said, a softness touching her voice. The cool breeze of the night swept a loose strand of hair from her face, and she tucked it behind her ear.

"Great. Then it's a date," he said, grinning.

"Yeah," she said as her heart exploded into a thousand pieces. "It's a date."

CHAPTER 15

The next evening, Cameron and Harper indulged in fish tacos and fried oysters from a local dive, then drove out to the East Jetty where they could be alone. After carefully navigating the uneven terrain, they found a suitable place to sit and talk, while basking in the warmth of the setting sun.

"Sunsets really are better by the ocean," Harper remarked, gazing westward as the sun edged toward the horizon.

Cameron nodded in agreement. "I won't argue with you there."

Harper looked away from the horizon and into Cameron's eyes. "You ever wonder what else is out there?" she asked, her voice barely a whisper against the lapping sound of waves against the rocks.

"Beyond the horizon you mean?"

She nodded, biting her lower lip. "Yeah."

"All the time. There's a whole world out there," he said, focusing back on the distant horizon where the sun was becoming a slender arc of glowing ember.

"Do you think we'll ever see the world? Or are we bound to our own little corners of the globe?"

"I know I will," he said confidently.

"Really? How can you be so sure?"

"Because, when summer's over, I'm off to school at the U.S. Naval Academy in Annapolis. Ever since I was little, my dream has been to become a fighter pilot."

"That's ambitious," said Harper, thinking there was no way she'd ever get in a plane, let alone one that traveled faster than the speed of sound.

"What about you—what are your plans after this summer?"

"I'm headed to New York," she said proudly. "I'll be attending Parsons—it's a fashion design school in Greenwich Village."

"Speaking of ambitious ... So you want to be a fashion designer?"

"Yes," she answered. "I do. But I worry about making it in a place like New York. I've never been anywhere bigger than Cincinnati before."

"You'll do fine. Just remember, we're only bound by the limits of our imagination," he said. "And by our willingness to step outside our comfort zone."

Harper smiled slightly, wishing that, if only for a second, every young man could be like Cameron. "You're starting to sound like Sidney," she said, recognizing the similarities between them. "She's always trying to get me to live outside my comfort zone."

"Sidney sounds like a smart girl."

"Yes, she is. Not to mention pretty, and funny, and ..." Harper stopped, realizing that as much as she had grown in the past year, she could never measure up to Sidney.

"Do I detect a hint of jealousy?"

"No," Harper replied automatically. "I'm not jealous of her. Not anymore. It's just ... I'm aware that she has qualities that I'll never possess."

"Don't sell yourself short." Cameron watched while she fidgeted with the locket hanging from her neck. "You have plenty of admirable qualities."

"Oh yeah—like what?"

"For starters, you're beautiful."

She rolled her eyes and said, "Thanks, but we both know I'm not going to be competing for the Miss America title anytime soon. Besides, most girls I know fit into one of two categories—pretty or smart—and I fall squarely into the latter."

"I don't see how that can be true, considering you just told me Sidney is both pretty and smart."

Harper was stumped, her brows furrowed in thought. "That's ... that's different," she managed to say, although she herself wasn't quite sure how. "Sidney is the exception, not the rule."

"From where I'm sitting, you're pretty exceptional too," he said, his eyes on her. "You're obviously smart. Anyone who talks to you for two minutes knows that. Plus, you're funny and sarcastic and thoughtful. But you're also beautiful, whether you believe it or not. And if you do ever compete in the Miss American pageant, you'll get my vote."

Was he serious? Or was this his moment to turn on the charm. Suddenly, she couldn't think straight, as if his words had cast some secret spell on her.

"Wait," Harper stuttered, "are you just trying to be nice?"

"No." He shook his head. "I'm not trying to be anything, except honest."

She looked away, attempting to hide the flush that threatened to creep across her cheeks. She had never considered herself as anything more than ordinary compared to Sidney—a fact she always accepted. But Cameron's words made her reconsider this notion. "I'm sorry," she said, feeling foolish for thinking he was anything but sincere. "It's just that I haven't had the best luck with guys, so when I hear you say things like that, I want to believe you, but I can't help but be skeptical."

"I understand," Cameron replied, nodding sympathetically. "It's okay to be skeptical, but it doesn't change the truth. Besides, everyone has their bad experiences, Harper. Trust me, I've had a few of my own."

"Is that the real reason you don't go on multiple dates— because of past trauma?"

"That's part of it. But mostly I'm just not interested in investing a lot of time in someone who isn't the one. Call me old-fashioned, but I hope to find someone different, someone interesting, who I can get to know on a deeper level."

Harper could hardly believe her ears.

"That doesn't make me sad, does it?"

"No." Harper shook her head. "It's worse; you're a hopeless romantic." Cameron laughed at that. "I hate to break it to you, Cameron, but those kinds of stories only exist in fairytales."

Cameron leaned back on his arms, gazing up at the slowly darkening sky. "My parents had that kind of love."

Harper raised an eyebrow cynically. "Had? As in, past tense? Point proven." A sense of satisfaction washed over her, knowing she had won the argument.

Cameron's expression turned pained as he looked away from her. "You're wrong," he said, turning back to her. "Their relationship didn't end because they stopped loving each other. It ended when my mother died." With that, he got to his feet and began walking back toward the beach.

The smile slipped from Harper's face. "Hey," she called out, chasing after him. "Wait!"

But Cameron didn't turn around, his tall silhouette growing smaller as he moved toward the crimson horizon.

When Harper finally caught up to him on the beach, she

offered a sincere apology. "I'm truly sorry. I had no idea."

"Yeah, well ..." Cameron's voice trailed off, leaving the silence to hover around them like an unwanted guest. "When I told you I had my reasons for liking *Little Women* so much, it's because it was her favorite. While most kids were being read stories of hobbits and dragons, I enjoyed hearing about four sisters navigating life's complexities. Her favorite was always Jo, but she was a lot like Beth—the cricket on the hearth. And it wasn't until she died that I realized the magnitude of the silence and shadow she left behind." He stared into the distance, tears threatening to spill from his eyes. "Even now, every word I read from that book echoes with her voice, and somehow it makes me feel close to her."

Harper bit her lip, not sure what to say, or if she should even say anything at all. Feeling brave, she reached out, gently placing her hand on Cameron's tensed forearm. He flinched slightly at the contact but didn't withdraw, his gaze still fixed on some unseen point in the distance. Harper swallowed hard, her throat dry and tight. "What happened to her?" she asked gently.

"She died when I was twelve," he said, his voice laced with sadness. "When the helicopter she was flying went down during a training exercise."

Harper swallowed hard. "So she was in the military?"

Cameron nodded, his eyes still fixed on the water. "She was a Navy pilot. She loved it. Said flying made her feel free."

Free. Harper turned that word over in her mind as Cameron continued speaking.

"Her favorite thing was to fly over the ocean, just as the sun was setting. She said it was like watching a painting come to life." His voice seemed to echo the words with a tender reverence, creating an image of a strong and enchanting woman. "She loved her job, loved serving her country. But more than anything, she loved her family. My dad was her rock, her anchor. And me ... I was her dream."

Harper found herself speechless, not knowing what to say or how to react. Cameron's pain seemed to hang in the air between them like a prickly fog, stinging her with its intensity. She could almost feel his heartache—it was a living entity, something that had crawled under his skin and seemed to be slowly eating away at him from the inside.

"Cameron," she whispered. "I'm so sorry. I should never have been that insensitive."

He turned to face her, his eyes an abyss of immeasurable sorrow. "It's okay, Harper. You didn't know."

"And that's why you've joined the Navy, isn't it?" Harper deduced. "To carry on your mother's legacy."

Cameron didn't answer right away, his gaze drifting back to the inky blackness of the water. "In a way, yes," he finally admitted. "But it's not just about carrying on her legacy. I want to live a life that will make her proud."

"And you think military service will make her proud of you?"

"Yes, I do," he answered resolutely. "She told me so herself."

"And what about after your service? Have you thought about that?" Harper found herself surprised at her own curiosity, surprised that she wanted to know more than just the surface details of Cameron's life.

"My plan is to retire from the Navy, which means I'll need to serve at least twenty years. After that, I can do whatever I want—maybe teach others how to fly."

"And what about a family? Don't you want to get married and have kids?"

"Of course I do. I realize it will be hard, and that I'll need to find the right kind of girl, someone who isn't afraid of the challenges that come with a long-distance relationship. But my parents made it work, so it can be done."

Harper thought about his words, the raw honesty in them resonating with something deep within her. His dreams were not just echoes of a lofty ambition but an intricate mix of duty, honor, and personal fulfillment. A realization washed over her. She was drawn to this boy with far-off dreams and a heart full of determination. His stoicism, his resolve—they were like a lighthouse in the turbulent weather of her own life. But there was an earnestness about him, a sincerity that echoed in the silence between them, and it pulled at something within her.

***

When Harper walked through the front door of the beach house, Sidney was waiting for her, lounging in her favorite wicker chair. "So, how did it go? I want to hear all about it."

Harper discarded her purse on the table, then kicked off her sandals and plopped down in the recliner. "Things were going fine until I opened my big fat mouth."

Sidney's face fell. "Oh no, what did you say this time?"

Harper sighed and told Sidney everything.

"You're right," said Sidney, shaking her head in disbelief. "Making a joke about someone's dead mother is bad, even for you."

Harper heaved a sigh. "Thanks, Sid. You always know how to make me feel better."

"Anytime," Sidney replied with a smirk and a flick of her hair. "So, aside from offending him, what else happened? Did he kiss you?"

Harper paused as she replayed the evening in her mind. "He told me about his dreams. His ambitions." Her voice was soft, tinged with a reverence she hadn't realized she was capable of feeling for someone else's aspirations. And it was then that Harper realized she'd been caught in the undertow of his spirit, dragged into a current that was entirely Cameron. She blinked rapidly, trying to dispel the sudden fog that had settled over her. She hadn't expected to feel this way, to be so touched by his stories, his dreams.

Sidney tilted her head, a look of surprise crossing her face. "Really? And how did that make you feel?"

Harper closed her eyes, trying to find the right words. "I was touched, Sid." She replied. "His dreams ... They're not about money or fame. They're about honor, duty ... fulfillment."

"So you were wrong about him, weren't you?"

"Yeah," she conceded. "I suppose I was."

CHAPTER 16

One day passed, then another. By the third day, when Cameron didn't show up for work, Harper had a sinking feeling that something was wrong. So she went looking for someone who could tell her about his whereabouts.

"If you're looking for Cam, he's not here," said Trevor as he loaded some supplies into the guard tower.

"Where is he?"

"At home, sick. He's called off work the last two days."

"I hope it isn't serious."

"Nah, I think it's just a cold. I'm sure it's nothing to worry about. If you want, I'll tell him you were asking about him."

"Thanks, but I think I'll go and see for myself," Harper said, her mind already mapping the quickest route to Cameron's place.

***

"Harper, what brings you here?" Cameron asked as he cracked open the door and peeked out.

"Trevor said you were sick, so I wanted to make sure everything was okay."

"You were worried about me?"

"More like mildly concerned," she said, concealing the depth of her worry.

Cameron's lips curved into a small smile as Harper shifted

nervously, holding onto a paper bag from a nearby deli.

"I brought some soup and sandwiches," she murmured. "Trevor said this place was your favorite."

Cameron's eyes lingered on the bag in Harper's hands, his eyebrow raised in surprise. "He's right. That's very sweet of you. Wanna come in?"

A blush bloomed across Harper's cheeks as she nodded vigorously. She fumbled with the bag that smelled like chicken noodle soup and freshly baked bread before turning sheepishly toward Cameron and extending it toward him.

Taking the bag, Cameron looked past Harper to the steely gray sky visible behind her. Rain was starting to patter with a steady rhythm. "You didn't have to do this," he said quietly as he showed her inside. "Especially not with this weather."

"But I wanted to ..." Harper mumbled, determination lighting her eyes. "You're sick, Cameron. Someone needs to take care of you. Otherwise, it could lead to pneumonia. I had it when I was little, and believe me, it's not something you want."

"I don't think it's that serious," he said on his way into the kitchen. "But just in case, my grandparents are around."

Harper glanced around the house. "Are they home?"

"Not right now," Cameron said, setting down the bag and rummaging through its contents. "My grandmother had a doctor's appointment, so she and my grandpa won't be back for a while." He poured two bowls of soup and invited Harper to join him.

They sat at the table, enjoying their lunch and engaging in casual conversation about the weather.

When they had finished eating, Cameron rested his chin against the back of his hand and watched Harper in the pale light streaming in from the kitchen windows. "Thank you," he said finally. "Not just for the soup, but also for your concern."

Harper nodded. She felt a warmth spreading through her chest but quickly brushed it off. Ignoring the sudden silence that filled the room, she got up and began carrying their dishes to the sink.

As she moved around Cameron's kitchen, her gaze fell upon a photograph magnetized to the fridge—it was an old one, with faded colors and slightly frayed edges. In it was a much younger Cameron, his arm slung around the shoulders of a woman who bore a striking resemblance to him. His mother, Harper assumed.

"Is this you?" she asked, pointing to the photo.

Cameron looked up from where he sat at the table. A soft smile touched his lips as he saw what she was indicating. "Yes. And that's my mom," he admitted, pushing himself up and walking over to join Harper by the fridge.

"You look like her," Harper commented, looking from Cameron's face to the photograph.

Cameron gave a slight nod, his fingers tracing the edge of the picture delicately. "So I've been told."

A comfortable silence ensued. Despite the melancholic undertones, there was something undeniably intimate about sharing this quiet moment together.

Cameron cleared his throat, pulling Harper from her reverence of the photograph. "She would've liked you, I think," he said, his voice softer than before. "My mom ... She always had a way of knowing who the good people were."

Harper grinned, then gently returned the photo to the fridge and looked at Cameron. "Do you miss her?" she asked quietly.

Cameron smiled sadly, nodding. "Every day."

Rain lashed out against the window. It seemed as if nature was adding its own melancholy soundtrack to their conversation.

Unsure of what more to say, Harper reached out and squeezed Cameron's arm. He gave her a grateful glance before pulling away and returning to the table. Harper followed, her thoughts turning in her head like the gloomy clouds outside.

"My mom ... she loved the rain," Cameron said, his eyes misting over. "She used to say that it was nature's way of washing away the sorrow and pain of the world."

Harper listened to Cameron's words, her heart aching for him as she watched him lost in his memories.

"She would dance in it," he continued, remembering. "With me or my dad. Or alone if we were foolish enough to stay inside. I used to worry about her getting struck by lightning, but she would say, '*I am not afraid of storms, for I am learning how to sail my ship.*'"

"Another line from *Little Women*," Harper interjected.

Cameron breathed an easy laugh. "She knew that book inside and out."

Harper smiled at the image Cameron painted with his words—a woman dancing freely in the rain, radiating happiness. She found herself wishing she could have met this woman who had left such a strong mark on Cameron.

"She sounds like she was a wonderful woman," Harper said softly, meeting Cameron's eyes. They were still watery, but the pain she saw in them was slowly replaced by fondness, admiration even.

"She was," Cameron confirmed with a nod. "Maybe one day you'll dance in the rain too," Cameron suggested.

"Maybe I will," Harper replied. She could almost picture

it—herself dancing in the rain, without a care in the world.

Cameron grinned, pleased by her answer.

"And maybe," Harper continued, a slight teasing edge to her tone. "I'll convince you to join me."

Cameron's grin broadened, and he shrugged noncommittally. "Now that would be a sight."

Harper continued to watch the rain, her thoughts floating along with the droplets that slid down the windowpane. After a minute, she noticed Cameron fighting a yawn, so she suggested it was time for her to leave.

Cameron was about to protest but Harper cut him off with a pointed look. "No arguments, okay? I'm only here for a few more weeks, and I don't want to waste a minute of the time we have left."

"Yes ma'am." He saluted her, then walked her to the door. "Thanks again, Harper. I feel better already."

"You're welcome," she replied with a small smile, tucking a loose strand of hair behind her ear. "I'm glad I could help."

***

The next day, Cameron was back at work, looking as good as new.

"That chicken noodle soup must have done the trick," said Harper, giving him the once over with her eyes.

"It was either that or your threat to make me dance in the rain," Cameron replied, his grin infectious. Harper laughed, shaking her head at his teasing. "But seriously ... thank you for yesterday," said Cameron, his voice sincere. "You really lifted my spirits."

"You're welcome," Harper replied. "And I'm glad you're

feeling better."

"So am I, because I was thinking ... everyone's going to the beach after work, and I was hoping you'd come with us."

Harper hesitated. "I don't know. I sort of promised Sidney I'd do something with her tonight."

"Why don't you bring her with you?" Cameron suggested. "It'll be fun. We'll build a bonfire, roast marshmallows. Maybe even have a little beach volleyball. And if we're lucky, Trevor might play us a tune on his guitar."

She bit her lip, mulling over his idea. It was true; it would be an excellent way of introducing Sidney to Cameron and his friends. Yet the thought of combining two parts of her life unsettled Harper for reasons she didn't quite understand.

After a moment, she agreed, her desire to see Cameron again overriding her reservations. "Count us in."

***

"So Cameron tells me you want to be a fashion designer," said Trevor later that evening while sitting around the bonfire. "No offense, but that sounds like a long shot."

Harper considered that. "Sure, but I know with hard work and perseverance, I can make it happen."

Trevor leaned back in his chair and smiled. "Most people our age have no idea what they want to do with their life. They're more concerned with parties and breaking curfew than maintaining a respectable GPA and planning for the future. But it sounds to me like you've got it all figured out."

Harper blushed, flattered by Trevor's words. But in truth, she didn't feel like she had anything figured out at all. "I wish," she confessed, wiping a stray lock of hair away from her eyes.

"But I guess all we can do is keep trying, right?" She took a sip of Coke and asked, "What about you? What are your plans after summer?"

Trevor tilted his head in confusion. "Cameron didn't tell you? I'll be joining him at the Naval Academy."

"Does that mean you're going to be a pilot too?"

"That's the plan." He paused, his expression becoming more serious. "Honestly, I'm just thankful I got in. If it hadn't been for Cameron, I'd likely be stuck at home for the next four years, forced to attend the University of Louisville. Not that it's a bad school or anything but it isn't the Naval Academy. He really did me a solid."

"What do you mean?"

"Well," he said, lowering his voice. "I'm ashamed to admit it, but I've been known to procrastinate. I nearly missed the application deadline, but Cameron stepped in. He drove all the way to my house, and we pulled an all-nighter, just to finish the paperwork."

Harper was shocked. She had suspected Cameron to be a loyal friend but hadn't realized the depths of his loyalty until now.

"He must really care about you."

"Yeah, he does. It's comforting to know he's always got my back."

"I know what you mean," said Harper, thinking of Sidney. "Sid and I are the same way. We're not family like you and Cameron, but we're best friends, which I suppose is the next best thing." She looked up and saw Sidney laughing and having a good time. Despite her initial hesitation to invite her, Harper was glad she did.

When Cameron joined them a few minutes later, Trevor

got up and excused himself, giving them time alone.

"You and Trevor seemed to be getting along," he said, and sat down beside her. "I hope he didn't talk your ear off."

"No." She shook her head. "But he was singing your praises. You didn't put him up to that, did you?"

A smile made its way onto Cameron's face. "Nah. But he's good at that—making things sound greater than they really are."

"How come you didn't tell me he was going to the Naval Academy with you this fall?" Harper asked.

He shrugged. "I don't know. I just hadn't got around to it, I guess."

Harper scooted forward a few inches, letting the heat from the fire warm her hands. "Tell me something. Did you really drive all the way to Louisville, just to help him with his application?"

Cameron chuckled, taking a sip of his Coke before answering. "Yeah, I did. It was probably a bit over the top, but I couldn't stand to see him throw away such a golden opportunity."

"I don't think there are many people out there that would have done something like that."

Cameron shrugged a shoulder. "Maybe. But Trevor is family, and to me family is everything." He paused, then said, "Besides, Trevor's the one who came to stay with me after my mom died, and I promised him then that if there was ever a time he needed me, I'd be there for him, no questions asked. So when he called and said he was in a bind, I just kept thinking about the promise I made to him, and how I needed to keep it."

Harper marveled at his devotion, a sharp contrast to all the broken promises—party invitations, phone calls, being stood up at homecoming—she had experienced in her own life. "And I thought this whole time that promises were only made to be broken."

Cameron leaned back, a contemplative look on his face. "They may seem harmless, but promises are powerful things, Harper. They're the glue that holds relationships together. Without trust and the willingness to keep our word, what do we really have?" He paused, letting his words sink in. "When I was a boy, my mom warned me not to make promises under any circumstances. That I would only be setting myself up for failure. But said if I was foolish enough to make one, be man enough to keep it. So that's how I've tried to live my life. I rarely make promises, but when I do, I always follow through."

Harper pondered his words as she traced her finger over the condensation on her Coke bottle.

The soft strum of a guitar prompted Harper to look up at Trevor playing an impromptu tune.

"He's pretty good." She watched in silence as his fingers moved with an effortless grace across the strings.

"Music runs in his blood," said Cameron. "His parents are both musicians. That's how they met—playing in a band when they were in college."

Harper's eyes stayed locked on Trevor, the dancing light of the fire flickering on the strings of his guitar. Every note, every chord, mirrored something deep within her that she could not name. "It's beautiful," she murmured. "Almost haunting."

Cameron nodded quietly in agreement, watching the firelight play on the soft contours of her face. "Sometimes, I think that's why he plays—to convey emotions too complicated for words."

Trevor's tune drifted to a close, the last note hanging in

the air, as palpable as the silence that followed. The warmth of the fire and the sweet lull of the guitar created a cocoon around them, shutting out the cool night.

"Hey, what are you doing on Saturday?" Cameron asked after everyone applauded.

"Nothing. Why?"

"Because there's somewhere I want to take you. It's a surprise."

"Okay," she answered tentatively. "Do I need to bring anything?"

He shook his head. "Just yourself, and an open mind."

CHAPTER 17

On Saturday, Sidney stood in the kitchen of her parent's beach house, searching the cabinets for something to eat. "Will you be joining me today or am I flying solo again?" she asked as she poured herself a bowl of Frosted Flakes.

Harper looked up from her plate of bacon and eggs. "Actually, I told Cam I'd spend the afternoon with him. You're cool with that, right?"

Sidney sighed and said, "I guess I don't have any other choice. Maybe I'll see if Mom can take me shopping. I'm dying to get some new shorts, and maybe a couple of T-shirts from Innerlight." She reached for the milk. "So what's this make— three, four days in a row you guys have spent together?"

"Five, actually." Harper breathed an easy laugh. "But who's counting, right?"

Sidney sat down at the table and started eating. "You must really like this guy."

Harper smiled reflexively, recalling the near kiss from the day before. "What can I say? There's just something about him. He and I just ... click."

"Well, I'm happy for you—you deserve it. Just don't fall too hard," Sidney warned. "We're only here for a couple more weeks, then it's back to reality." She spooned in another bite of cereal, then asked, "So where is he taking you today?"

"I don't know. He said it's a surprise."

Sidney raised an eyebrow. "For your sake, and his, let's just hope it doesn't involve heights."

After breakfast, Harper donned her teal Key West t-shirt—the one that brought out her eyes—and her cutoff denim shorts, then slid into her tennis shoes. After applying a spritz of perfume, she grabbed her shades before leaving the house to meet Cameron.

They got lunch from a local fish house, then Cameron drove Harper inland to a flat strip of land carved out of the forest.

"Here we are," he said, announcing their arrival.

Harper glanced out the window, her eyes locking onto a large metal building in the distance. "Where are we, exactly?"

"It's a surprise, remember? And to keep it that way, I'd like you to wear this." He pulled a blindfold from the center console and gave it to her.

Harper gave him a wary look.

"I know it's a little dramatic but trust me."

"How will I see where I'm going?"

"Don't worry. I'll hold your hand until we get there."

Slowly, they made their way across the field. Harper felt grass beneath her feet, then gravel and concrete, before grass again. All the while, her insides churned as she tried to imagine why Cameron would have brought her to such a place.

"Okay." He brought her to a stop and slowly removed the blindfold. "Open your eyes."

When Harper opened them, the first thing she saw was a single-engine Piper aircraft with the nose and tail painted red. She stood there, staring in disbelief.

"I don't understand," she mumbled. "You don't really expect me to get into that thing, do you?"

"You said you wanted to see the area, so I thought, what

better way than from the air?" His expression burned bright with anticipation.

Harper looked around, finding the field empty. "Who's going to fly it?"

Cameron pulled a set of keys from his pocket and dangled them in front of her. "I am."

"You? But you're not a pilot."

"Actually, I am." He carefully inspected the rudder, flaps, and the aileron. "I've had my private pilot's license for over a year, but I've been flying for much longer."

Harper could hardly believe what she was hearing. She knew Cameron was adventurous, but this was on a whole new level.

"So what do you say?" He brought his gaze back to her, his eyes dancing expectantly.

"I ... I don't know."

"Come on. You trust me, don't you?"

Trust had nothing to do with it. "It's not that. It's just ..." Fear pulsed through her.

"I won't let anything bad happen to you, Harper. Promise." Cameron took her by the hand, and he led her toward the cockpit. When she was safely inside, she put on the headset and listened as Cameron went through the pre-flight checklist, his voice calm and confident.

After getting the all-clear from the tower, they taxied to the end of the runway. When they were in position, Cameron turned toward Harper, dropping the aviator sunglasses over his eyes, "Ready?" he asked.

Harper nodded, doing her best to maintain her composure. But on the inside, she was trembling like a bird in a cage.

Cameron increased the throttle and the plane roared to

life, a metallic beast shaking before its leap into the air. The scenery outside blurred, the runway lights streaking past like fallen stars.

As they began to take off, Harper clutched Cameron's thigh, experiencing a rush of excitement like she had never felt before. The feeling of being lifted off the ground and soaring through the air was both exhilarating and terrifying. With her free hand, she gripped the armrest, her heart racing as they climbed higher into the sky.

When they reached cruising altitude, Cameron steadied the plane, then turned to her and asked, "What do you think of the view?"

"Amazing!" she said, venturing a look at the beach below. "The world looks so small from up here."

"Do you know where we are?"

Harper surveyed the landscape below—the stretches of sand, bodies of water, the network of roads that spread out in all directions. Finally, something familiar caught her eye. "There's the park," she said, pointing to the undeveloped section of dunes and scrub brush. "And the boardwalk where you took me on our first date." She looked closer. "And there's the beach club." Her voice rose with excitement.

"Hey, you're pretty good at this," he complimented as they glided above the shoreline.

Beneath them, the houses and hotels dotting the coastline passed by in a dizzying array of color. Harper found herself entranced, her eyes drinking in every detail.

"Now that you've acquainted yourself with the area, how do you feel about taking the controls?"

Harper's heart jumped into her throat. "No way!"

"Come on. Just put your hands here," he said, guiding her

to the controls. His fingers, surprisingly gentle, curled around her own. The cold metal of the yoke did little to stave off the warmth that threatened to envelop her. His scent, a mix of leather and a subtle hint of spice, filled her senses. "Now, pull back slightly."

Despite her trepidation, Harper followed Cameron's instructions, and in no time she had control of the plane. "Wow! Am I actually flying?"

"You're a natural." The plane eased upwards, moving in sync with Harper's touch. Beneath her fingers, the controls vibrated gently, like a living entity responding to her command. She glanced over at Cameron. His lips held a soft, encouraging smile. "See? Nothing to worry about."

They flew on, the hum of the plane's engine the only sound filling the space. Harper couldn't suppress her grin as she held on to the controls, flying high above the sprawling canopy.

"You know, there's something about being up here that makes everything seem clearer," said Cameron. "It's like all the worries and stress of life disappear when it's just you and the sky."

Harper nodded in agreement, feeling a sense of peace wash over her. She had never felt anything like it before. It was as if all the worries that had plagued her since childhood—the fear of not fitting in, the overwhelming loneliness she often felt, her own self-doubt—were left behind on the ground. Up here, in the sky, she was free.

As they flew on, Harper stole glances at Cameron. She felt her heart skip, and she couldn't deny the attraction she felt toward him.

They flew as far as Pensacola Bay before turning and heading for home. And as the plane touched down and Cameron brought it to a stop, Harper breathed a sigh of relief.

"That was incredible," she said, the adrenaline still coursing through her veins. "Thank you so much for letting me take control."

"Anytime." Cameron grinned. "Oh, and I have something special for you." He reached into his pocket and pulled out a tiny pair of golden wings. "Everyone gets a pair of wings after their first flight," he explained, handing them to her. "Keep these as a reminder of the day you conquered your greatest fear."

The tiny pair of golden wings glistened in the sunlight. Harper stared at the delicate gift with awe, cradling it gently in her trembling hand. "Thank you," she said, hardly believing that she had flown, had risked everything and soared above the clouds. When she attached the gold wings to her T-shirt, she removed the headset and unfastened her safety belt with a sense of accomplishment. "I can honestly say this has been the best day of my life."

Cameron beamed. "It isn't over yet. I still have one more surprise for you."

They made it to the beach just in time to watch the sunset. Cameron dragged two chairs from his grandparents' deck and placed them in the sand, then started a fire. When the sun was gone, he filled a cooler with drinks, then spread out a blanket and brought out a basket of sandwiches and chips.

"Today was pretty great, right?" he asked.

"Oh yeah," she answered, feeling a little spoiled. "Is this how you treat all the girls?"

A smile pulled at the corners of his mouth. "No. Just you."

"So you've never taken another girl flying with you before?"

"Never."

Even after spending the last two weeks with Cameron,

Harper still found it hard to believe that he hadn't had dozens of girlfriends.

"So what makes me different than the others?"

"It's simple," he answered, without skipping a beat. "I like you. And I believe if you like someone you should show them who you are ... what makes you happy ... what brings you joy. For me, it's all about flying and the beach and looking out over the water at the sunset. And I wanted to share a little of that with you."

His words melted her heart, and it took her a minute to compose herself. "You know, you're not like anyone I've ever met ... not like I thought you'd be at all."

Cameron gave an easy laugh. "I'm just glad you gave me the chance to show you who I really am."

The fire crackled and the stars twinkled above them as they continued to talk and laugh. The conversation flowed easily between them, and the attraction Harper felt toward Cameron only intensified. She felt drawn to him, to the way his eyes sparkled when he talked about flying, or the way his laugh echoed through the warm night air.

When they had finished eating, Cameron stood up and extended his hand to her. "Let's take a walk."

Harper took his hand, and they wandered along the beach, the waves lapping at their feet.

"Harper, I know we haven't known each other very long, but I feel like there's something between us. Something special," he said, his voice low and sincere.

"I feel it too," she said. "I was telling Sidney the same thing this morning."

Cameron stepped closer to her, his hand reaching up to brush a lock of hair behind her ear. "I don't want to push you, but I can't help the way I feel. I want to kiss you, Harper, if that's okay."

Harper's breath caught in her throat. She had never felt such a strong connection with anyone before. Without a word, she leaned forward, and their lips met in a soft, gentle kiss.

The kiss was electric, sending shivers down Harper's spine. She wrapped her arms around Cameron's neck, pulling him closer as their lips moved in perfect harmony. The sound of the waves crashing against the shore faded into the background as they lost themselves in the moment.

Cameron's hands wandered down to the small of her back, pulling her even closer. Harper let out a soft moan as he deepened the kiss, exploring her mouth with his tongue. She had never felt so alive, so wanted. It was like she had been waiting her whole life for this moment, and now that it was here, she never wanted it to end. They broke the kiss, both gasping for air, and Cameron stared down at her with such intensity that she felt a shiver run through her body.

"Harper, I can't explain it, but I feel like I've known you forever," he said, his voice thick with desire.

Harper nodded, unable to find her voice. She felt the same way. It was like they were meant to be together.

Cameron took her hand and led her back to the chairs and the fire, where they sat and talked for hours. Finally, just before midnight, they decided it was time to go. Cameron walked her back to the beach house, and they stood there on the porch, neither of them wanting to say goodbye.

"I had a really great time today," Harper said, feeling a little shy all of a sudden.

Cameron smiled at her. "Me too. Want to do it again tomorrow?"

Harper grinned. "Of course. Same place, same time?"

"You already know me too well," he said, then smiled.

At the door, Cameron leaned in to kiss her once more, and Harper felt herself melting into him. When they finally broke apart, she said goodnight then went inside, her heart racing. She couldn't wait to see Cameron again, to feel his touch and taste his lips once more.

***

A few days later, Cameron used his day off to take Harper out on his grandfather's boat. They left the marina just after ten and headed west along the coast.

"So you can fly, drive, and operate a boat," said Harper. "Is there any type of machinery you don't know how to use?"

Cameron grinned slyly. "I've never driven a Zamboni," he joked.

Harper rolled her eyes playfully. "So where are we heading today?" she asked as she scanned the horizon.

"Crab Island," Cameron answered as he expertly steered the boat around a navigational buoy. "It's where all the locals go to hang out and relax. You're going to love it."

As they forged ahead, the sea took on a deeper shade of turquoise, revealing a mesmerizing underwater world beneath the surface. Harper leaned over the boat, taking in every little detail—the playful dance of fish darting in and out of crevices, the rays of sunlight filtering through the water. "I've never seen water so clear," she marveled.

"Just wait," said Cameron.

Just then, a playful breeze swept through Harper's dark hair, tossing loose strands over her sun-kissed cheeks. Cameron watched this from the corner of his eye, a soft smile adorning his chiseled face.

When they reached the East Pass, Cameron cut back on the engine and pointed the boat toward a narrow sandbar visible in the distance where a dozen boats were already moored.

"Is that it?" Harper asked as she put her hands on the bow and leaned into the wind.

"Yes." Cameron nodded. "That's Crab Island."

"Wow!" Harper gasped, her eyes wide with anticipation. She had never seen anything quite like it.

Cameron allowed himself time to take in the view before he turned off the engine and drifted toward a vacant buoy. When he'd secured the boat, he tore off his shirt and dove headfirst into the clear water.

Harper watched him in surprise, a playful smile breaking across her face. She hastily kicked off her flip-flops, hoisted herself onto the side of the boat, and dove in after him. The water was refreshingly cool, a stark contrast to the relentless heat of the Florida sun. Cameron resurfaced with a triumphant whoop, shaking droplets of water from his dark hair. Harper emerged moments later, her face flushed and bright.

"Ready to find some rays?" Grabbing a pair of goggles from the boat, Cameron led Harper to the edge of the sandbar. As they submerged beneath the surface, they were greeted by a whole new world of aquatic splendor. Streaming beams of sunlight illuminated schools of fish that darted along the flats, their scales shimmering in a rainbow of hues. Sea turtles gracefully swam by, their ancient eyes observing the intruders nonchalantly. As they ventured further, small white and black stingrays skated across the sandy ocean floor like silent, flying saucers.

"Look!" Harper signaled, her voice bubbled and distorted beneath the water as she pointed toward a particularly large ray gliding past them. Its twin tails fluttered lazily behind it.

Cameron followed her pointed finger and gasped, his breath rippling out in bubbles around his face mask. The ray was massive, its wingspan easily dwarfing both of them. The sight was mesmerizing, a moment of pure serenity in the chaos and color of the underwater world.

Above the surface, the noise of the beachgoers was muffled by the blanket of water that enveloped Harper and Cameron. They were in their own bubble, isolated from the world above with only the sound of their breathing and the occasional click of a dolphin's sonar to fill the silence.

Cameron reached out a hand, fingers stretching toward the magnificent creature. Harper watched, her eyes wide, as the ray seemed to acknowledge their presence with a slow, sweeping gesture of its wing. It came closer, allowing Cameron's hand to graze gently over its smooth surface. Emboldened by Cameron's success, Harper reached out too, her heart pounding in her chest as she felt the ray's skin under her fingertips. It was smoother than she'd imagined, cold and slightly rubbery.

Suddenly, the ray turned, its large eyes regarding them calmly before it swam off into the blue expanse.

When they surfaced, Harper beamed a smile. "That was incredible!" she said, wiping the hair from her face. "My heart is still beating like a drum."

Cameron laughed. "Mine too," he admitted, his grin matching her own. He tilted his head back, his wet hair slicked back and framing his face.

They swam back to the boat, storing their snorkels and climbing back aboard. As they huddled together on the sun-warmed deck, Harper asked, "Did you see when it looked at us?"

"I did," Cameron nodded as he reached for the cooler. He lifted the lid and grabbed two sodas, handing one to Harper.

"Thanks," she said, then popped the top and took a sip. "Ah." She smacked her lips. "So what do you want to do now?"

"Whatever you want," he said. "Today is your day."

Harper's cheeks flushed under the weight of his gaze, but she quickly hid it behind her smile. "Well then ..." She took another look around. "This place is so beautiful, I don't want to leave. Why don't we hang out here this afternoon?" She tossed her hair back and stretched out on the deck, tilting her face toward the sun and closing her eyes.

Cameron chuckled softly. He took a drink from his own soda and said, "That can absolutely be arranged."

Time seemed to slow as they lay side-by-side, letting the sun dry their skin and the soft rock of the boat lull them into relaxation. Harper's breathing deepened as she slipped into a light doze, the sounds of the sea a soothing melody to her ears. Every now and then, Cameron reached out to gently brush a stray lock of hair from her face.

"You really are the most beautiful girl I've ever met."

The sound of his voice stirred her awake. "I doubt that," she murmured. "But thank you for saying so."

"No, really," Cameron insisted. "And not just on the outside ... but inside too."

Harper rolled her head to the side and looked at him, her blue eyes wide and vulnerable, her lips slightly parted.

"Harper ..." he started, his voice husky. "May I ...?"

His question hung in the air like a secret, and Harper found herself breathless with anticipation. She simply nodded, giving him silent permission.

He reached out, cupping her face gently between his hands. His thumb brushed across her lips, sending a shiver of anticipation down her spine. He leaned in closer, his breath hot on her skin, his eyes searching hers for any trace of hesitation. But all he could find was a soft glow of acceptance that beckoned him closer.

His lips pressed softly against hers, an innocent kiss that ignited a fire within them both. It was sweet and tender, their breaths mingling in the warm air. The world shrank away until all that was left was this moment, this connection.

He pulled back slowly, his lips lingering before he drew away completely. His thumbs drifted to her cheeks, feeling the warmth rising in them as her eyes fluttered open.

"Cameron." Her hand rose to his cheek, her thumb tracing his lower lip as if trying to memorize the feeling. "That was ..." She trailed off, words failing her.

"Good," he finished for her, his voice a hushed whisper.

"Better than good." Her hand lingered on his cheek, the heat of his skin a comforting contrast to the cooling evening air. "It's moments like this that make me never want to leave this place."

"I know what you mean. I wish we could stay in this moment forever, just the two of us."

"But we can't, can we?" she said, her voice echoing his melancholic tone. Her fingertips traced the line of his jaw, a tender touch that spoke volumes.

Cameron shook his head, a small smile playing on his lips. "No."

"What will happen when we go our separate ways ... to us, I mean?"

"Honestly, Harper," he began, his voice steady but filled with a hint of sadness. "I don't know. Falling in love with you this summer was not part of my plan."

She held her breath, her thoughts ran at his words. "Love," she managed to say. She sat up and stared at him for a long time before speaking. "You're in love with me?"

"Yes," he answered without hesitation. "I thought you knew that."

Harper bit her lip, the harsh sting grounding her in reality. She wanted to laugh, to cry, to scream—anything to show this excitement welling up inside her. She felt like a snow globe that had been shaken violently, the little pieces of her heart swirling in a chaotic storm. "I ... I don't know what to say, Cameron," she finally admitted, unsure of which emotion held dominion over her in that moment—shock, disbelief, or a strange, terrifyingly fragile happiness. "I've never been in love before, so I don't know what it feels like, but ..."

"This." He guided her hand to feel the steady beat of his heart. "It feels like this."

Harper was at a loss for words, her eyes darting from Cameron's face to their entwined hands on his chest. She could feel the strong rhythm of his heart against her palm. Each beat was a testament to his words, pulsing with truth, with life, with love.

"Then I love you too," she said, putting his hand to her chest.

Cameron exhaled as the corners of his mouth quirked upward in a smile.

***

As the sun disappeared below the horizon, Cameron released the boat from its moorings, and they set off for home. The trip back was quiet, peaceful, both of them savoring the perfect day.

When darkness had fallen, they drove to the park and sat in the lot beneath a blanket of stars. It was the perfect ending to what had already been the perfect day.

"What will you do next summer?" Harper asked as she leaned her head on Cameron's shoulder. "Will you come back here?"

"No." He shook his head. "My summers from this point forward are spoken for."

"So this is it?" Harper frowned, her heart aching with the realization of their impending separation. "This is our one and only summer together?"

"Yes, but hopefully not the last time we'll be together," he said. Cameron pulled Harper closer, wrapping an arm around her shoulder. "I mean, I hope that we'll find a way to see each other again, regardless of where we are or what we're doing."

Harper nodded against his shoulder, her heart beating in tandem with his. She knew that nothing would be the same after this summer—Cameron had become a part of her in a way no one else ever had before, so she clung to the hope that this was only the beginning for them.

"I'd like that," was all she said, but her heart was screaming for more. She wanted to tell him that she would cross oceans, climb mountains, do anything just to see his face again. But instead, she sat there, listening to the distant waves crash against the shore.

CHAPTER 18

Present day

"And that's when I knew," said Harper, pulling her knees to her chest, "that I was in love with him."

Sidney swooned. "I know you've told me that story before, but it gets me every time. I'm still shocked you agreed to go flying with him."

"Me too, but he always had a way of making me feel comfortable, even when I should have been scared out of my mind." She sighed, thinking back to all the adventures they had shared over the years.

As the storm rolled on, Harper poured herself another drink and gulped it down before pouring another.

"You might want to slow down," Sidney advised.

Harper gave a bitter laugh, "Oh, don't worry about me, I can handle my liquor." With that, she lifted the glass to her lips, took a big gulp, and grimaced as the alcohol burned its way down her throat. Sidney watched her with stern eyes, as if she were analyzing each twitch of Harper's face.

"Can you now?" Sidney finally replied with a smirk. She walked over to the window, peering out into the deluge. "Being here is difficult for you, isn't it?"

Harper didn't answer right away. "Yes," she admitted, finding clarity amidst her intoxication. "Don't take this the wrong way, but I was thinking how this should be my wedding. Being here, the memories I have ..."

"You mean of you and Cameron?" Sidney sat down beside her. "You're not upset with me for having my wedding here, are you?"

"No." Harper shook her head. "Not at all. That's not what I meant. This place means as much to you as it does to me. It's just that this is a place of firsts for me—first kiss, first time I fell in love, first time I ..."

Sidney nodded in recognition. "You don't have to explain, Harper. I understand." She reached out and gently squeezed Harper's shoulder, trying to offer some comfort. "There's no easy way to revisit the past, especially when it's a place you associate with someone you loved deeply."

Harper stared into her glass, her mind racing back to that last night of summer vacation. She remembered the way Cameron had looked at her, the heat in his eyes as he touched her. It was intense, passionate, and unforgettable. And as she closed her eyes, she relived every moment of that unforgettable evening, the memory still so vivid and powerful, as if it could have happened just yesterday.

12 years earlier

Warm light spilled from the windows of Cameron's grandparents' house, casting a welcoming glow on the lush garden outside. Inside, the atmosphere was intimate and cozy, with soft music playing in the background.

Knowing this was their last night together, Cameron had pulled out all the stops, enlisting the help of his grandmother in preparing a delicious meal.

As Harper entered the cozy coastal cottage nestled among the swaying palm trees, she was greeted by the delicious aroma of home-cooked food. The scent of fresh rosemary and thyme mingling with the mouthwatering smell of roast chicken made Harper's stomach rumble.

"And this is Harper," said Cameron, introducing her to his grandparents.

"How do you do?" Harper said politely.

Cameron's grandparents greeted her with genuine warmth. His grandfather, Kenneth, had on a pair of neatly pressed khakis and a white golf shirt. A sprightly man with wise eyes and a forthright demeanor, he extended a weathered hand toward Harper. "Pleased to meet you, Harper," he said, his voice strong and firm.

In response, Harper gently rested her hand in his, feeling the lines of a life lived fully carved into his skin. "The pleasure is mine," she replied, her smile warm and sincere.

Cynthia, Cameron's grandmother, was a picture of poise and elegance in her frilly lavender dress. She had an ageless beauty about her; her hair, silver as the moonlight, was neatly coiffed, framing her face and accentuating her blue eyes. "You're even lovelier than Cameron described," she said, her voice laced with a gentle chuckle that reminded Harper of a melody from a forgotten song.

Harper blushed but managed to thank her for the compliment.

As they walked through the living room, Harper studied the photographs decorating the walls, many of which featured Cameron and his mother. There were black and white images of holidays past, color photos of various family gatherings, and a particular portrait that caught Harper's eye: a younger version of Kenneth and Cynthia on what looked like their wedding day. They stood arm-in-arm, smiles beaming from their youthful faces under an arch of flowers.

In the dining room, a giant curio cabinet held various trinkets and antiques. Among them was an American flag displayed in a shadow box. Above it was a photograph of Cameron's mother along with her war medals. It was a sobering reminder that Cameron's mother had been a soldier, a hero in her own right, and had given the ultimate sacrifice. Harper felt a twinge of sadness at the thought.

As Harper and Cameron made their way outside, Kenneth and Cynthia eased back inside, giving them privacy. As they sat down to dinner on the back porch beneath the lights, Harper noticed how the candlelight accentuated the planes of Cameron's face, highlighting his strong jawline and the intensity of his deep blue eyes. In that moment, she felt a connection between them that defied explanation. It was as if the universe had conspired to bring them together, setting the stage for a love story that would echo through the ages.

"Harper," Cameron said gently, pulling her out of her reverie. "You look like you're a million miles away. Is everything okay?"

"Sorry," she replied with a self-conscious laugh. "I guess I was just lost in thought."

"Anything in particular?" he asked, his eyes searching hers for an answer.

"Actually, I was thinking about us," she confessed, feeling a warmth rise in her cheeks. "This night feels so special, and even though I'm leaving tomorrow, I can't help feeling like this is the beginning of something amazing between us."

Cameron reached across the table to take her hand. His

touch was tender and reassuring, as if he understood the vulnerability that lay beneath her words.

"I agree," he said softly, his voice barely audible above the soothing music. "I felt it the first time I saw you."

"You mean when I was flailing about in the water that day?"

He chuckled. "No. I had seen you the day before, out by the pool."

Harper's heart fluttered at his admission. "You did?"

He nodded, his eyes never leaving hers. "Yes. I remember seeing you there, basking in the sunshine, the book in your hand. And there was just something about you," he confessed. "Something that caught my eye."

"You caught my eye the first time I saw you too," she said. "It was the way you looked in those red lifeguard shorts."

Cameron blushed, a boyish grin spreading across his face. "Then I guess it's safe to say that it was love at first sight—for us both."

Harper considered that. "Yeah, I guess you could say that."

As they continued their dinner, Harper and Cameron found themselves sharing stories from their past, the laughter between them growing more frequent and the conversation flowing effortlessly. With each anecdote, they discovered more common ground and a deeper understanding of the other's soul.

After finishing their meal, Cameron led Harper out onto the beach, where the gentle breeze carried the scent of saltwater and the distant sound of crashing waves.

"Would you like to take a walk?" he asked, offering his arm to her.

"Sounds like the perfect way to end the evening," Harper

replied, taking his arm and feeling an all-too-familiar flutter in her stomach.

As they strolled along the shore, the moonlit sky cast a silvery glow on the water, creating a serene atmosphere that lent itself perfectly to the intimate nature of their conversation.

"I find myself wishing you and I had grown up together," Harper mused. "That we'd known each other from the start."

"You know, I've thought the same thing," he admitted. "But then I realized something."

"What's that?"

"That maybe our paths crossing now was intentional. Maybe we weren't supposed to be a part of each other's past, because we're meant to be each other's future."

Harper's eyes widened. She hadn't thought of it that way before—the idea that their meeting wasn't a missed chance, but rather, a destined encounter. "Maybe you're right."

They walked on in silence for several moments, neither of them saying a word.

The moonlit waves seemed to dance along with their thoughts, each crest and fall reflecting the ebb and flow of their burgeoning feelings.

"Let's make a promise," Cameron began, turning to face her and taking her hands in his. "No matter where life takes us, we'll always keep this night in our hearts. That we'll remember the way the moonlight danced across the water, the way your laughter blended with the sound of the ocean, and how this moment feels, right here and now."

Harper looked at him, moonlight illuminating the earnestness in his eyes, and she remembered what he'd told her about the consequences of making promises. But this wasn't just him putting on a charming act, he was genuinely sincere.

A lump formed in her throat as she realized the gravity of his words—they weren't just fleeting teenage promises, but a pledge of a lasting bond.

"I promise," she said, allowing herself to hope beyond hope that this was only the beginning of the rest of her life.

In the distance, the once-clear sky began to change, dark clouds gathering on the horizon like a veil being drawn across the heavens. The wind picked up, rustling the nearby dunes and carrying the scent of the impending storm. The wind howled around them, whipping Harper's brown hair against her face, stinging her cheeks as she peered into the tempestuous sky. The first rumble of thunder rolled in from the distance, and she felt its vibrations course through her body.

"We should head back," Cameron urged as the first raindrops fell. He surveyed their surroundings. "This is the last place you want to be during a thunderstorm."

As they hurried along the beach, their hands clasped tightly together, lightning streaked across the heavens like jagged veins of silver fire, illuminating their path for brief moments before plunging them back into darkness. The ominous flashes cast deep shadows on the sand, transforming the once-idyllic landscape into an eerie dreamscape.

"Over there!" Cameron shouted. Out of the darkness, a lifeguard shack emerged, offering an unexpected refuge.

Cameron forced open the door and they went in. Inside, the small space was cozy and warm.

"Are you all right?" Cameron asked when they were out of harm's way.

"Fine," she answered. "Just cold."

Cameron found a lantern and lit it, then he took a large blanket and wrapped it around Harper, pulling her close.

"Better?" he asked as they fought off the chill.

"Yes, thank you," she murmured.

As the storm raged on, Harper and Cameron sat in the dimly lit lifeguard shack, their bodies pressed close together. The light from a single lantern cast warm shadows across their faces as they leaned in, their voices barely audible over the pounding rain and the crash of waves outside.

"Harper, I love you," Cameron whispered, his words trembling like leaves in the wind. "I should have told you every day, every moment we were together."

The raw honesty in his confession sent a shiver down her spine, and she clung to him, feeling the steady beat of his heart against her chest. "I love you too."

As if drawn by an invisible force, their lips met in a tender, longing-filled kiss.

Tenderness gave way to passion as they explored each other's bodies, their feverish touches revealing the depth of their desire. The weather outside seemed to mirror the tumult within them, the thunder echoing the pulse of their hearts while the lightning illuminated the dance of their entwined forms.

In the midst of it all, Harper and Cameron discovered a sanctuary in one another, a place where their love could take root and flourish despite the odds.

***

The first golden rays of sunlight pierced through the gaps in the wooden walls, casting a warm glow over Harper's face as she stirred from her slumber. She blinked against the light, taking in the sight of Cameron lying on the blanket beside her, his chest rising and falling with each steady breath. Her heart swelled with love, but it was bittersweet—the knowledge that she must leave Destin and say goodbye to him weighed heavily upon her.

"Morning," Cameron murmured, his voice thick with sleep. He opened his eyes, meeting Harper's gaze with a warmth that made her chest ache.

"Good morning," she replied, forcing a small smile. As much as she wanted to revel in the afterglow of their night together, the daylight haunted her thoughts, reminding her of their impending separation.

They rose from their makeshift bed, pulling on clothes that still held the scent of saltwater and rain. The storm had passed, leaving behind a clear sky that mocked their inner turmoil. Cameron reached for Harper's hand, entwining their fingers as they stepped out of the lifeguard shack and onto the beach.

"Harper," he said, his voice cracking. "I don't want you to go."

"I don't want to either," she admitted, tears welling in her eyes. "But I have to."

They walked along the shoreline, the waves lapping gently at their feet, erasing the footprints they left behind. Seagulls soared overhead, their mournful cries echoing the sorrow that filled Harper's heart.

"Listen," said Cameron. "About last night. I want you to know that I meant every word I said, every touch ... What we shared, it was real, Harper. Nothing has ever felt more real."

Tears spilled from her eyes. "I know," she whispered. "I meant what I said too." After composing herself, she said, "Hey, I was thinking ... New York and Annapolis aren't that far apart. What if I were to come and visit you sometime in Maryland? Or what if you came to see me in New York?"

"Yeah," said Cameron. "I'd like that."

"Then it's settled," Harper said, brushing away her tears with the back of her hand. "This isn't goodbye; rather, until I see you again."

"Until I see you again," Cameron said, then kissed her one last time.

CHAPTER 19

Present day

By the time the rain finally stopped, Harper and Sidney were three sheets to the wind, so they ordered room service and watched movies until they sobered a little.

"So what do you want to do now?" Sidney asked as she tossed aside the last bite of pizza crust.

Harper slouched back on the bed, her eyes heavy with exhaustion. "I don't know," she sighed, flicking a stray olive off the duvet. "Go to sleep, I guess."

Sidney shifted in her seat, her gaze drifting over to the open window revealing a night sky filled with stars. "It's still early," she protested, although the yawn she tried to stifle seemed to betray her own fatigue. "Let's get dressed up and go out."

Harper tilted her head to glance at Sidney, an amused grin playing on her lips. "Out? After the day we've had?"

Sidney grinned back sheepishly, shrugging her shoulders. "Why not?"

Seeking a compromise, Harper suggested they go to the rooftop bar instead.

"Sounds fun," said Sidney.

An hour later, Harper and Sidney found themselves on the top floor of the hotel, sipping cocktails and enjoying the refreshing ocean breeze.

"See," said Harper, taking in the view. "This is much better than going out. There's music, no traffic to contend with, and our rooms are literally down the hall."

Sidney brought her cocktail to her lips and swallowed a bitter gulp. "I suppose you're right," she conceded, her gaze shifting toward the endless ocean that glittered under the pale moonlight. "You know what this reminds me of? The night we hung out with Cameron and Trevor at the bonfire. Do you remember?"

Harper nodded, peering out toward the beach where the echo of laughter and music from a distant party wafted up to meet them.

"Yes," Harper replied, "I remember. That's the night Trevor played that tune on the guitar."

"That's right," Sidney mused, as if reminiscing about a long-forgotten memory. "That was such a nice surprise, wasn't it?"

Harper nodded in agreement. "Almost as nice as when Cameron showed up to surprise me on my twenty-first birthday." Harper's memory dredged up the image of a tall, chiseled Cameron, arriving just when it was time for her to open her gifts. Sidney had arranged for him to be there, knowing how much Harper was in love with him at the time.

Suddenly, Sidney's phone buzzed. She pulled it out and squinted at the screen, her brow furrowed in surprise. "It's Todd."

"Todd?" Harper checked her own phone. "At this hour?"

"Maybe he's found a house for me. I told him to call the minute something came up," explained Sidney as she excused herself.

Despite her buzz, Harper's mind kicked into overdrive.

What was Sidney really up to? Harper went immediately to the one place she promised herself she would never return with Sidney—the topic of infidelity. "No," she said, trying to shake away the doubt. "She wouldn't go down that road again, would she?"

It had been a long time since Sidney's last indiscretion, a moment in their past that Harper had tried to erase from her memory. But there it was, surfacing again. The past had a way of doing that to Harper, finding the perfect moment to rear its ugly head.

Curious, Harper got up and followed Sidney into the hallways, careful not to call any attention to herself. She stopped at a corner and leaned in close to eavesdrop on her conversation. "I don't know," Harper overheard Sidney say. When the other person responded, she whispered back, "No, I don't think so. But you can't keep calling me ... Fine, just text me next time ... Okay. Bye."

Harper quickly made her way back to her seat before Sidney could see her.

"Is everything okay?" Harper casually asked as Sidney returned.

"Right as rain. Now, where were we? Oh right, your birthday party." She raised a finger. "Not to gloat, but I still think that was one of my best surprises. I mean, you had no idea what I was up to, did you?"

Harper's doubts about Sidney faded a little as she smiled at the memory. "I'll admit, you really outdid yourself that night. Never in a million years would I have guessed Cameron would be there. But of course,"—her smile faded a little—"I also never would have thought that the day would come when Cameron and I wouldn't even speak to each other, but look at us now."

Harper's smile disappeared completely, buried under the weight of her memory.

"I know what you mean," said Sidney. "Everyone saw how close you and Cameron were. Despite the odds, we all thought you two would make it."

"I thought so too," said Harper. "We were committed to one another, and to our future, and despite the distance, we made it work the best we could." Sidney nodded as Harper's eyes misted over. "Of course, nothing lasts forever, and in the end, it became too much for either of us to bear."

"Remind me," said Sidney. "Who was it that decided to end things? You or him?"

"The first time, or the second?"

"First," said Sidney.

Harper shook her head, a bitter chuckle at the edge of her voice. "Neither of us, really. It was more like ... like an inevitability, a foregone conclusion that had been hanging over us for months." She reached for her glass and found it empty; ordered another with a motion of her hand. "In fact, I think we both came to the realization that it was over at the same time."

Harper took a deep breath, recalling the moments that had led to their eventual breakup. She explained that it wasn't one big thing, but rather a series of small events that slowly drove them apart. "Death by a thousand paper cuts," as she put it.

Sidney sat quietly, allowing Harper the space to continue.

Harper traced the rim of her now-refilled glass with a finger, the clinking sound punctuating her somber reminiscence. She drank the tart liquid, its warmth spreading through her veins and providing a temporary comfort. "Regardless," she started, her voice nearly a whisper, "I always regretted not trying to hang on just a little longer, try a little harder ..." Setting her drink aside, she folded her hands on the table and sighed, the air conveying an unspoken story of a love that had once been.

"I wonder if he feels the same way?" Sidney asked.

Harper stiffened slightly, masking her avoidance with a shrug. "I don't know. But since he won't return any of my texts, I have to assume the answer is no."

***

Harper called it a night sometime after three and retreated to the comfort of her room, hoping to find some much-needed rest. The day had taken its toll on her, pushing her to the brink of exhaustion. As she sank into her comfortable bed, she couldn't resist the pull of her phone and checked her messages one last time. A warm message from her mother brought a smile to her face, while an update from Marco assured her that everything was going smoothly at the office. But there was still no word from Cameron.

Turning off the light, Harper lay in the dark, listening to the hum of the fan. "Where are you, Cameron?" she whispered into the darkness as she drifted off into a restless slumber.

CHAPTER 20

When Harper woke the next morning, she was greeted with a splitting headache and the bitter taste of tequila on her tongue. Working to open her eyes, she glanced at the clock on her nightstand. It was already past eleven. Groaning, she buried her face in the pillow.

"Never again," she muttered to herself. She repeated it like a mantra, in hopes that she could fool herself into believing it.

With a sigh, she rolled onto her back and stared at the ceiling, her mind a muddled mess of vague memories. With a wince, she managed to sit up, the world tilting as if she were on a merry-go-round. Harper reached for the mini fridge door and grabbed a bottled water. The cold liquid sent a painful jab through her temples like an ice pick to the brain, but she welcomed the shock of clarity that followed.

Fumbling for her phone, she squinted at the bright screen to see a barrage of missed calls and unread messages. She hoped to see Cameron's name among them, but to her disappointment, they were mostly from Sidney, except for one.

"Call me when you get a minute—no rush," read the message from Marco.

She dialed his number right away. "Hey Marco," she said in a raspy voice. "Is everything okay?"

"Yeah, everything's fine," he replied. "I just wanted to check in ... make sure you're having a good time."

"Yes, I am." *Except for this mega hangover.* "We're having

a blast."

"I'm glad. Listen, I got a call this morning from a young lady named Megan Gaston—she said you told her to get in touch with you."

"Right. She's the girl I was telling you about—the one I met in the park last month. I think she'd be perfect to take Sophie's place when she leaves next spring. Could you do me a favor and show her around the office, let her meet everyone?"

"Of course, I can do that," Marco responded, a note of hesitation in his voice. "Are you sure about this though? I mean, you've only met her once and ..."

"I'm sure," Harper insisted. "So don't scare her away. Just be your usual charming self."

"Consider it done," he chuckled.

"Any word from Eleanor?"

"Actually, I haven't heard a peep from her, knock on wood."

"That's what I like to hear," Harper replied. "Well, it seems like you have everything under control. But if anything comes up—"

"Yes, yes," he interrupted. "You'll be the first to know."

When Harper ended the call, she let out a long, husky sigh, dropping the phone back onto the nightstand with a clatter that echoed loudly in her throbbing skull. At least one aspect of her life felt stable. Her love life, on the other hand ... Who was she kidding? Cameron would probably never call again after what she had done to him. A pang of regret twisted in Harper's gut, like a knife milling around, and not just from the hangover. But she did her best to ignore it, forcing herself out of bed.

Legs wobbly, she stumbled toward the bathroom, pausing only to glance at her disheveled reflection in the mirror. Her mascara was smudged, and her hair tangled, evidence of the reckless abandon of the night before. With a sigh, she turned on the faucet, splashing her face with cold water.

After getting dressed, she joined Sidney in the ballroom to finish decorating for the wedding.

"Well, well, well," Sidney said as Harper walked in. "Good morning ... or should I say, good afternoon."

Harper checked the time on her phone and groaned. "How is it you're so perky? You drank as much as me last night."

"You forget I was in a sorority," Sidney answered with a smirk.

"Clearly," Harper retorted, stumbling toward a table laden with tulle and flower arrangements. She picked up a stray hydrangea and twirled it absently between her fingers.

Sidney raised an eyebrow, crossing her arms over her chest. "Did you sleep well?"

"Does passing out count?" Harper replied.

Sidney shook her head, a grin pulling at her lips. "You'll be fine once you get some food in your stomach. I took the liberty of ordering lunch for us." She checked her watch. "It should be here any minute."

Harper only grumbled in response, allowing the hydrangea to slip from her fingers and flutter down onto the table. Turning toward the grand windows of the ballroom, she squinted against the afternoon sunlight that streamed in. "Did I dance on a table last night?" she asked as glimpses of the previous night began flooding back.

"The table, in the elevator, in the hallway outside your room. You put on quite a show."

Harper groaned. "Sorry. That's completely out of character for me." She turned back to Sidney, her head pulsing against her temples. "Which is why I'm never drinking tequila again as long as I live."

Sidney chuckled. "Don't sweat it. It was all good fun. And I was right there to make sure you didn't do anything stupid. Besides, it was nice to see you cut loose for a change. I haven't seen you do that in years."

"Yeah, well ..." Harper wandered back to the table, and sat down. "Ever since I got here, I haven't really felt like myself." She shook her head slowly, trying to clear the fog. "Being back here is even harder than I expected."

Sidney took a break and sat down across from her. "What do you mean?"

"There are too many memories here," she said as the fog lifted. "Little ghosts lurking around every corner. I thought I could handle it, but clearly, I wasn't ready."

Sidney's brown eyes softened as she studied Harper. "Is this about Cameron again?"

Harper looked down at the table, her fingers tracing the intricate lace pattern on the tablecloth. "He's just ... everywhere. I thought time would have faded the memories, but it hasn't." She stared at the tablecloth, her gaze unfocused and distant.

Sidney reached across the table, her hand covering Harper's. "Harper, you loved him. It's normal to feel the way you do. This place meant so much to both of you. You can't expect to come back here after all these years and not feel anything. But it's also a necessary part of the healing process Dr. Andrews has talked to you about."

Harper swallowed hard, her throat tight at the mention of love. She withdrew her hand and fiddled with the edges of the tablecloth. "I know, but maybe Dr. Andrews was wrong ... Maybe I'm not ready to face this."

Sidney looked at Harper, her eyes sincere and unwavering.

"Harper, it's not about being ready. It's about taking one step forward even when you're scared. Healing isn't an easy road, but I know you have the strength to walk it." She reached out again, this time gripping Harper's shoulder. "And remember, you're not alone on this journey."

Harper nodded in agreement, Sidney's words echoing that of Dr. Andrews. "You're right," she said, and took a breath. "You're always right."

Sidney flashed a teasing smile. "And don't you forget it."

When Harper's hangover had finally worn off, she and Sidney moseyed down to the beach to bask in the afternoon sun. The sand, warm and silky to the touch, left a powdery dust on their bare feet as the two made their way to the shoreline.

Sidney had a sun-kissed complexion that glistened under the radiant sunlight, offset by her slightly disheveled hair with its sun-bleached streaks. Harper, on the other hand, sported a skin tone that seemed pale in contrast. Her dark waves tumbled down her back, catching little flickers of sunlight as they danced in the soft breeze. With their beach towels draped over their shoulders, they picked a spot by the water, distant enough to enjoy the peacefulness yet close enough for an occasional cool splash.

"This is more like it," said Sidney as she stretched out on her stomach.

"I couldn't agree more," said Harper, settling next to her friend and splaying her fingers in the sand. The grains, tiny as they were, held a world of warmth within their minuscule bodies. She wriggled her toes under the surface, relishing the sensation of the tiny particles tickling her skin.

Above them, the drone of an airplane could be heard as it flew east along the coast. Harper smiled as she remembered her first time soaring above the Emerald Coast. But just as she was about to indulge in yet another memory, Sidney's phone pinged, breaking Harper's concentration.

"Is that Jason?" Harper asked reflexively.

"Um ... no," said Sidney, squinting at her phone.

"Let me guess." Harper cut her eyes to Sidney. "Todd?"

"Uh-huh." She tapped the screen furiously, as if crafting a response, then showed Harper her phone. "Look at this charming farmhouse that just came on the market." The image on the screen was that of a quaint, two-story farmhouse sitting in the middle of a lush green field dotted with wildflowers. It looked like something from a postcard. "It's beautiful, isn't it?"

"It's lovely," Harper replied, momentarily second-guessing her suspicions of Sidney's potential infidelity.

When Sidney finished texting, she stowed away her phone in the beach bag and rolled over to tan her front side. For a long time, they lay there, soaking up the rays. But eventually, Harper's curiosity got the best of her.

"Are you and Jason ... okay?" Harper asked tentatively.

"Of course we are. Why do you ask?"

"I don't know ... It's just ... him not being here, and then these calls and texts you've been getting ... from Todd. Are you sure there's nothing else going on?"

Sidney propped herself up on her elbow and gave Harper a pointed look. "What are you implying?"

"I'm not implying anything. I'm just ... You know what, never mind." Harper rolled onto her side, facing away from Sidney.

But Sidney wouldn't let it go. "If there's something you want to ask me, Harper, just ask it."

Harper hesitated, biting her lower lip. She drew a slow

breath before turning back toward Sidney. "Are you seeing this Todd guy behind Jason's back?"

Sidney leaned away, her eyes wide with surprise and a touch of hurt. "Are you serious?" Sidney finally managed to sputter out. "Do you really think that little of me?" The jovial atmosphere around them seemed to have vaporized, replaced by a thick layer of tension. "Like I told you before, I've changed."

Harper sat up, wincing at Sidney's harsh tone. She wished she could take it back, swallow the words she'd spat out so thoughtlessly. But given Sidney's past—the infidelity, the heartbreaks—she couldn't shake off the nagging suspicion. "Oh really?" Harper shot back. "When, exactly, did you change? Was it after Scott McCormick, the guy you cheated on in high school? Or was it Zach Marshall, your boyfriend from college? Or maybe it was Steven Milner, who you swore was the love of your life. You cheated on him for an entire year before he found out what was going on."

"That was different, and you know it," Sidney protested, her face red with anger. "First of all, I was young then, and stupid ... and second, Steven cheated on me at the same time. God, Harper! I can't believe you would bring that up again, or that you think I'm still the same person I was back then." She hastily gathered her things and stood up. "You know, you may have a fancy penthouse in New York and be a high-powered fashion executive, but deep down you're still the same insecure, jealous girl you've always been."

"Oh yeah, well at least I'm not sleeping around behind everyone's back," Harper growled, her chest heaving as she struggled to keep her emotions in check.

For a moment, there was a bone-chilling silence between the two women. Only the sound of the waves crashing on the shore punctuated their lingering tension. Sidney's eyes flashed with a hurt that she was failing to keep concealed, but her voice was steady when she finally spoke.

"Look, Harper, I can't change my past. Yes, I made mistakes, and yes, I hurt people. But that was years ago. If you can't see that I've changed, that I'm not that selfish girl anymore ... I don't know what else there is to say."

Harper watched as Sidney turned in the sand and began to move away, her feet sinking slightly into the wet sand with each step she took. Filled with regret and anger, Harper's heart pounded in her chest. She wanted to call out, to offer some sort of apology or explanation. Yet, resentment held her in its bitter grasp, and silence remained her only companion.

When they reconvened for dinner later that evening at the Beach Walk Café, Harper couldn't shake off the unease from their earlier conversation. They'd had fights before, but this one had cut deep. The usual jovial banter between them was replaced by an oppressive silence.

After taking some time to reflect on their earlier argument, Harper recognized she had overstepped and let her own feelings cloud her judgment. "I want to apologize ... for earlier," said Harper as she settled into her seat. "I crossed a line, and I shouldn't have."

Sidney's posture relaxed and she managed a small smile. "Me too. I shouldn't have snapped at you and said those hurtful things. I didn't mean any of it."

"It's okay," Harper reassured her. "And you were right. I was jealous of you ... am still jealous of you, if I'm being honest."

"Why?"

Harper sighed, her gaze fixed on the endless ocean stretching out before them. "Because you're so many things that

I'm not—extroverted, comfortable in your own skin, effortlessly brave. I've had to work really hard to embody those qualities, but it never comes easy," Harper confessed. "Plus, you've got it all—a successful career, meaningful friendships, and a fiancé that adores you. Meanwhile, my love life is nonexistent."

"This isn't a contest, Harper. It isn't about who gets married first. It's about finding happiness and being grateful for the opportunities we've been given. And yes, some days I feel like I'm on top of the world. And I'm truly blessed to have someone like Jason, but,"—she turned her eyes to Harper—"I've had to kiss a lot of frogs to find my prince. You understand that better than anyone. But if either of us has reason to be jealous of the other, it's me."

"You? Jealous of me?" Harper laughed out loud.

"Yes, Harper. I am jealous of you," Sidney confessed. "You possess something that I've always admired and longed for—a depth of empathy and understanding. You have this profound ability to feel with your whole heart and make connections on a much deeper level than most. You see through people, Harper, like they're made of glass. And that ... that is something I could never do. I may seem fearless on the outside, but deep down, when it comes to getting close to someone, I run. I run because it scares me. But you," Sidney continued, her voice barely rising above the whisper of the ocean breeze, "You don't run ... You embrace it. You feel, you heal, and you grow. And that's how I know that when the right person comes along, you'll have a love that will be envied and talked about long after the last kiss is over."

Harper swallowed, feeling a lump form in her throat. She was taken aback by Sidney's revelation. In all the years they had been friends, Harper would have never imagined the seemingly invincible Sidney would ever look at her, Harper, with envy. "I ... I'm not sure what to say."

Sidney gave her a half-smile. "You don't need to say anything, Harp. I just wanted you to know."

"Thank you. That means more to me than you can imagine."

With their differences behind them, they shared a toast to maturity and the future, whatever it may bring. The evening was surprisingly cool, the breeze from the ocean gentle and soothing. They ordered their meals and fell into an easy conversation, both forgetting about their earlier heated exchange.

As they dined on the open-air patio, Harper's gaze drifted out to the vast expanse of the ocean.

"I don't want to put a damper on the evening, but this week feels like the end of an era," she said, her voice tinged with sadness. "Like we're closing the door on a part of our life that will never be open again."

Sidney took a sip of her water and pondered Harper's words before responding. "I suppose it depends on how you choose to see it. Yes, one chapter—the one where we're both single—is ending, but another one—one filled with marital bliss and starting a family—is just beginning."

Harper smiled, grateful for Sidney's eternal optimism. She always had a way of finding the silver lining, no matter how dark things seemed. Harper pushed around her plate of grilled salmon, lost in thought. "But what about our friendship? With you moving back to Kentucky, we won't be able to see each other regularly anymore."

"That's true, but we'll still be friends. Nothing in this world could ever change that. Besides, Lexington isn't that far from New York—less than two hours by plane. And who knows, maybe this new arrangement will finally make you realize that you belong in Kentucky with me. It would be just like it was when we were kids."

Harper allowed herself to imagine that was still possible. "Would it, though?"

The question hung heavy in the air, causing Sidney's smile to falter slightly. She seemed to be searching for the right words. "No," she finally admitted with a sigh. "I guess not ... Not exactly."

Harper nodded solemnly, her fork now idle beside her half-eaten dish.

"But that doesn't mean it won't be great in its own way," Sidney continued optimistically. "After all, once you find someone to settle down with, we can start our own families and become soccer moms, and heads of the PTA. Can you imagine?"

Harper cringed at the thought. Once, perhaps, she may have dreamt of such a life. A house with a white picket fence, children playing in the yard, the aroma of freshly baked cookies filling the air. But the Harper of today had different aspirations.

"You're assuming there's someone out there who wants to be with me," she mused.

"Don't you?"

Harper considered Sidney's question before responding. "I don't know, Sid. I truly don't know," she said, unable to shake the uncertainty that lingered in her heart. "For a while, I've been clinging to this belief that someday Cameron and I would find our way back to each other, like we did before. But now"—her frown deepened as she glanced at her blank phone screen—"I realize that will never happen."

"Never say never," said Sidney. "There's still hope. There's still time. If it happened once, it could happen again."

CHAPTER 21

Three years earlier

"Harper?" The sound of his voice cut through the chaotic noise of the busy airport. Harper's heart skipped a beat as she turned to see Cameron standing there. Her eyes widened in disbelief as she rushed over to hug him. "Oh my God! What are you doing here?" She held him at arm's length, taking in his appearance. He had changed very little since the last time she saw him, but there was a maturity to his features now, a worldliness that was underscored by the faint lines around his eyes. His sandy hair was short and neatly combed, and his smile held that same enigmatic charm that stirred forgotten parts of her heart.

"I'm on my way to Cyprus," he replied with an uneasy smile. "To rejoin Trevor and my squadron. You?"

"I just got back from attending a fashion show in Milan." Harper couldn't stop smiling. "Are they letting you fly? I thought I heard they had grounded all flights until tomorrow on account of the blizzard."

He frowned. "Yeah, it looks like I'm stuck here for the night. I'm trying to work with the airline to find a place to stay, but by the looks of things ..." He glanced around at the crowded airport. "I'll be sleeping here tonight."

"Or you could come with me," she offered. "My apartment

isn't far from here, and I have a comfortable sofa that you can sleep on."

He hesitated, then gave her a grateful smile. "Are you sure? I don't want to impose."

"Trust me, you won't be any imposition," she reassured him. "It's the least I can do." She paused before adding, "What do you say?"

Cameron glanced at the growing line. "You drive a hard bargain," he said with a chuckle. "But all right, lead the way."

They managed to catch the last available cab and squeezed into the backseat. As it dropped them off in front of Harper's apartment building, she paid the fare and led Cameron inside.

"Thanks again for doing this," he said as they made their way inside her apartment.

"It's my pleasure," Harper replied with a warm smile. "Just make yourself at home."

He set down his bags in the living room and sank into the comfortable sofa. "This is a nice place you've got here. And you were right about the couch, it's comfortable."

"Thanks, I'm glad you approve." She removed her coat and gloves and placed them in the hall closet. "It's okay ... for now," she said as she joined him in the living room. "But now that I've started my own company, I hope to be able to afford a much better place soon."

"Your own company?" Cameron marveled at her. "At your age? That's quite impressive. Congratulations."

"Thanks," she replied, feeling the pride swell inside her. "It's small ... more of a boutique shop, for now. But I have high hopes for it."

"Well, I couldn't be happier for you. I always knew you had it in you."

Cameron had always believed in her potential but hearing him say it out loud made her heart soar.

She smiled, then tilted her head slightly, studying Cameron. "Are you hungry?"

"Starving."

"In that case, give me a few minutes, and I'll whip us up something." Harper headed toward the kitchen. "Any aversions?"

"Just something simple will do," Cameron responded, rubbing his stomach. "I'm not picky."

As Harper prepared a quick meal of stir-fried chicken and vegetables over rice, they chatted about their lives since they last saw each other. Despite the fact that they had decided to go their separate ways two years earlier, the conversation was easy and filled with laughter, a welcome respite from the long, stressful day.

While they ate dinner at her small dining table, Harper stole glances at Cameron. His hair had grown since the last time she saw him, framing his face in soft waves, and there was a hint of stubble along his jawline. His eyes were still the same shade of blue she remembered, filled with a light that always seemed to make her feel comfortable and at ease.

After dinner, they moved into the living room and continued their conversation. Still full of stories and laughter, they stayed up late into the night until dark circles appeared under Cameron's eyes.

"It's getting late," Harper observed, stifling a yawn. "I should let you get some rest."

In response, Cameron rubbed his eyes sleepily and stretched out on the sofa. "You're right," he agreed with a yawn of his own.

Harper rose from her chair, collecting the empty dishes. "I'll bring you some bed linens," she said, before disappearing into her bedroom. When Harper re-emerged, she was carrying a plush blanket and a fluffy pillow. Cameron chuckled at the sight. "This reminds me of when we were in college, and I'd crash at your place on weekends. Remember?"

Harper released an easy laugh, passing him the items. "That feels like a hundred years ago, doesn't it?"

With a nod, Cameron set himself up on the sofa, his body sinking into the cushions. He draped the blanket over himself and rested his head on the pillow.

"Need anything else?" Harper asked, pausing at the doorway to her bedroom.

Cameron shook his head, offering her a grateful smile. "No. I'm more than good. Thank you again. This beats the hell out of the airport."

"All right then," she responded with a gentle smile. "Goodnight, Cam."

Leaving the living room aglow with the dim light from a table lamp, Harper retreated to her bedroom.

Despite numerous attempts, Harper couldn't sleep, her mind consumed with thoughts of Cameron. Seeing him again had brought back emotions she promised herself she had let go of. She recalled their carefree days at the beach, his contagious humor, his striking appearance, and his deep, soulful gaze. The person sleeping just feet away was not only an old friend, but also someone who had once been her entire world.

Harper sighed, her mind painting a picture of Cameron as he settled into the sofa. She wondered if he felt the same as she did—if seeing her after all these years had brought up old feelings or just fond memories. A knot formed in her stomach at the idea of him harboring any lingering sentiments. Yet at the same time, there was an underlying anticipation, a tiny itch of hope that refused to be silenced.

She knew she had to quell these thoughts if she were to get any rest. Shaking her head to clear the thoughts away, she turned her back to the door and burrowed deeper into her blankets. As she closed her eyes, she could almost smell the salt and sea from their beach days, hear his laughter mixing with the cacophony of seagulls, feel the heat of his hand in hers.

***

Morning arrived sooner than either of them expected. In the kitchen, Harper was busy at the stove preparing breakfast when she heard Cameron stir in the living room. "Good morning," she called out without turning around. "Coffee?"

He stretched out on the sofa before responding with a groggy, "Yes please."

Over breakfast of scrambled eggs and toast with a side of bacon, they continued their conversation from last night. Through eyes still heavy with sleep but sparkling nonetheless, they shared more about their lives since they last met—their triumphs and heartbreaks, their misadventures and lessons learned. They spoke of the mundane, but the comfort of the ordinary felt soothing.

"I've missed this," Cameron admitted.

Harper paused, her hand stilling around her coffee mug. "So have I," she said, finding the courage to look him in the eye. "You could have reached out, you know."

Cameron looked down, a flicker of regret passing over his features. "I thought about it," he confessed, tracing the rim of his coffee cup with a finger. "I just ... I didn't know if you would want to hear from me ... after the way things ended."

Suddenly, Harper found her throat thick with sadness. She recalled their last meeting, the things they had said, the heart-rending silence that followed. She remembered the shock in Cameron's eyes when she told him to leave, the profound pain that mirrored her own. It was a memory that had haunted her, a bitter reminder of their once shared happiness turned sour.

She set her mug down, her fingers trembling slightly on the ceramic. "I'm sorry, you know, for how we left things."

"So am I."

Harper watched as Cameron's jaw tensed, his eyes reflecting a sea of mixed emotions. She had always known how to read him better than anyone else.

"I never stopped thinking about you," he said softly. He looked at her, vulnerability evident in the lines around his eyes.

"I—" she started, then stopped, unsure of how to form the words that spun in her mind. She swallowed, her eyes locked with Cameron's. "I didn't either," she admitted finally.

Cameron's eyes widened slightly, and Harper braced herself for his response, her pulse pounding in her ears.

"I've always wondered," he started, his voice earnest and sincere, "if you ever regretted us parting ways."

There was a time when such a question would have drowned her in a sea of pain and regret, but today it only stoked the embers of a long-extinguished fire. She felt the weight of his gaze bearing down on her, but this time, she didn't look away.

"I did," she confessed, her voice barely more than a whisper. "For a long time, I thought we had made a mistake. But as time went on, it got a little easier. I guess it's true what they say about time healing all wounds." But the reality was far more complicated. Time had healed what it could, but she was left with scars—reminders of a love that had once burned red hot.

Cameron nodded, letting out a breath he seemed to have been holding. The lines on his face softened, as if Harper's words freed him from shackles of guilt and regret. "I guess we've both done a lot of growing up since then."

Harper nodded. They had been so young back then, their love both powerful and volatile, an uncontrollable force that had swept them along until they were left battered and bruised. Their separation had been a painful, necessary parting, an end to a chapter that never seemed to have a right ending. And now, here they were—two people with familiar faces and shared memories, having lived years apart from each other—face-to-face once again.

Cameron ran a hand through his hair. His smile faded, replaced by thin lips and a furrowed brow. "Do you think," he started, his words cautious as if they were stepping on a landmine, "our lives would be the same if we had stayed together? Do you think you would have been able to accomplish what you have?"

Harper's heart pounded an answer before her mind could formulate one. "I don't know," she admitted, her voice a soft echo in the increasing silence of the room. "But, given the circumstances, I think we made the right choice."

That truth seemed to hurt Cameron the most, causing him to recoil. His eyes darkened, shadows creeping in to obscure the spark of hope that had been kindling there. His jaw clenched slightly, the ripple of tension visible beneath the stubbled skin. "Right," he hollowly echoed, his gaze retreating away from her and back to the world outside the window. "So where do we go from here? I feel like it was more than a mere coincidence that brought us together at that airport last night. I mean, what are the odds you and I would land at exactly the same time, and find one another in a sea of travelers?"

Harper considered that, thinking that she stood a better chance of being struck twice by lightning than running into him again. "Why don't we start by being friends again," she offered.

"I'd like that. Maybe over time, we can figure out what the universe has planned for us."

A ghost of a smile tugged at Harper's lips at his mention of the universe's plan. "You always believed in that stuff, didn't you?" she mused, catching a lock of her hair between her fingers.

Cameron returned her smile slightly. "What can I say? I'm a hopeless romantic." The irony of his statement was not lost on either of them.

"That you are," Harper agreed, her voice absent of any mockery or ridicule. A nostalgic sentimentality washed over her, and she thought back to her younger self, brimming with naive optimism and star-crossed dreams.

"Remember that night on the beach—the shooting stars? You said they were a sign."

Harper laughed lightly. "I was a melodramatic eighteen-year-old. Everything felt like a sign back then."

Cameron chuckled, nodding slowly. "You weren't wrong, though. I think those stars did mean something."

"Oh really?"

"They led us here, didn't they?"

"Here?" Harper questioned, her eyebrows raised in amusement as she gestured around the apartment. "Wow, that's a stretch, even for you."

Shrugging, Cameron grinned. "Hey, the universe works in mysterious ways," he retorted, a lopsided grin curving up his face. "But maybe they've given us a second chance, an opportunity to rediscover each other."

Harper smiled at Cameron's perpetual optimism, his unwavering belief in the unseen guiding hand of the cosmos. His words held that same warmth and comfort that drew her to him all those years ago. "Is that what you want?" she ventured, her eyes darting to his in a silent challenge.

"Yes," he said without hesitation. "It's all I've ever wanted."

A swell rose within Harper at his admission. She willed herself to remain collected, to not let her softening heart be worn so blatantly on her sleeve. Yet, the earnestness in Cameron's gaze was a force to be reckoned with.

"But what has changed?" Harper asked, recalling the reason they agreed to split in the first place. "I'm still here, and you're still ... somewhere else."

Cameron's smile faded, giving way to resignation. "About that," he said, looking as if he was wrestling with something. "I've been thinking about leaving the military."

Harper blinked in surprise. That was the last thing she'd expected to hear him say. The military had been a part of Cameron's life for as long as she could remember, as ingrained in his identity as his innate sense of duty and honor.

"Why? I thought you were going to make a career of it?"

Cameron sighed. "I was, yes," he said with a nod. "But I feel like it's taken too much from me—freedom, opportunities, family ... you."

Harper's heart pounded in her chest with a sudden intensity that left her disoriented.

"Besides," he continued, "I've done what I set out to do,

and I don't feel as if I have anything left to prove."

Harper stared at him, speechless, her mind a whirl of thoughts. Cameron had always been so passionate about his military career, about making a difference in the world. It was part of what she loved about him, that sense of purpose and dedication. But if he was considering giving it up, then maybe he really did want a second chance.

"But it's not that easy, Cam," Harper finally managed to say, her voice barely more than a whisper. "You can't just ... change direction like that. Leaving the Navy isn't like quitting a regular job. And what about your commitments? Are you really going to back out and break your promises? That doesn't sound like the Cameron I know."

"Maybe I don't want to be that person anymore. What if I want to reinvent myself? Look," he said, his eyes boring into hers. "I squandered an opportunity with you once. I swore to myself if I ever got another chance that I wouldn't make the same mistake twice."

Tears welled up in Harper's eyes, threatening to spill over. She did not anticipate this; his words were a tidal wave crashing down, unearthing long-held hopes and dreams that she had buried deep within herself.

"But ..." Harper's words trailed off, lost in the maelstrom of emotion churning in her chest. She had always admired Cameron's steadfastness, his unyielding dedication to his duty. Could he really be considering giving it all up? For her? "This isn't like leaving a normal job. You can't just quit whenever you want. You're bound by contract."

"Yes," he said. "I agreed to eight years, which means I have four more years before I'm eligible for discharge. I know that seems like a long time, Harper, but in the overall scheme of things, it isn't."

Harper got up and eased into the kitchen, needing time to process her thoughts. "I can't help but wonder," she said suddenly, "if we hadn't crossed paths last night, would you still feel the same way?"

"Yes. I've had these feelings since the day we ended things. In fact, I just returned from visiting with my father—we discussed a career path for me when my military service ends. Don't you see," he said, rising to meet her. "Our running into each other wasn't just a coincidence—it was fate."

"I don't know if I believe in fate," Harper replied. "And even if I did, I don't know if I can just pick up where we left off. Breaking up with you was one of the hardest things I've ever had to do, and I don't ever want to go through something like that again."

"I know what you mean," Cameron said, his voice quiet but steady. "But this time can be different. We can be different."

Harper sighed, running her fingers through her hair. A part of her yearned to leap into his arms and forget all about the past. But another part—a considerable one at that—held back. It was an internal tug-of-war, a battle being waged within her very soul.

Cameron's eyes studied her. He took a step forward, reaching out to her, but stopped, his hand hovering in the air between them. He was giving her space, waiting for her to make the call.

In that moment, Harper saw all the hope and fear in Cameron's eyes. Despite her inner turmoil, she found that she could not look away. She saw the man he had been when they first met, his rigid discipline and unwavering dedication apparent in every aspect of his life. She also saw the man he had become, someone who had learned how to bend, how to compromise, and how to love unconditionally. But most importantly, she saw the man he wanted to be—the man he promised her he would be. It was a compelling image, one that stirred feelings of tenderness, hope, and the kind of fear only love could provoke.

"Okay," Harper said slowly, allowing herself to believe that there were chapters to their story yet to be written. "I'm willing to try if you are. But," she said, dropping her eyes, "there's something you need to know first." She turned away, anxiety and uncertainty creeping through her.

"What is it?" he asked. "Are you seeing someone else?"

"No, it's nothing like that." Harper took a deep breath, steadying herself for what she needed to tell him. "A few months ago, I started having stomach pains. I didn't think much of it, at first, but when they didn't go away, I went to see a doctor who ran some tests. It turns out that I have a condition called endometriosis."

The silence following her confession was so profound that Harper could almost hear the blood pumping in her veins. She couldn't bring herself to look up, afraid of what she might find in his eyes—pity, disappointment, or worst of all, indifference.

"Harper, I'm sorry you're having to go through this," he said, his voice steady and calm. "I had no idea."

"I don't think you understand," she said, then paused, gathering the courage to continue. "There's a high likelihood that I will never be able to have children."

He was silent again, but she pushed past the silence this time, determined to lay everything bare. "I understand if that changes things for you, if it changes what you want."

She didn't need to look up to feel the intensity of his gaze on her. Bracing herself for rejection, Harper was caught off guard by the tender touch of his hand on her cheek. He turned her face gently toward him. The quiet empathy in his eyes was like a balm to her raw nerves.

"It doesn't change anything, Harper," he said. "I love you for who you are, not for what you can or cannot give me. Children or no children, that doesn't change the way I feel about you."

His words echoed through her mind, the fear of his rejection slowly dissolving into sweet relief. Tears threatened to spill from her eyes as she looked up at him, feeling a mixture of vulnerability and gratitude.

"Thank you," she managed to whisper.

His thumb gently swiped a tear that had slipped past her defenses. "We'll face this together," he said, then pulled her into a tender embrace.

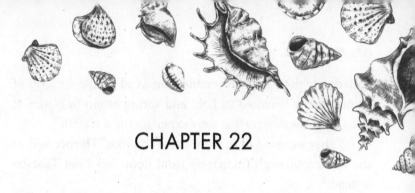

CHAPTER 22

After deciding to give their relationship another try, Harper and Cameron divided their time between her city apartment and his place in Maryland. When they weren't consumed with work, they spent long hours together, rediscovering each other. And by spring, they had settled into a comfortable routine.

Harper found solace in the quiet moments, stealing glances at Cameron as he read the morning newspaper, his brows furrowed in concentration, or how he absentmindedly stirred his coffee, his thoughts seemingly thousands of miles away. It was these mundane moments that taught Harper more about Cameron than any grand gesture could. She discovered his patience in the slow way he turned each newspaper page, savoring every article. She found his hidden anxiety in the unconscious way he bit his lower lip when the headlines were too grim.

Often, after dinner, they would go for long walks. Harper enjoyed these the most. Underneath the shared blanket of twilight, words between them flowed more freely. Comforted by the still of the night, they would walk hand in hand, footsteps in sync with each other. It was just like when they had first fallen in love, but now that they were older and had achieved things individually, it was even better.

As time went by, they found themselves unexpectedly laughing again. In these moments, Harper could feel a glimmer of hope seeping into their story—a subtle yet powerful presence underlying their renewed connection. And as the icy grip of winter finally loosened its hold and spring began to bloom, it wasn't just the flowers that were experiencing a rebirth.

"They were out of that hot sauce you like," Harper said as she walked through Cameron's front door. "So I got Tabasco instead."

From the kitchen, she heard Cameron's voice as he finished a call. When their eyes met, Harper knew something was off.

"Who was that?" she asked, setting the bags of groceries on the counter.

Cameron, his usually placid face a touch pale, cleared his throat and pushed off from the counter. "That was my CO," he said.

"Your CO?" Harper repeated. "What did he want?" She held her breath, fearing the worst.

"Al-Qaeda is making a resurgence in Afghanistan, and the Army has requested close air support ahead of their scheduled troop withdrawals."

The weight of the news settled heavily on Harper's shoulders as she processed his words.

"Harper, it means I'm being deployed again," Cameron confirmed.

Harper's heart jumped into her throat. Since deciding to give her relationship with Cameron another shot, this was the moment she had been dreading.

"When?" she asked, finding her voice.

"I ship out first thing Monday morning," he answered dismally.

Harper's breath hitched, and her grip on the bag of groceries tightened until her knuckles turned white. "But that's ... that's two days from now."

"Yeah, I know," he rasped, his voice heavy with dread. His eyes, usually bright and warm, were now clouded with regret.

Suddenly the room felt cold. Harper swallowed hard against a lump in her throat. "But you said the deployments were over. You said ..."

"I know what I said, but the situation has changed. I'm so sorry."

"H-How ... how long will you be gone?"

"Six months," Cameron said after a very long moment. "I don't know what to say."

The weight of his words crushed Harper. Six months. That was half a year, an eternity of moments and memories that they would have to endure apart. Cameron, on the other hand, looked as if he had been physically struck.

Knowing she had to be strong for both of them, Harper moved around the kitchen counter, placing herself in front of him. She reached up and touched his cheek. His stubble was rough under her fingertips. It was another reminder of how real this situation was.

"I know," she said softly, her hand lingering on his face. "It's not like you had a choice."

Cameron caught her hand in his, pressing a kiss to her palm. "But that doesn't make it any easier."

Harper nodded, fighting back tears. She thought about the sleepless nights ahead of her, the agonizing days filled with uncertainty and fear. But she knew better than to give in to despair just yet.

"Listen," she said, summoning every ounce of courage she had. "We still have the weekend. Let's try not to think about it right now, okay? Let's just enjoy the time we have left."

Cameron's eyes locked onto hers. He studied her face, as if

searching for signs of faltering courage or a hidden distress. He found none. Harper was standing tall, resolute.

But on the inside, she was dying, a silent agony twisting in her gut like a knife.

"Yeah, okay," he agreed.

Harper drew him into an embrace, holding him close as she committed the feel of him to memory.

For the next two days, they never left one another's side. They spent mornings in bed, afternoons hiking in the woods behind his house, and evenings gathered around the kitchen table, talking and laughing, and doing everything they could to delay the inevitable.

***

The night before he was to leave, Cameron found Harper sitting out on the porch, her knees pulled up to her chest, gazing out at the rain.

"Can't sleep?" he asked.

She shook her head, "Every time I close my eyes, I see you leaving."

He reached out, gently tucking a stray lock of hair behind her ear. "I wish things were different," Cameron said quietly. "I wish we never had to be apart."

"So do I."

Taking a seat beside her, Cameron slipped his arm around her shoulders, drawing her close as they listened to the soft patter of the rain. Harper turned her head, burying her face in his shoulder. Her tears were warm against the rough fabric of his shirt. He held her tighter, their bodies almost merging into one as they sought comfort in each other's presence.

"I'll miss you," she finally admitted, her voice a mere whisper over the sound of the rain.

"I'll miss you too," he replied, a hint of sorrow lingering in his tone. "More than you know." He so desperately tried to find words that would make it okay, that would soothe the profound pain they both felt, but words seemed so futile in the face of their impending separation.

Instead, an idea came to mind, something he hadn't thought of in years. "Remember how you threatened to make me dance in the rain?" he asked.

Harper looked up at him, the hint of a smile on her lips.

Cameron stood and offered her his hand. "I'm ready for that dance now."

Blinking at him in surprise, she hesitated before placing her hand in his. Cameron pulled her to her feet, leading her into the shimmering curtain of rain. Instantly, they were drenched—the cool water seeping through their clothes and soaking their hair, adding weight to their already heavy hearts.

Harper tilted her face up toward the sky, letting the raindrops fall onto her eyelashes before streaming down her cheeks. It almost felt like a baptism, the rain cleansing not only their physical selves but also their souls entwined in this bittersweet moment.

Cameron tentatively put his arm around her waist, pulling her closer as her arms went around his neck. They swayed to a rhythm only they could hear, their bodies moving in sync with each other under the deluge. It was a dance of love and sorrow, of joy and grief, all wrapped up in one.

Somewhere in the distance, a flash of lightning split the sky, reminding them of the spark that had brought them together all those years ago. The thunder that followed echoed their heartache, a poignant reminder of the beautiful yet tragic love they held for one another.

Cameron tightened his grip around her, pulling her even closer. He reached out and touched her face, a soft, fleeting touch. In that small, infinite moment, there was just them and the insistent drumming of rain around them. His lips moved against hers in a desperate plea. Harper responded in kind, her arms wrapping around his neck to pull him closer. The world outside fell away as they lost themselves in each other.

Without a word, Cameron swept Harper off her feet and into his arms, carrying her into the house. Only when they arrived at his bedroom did Cameron finally break eye contact with her.

He carefully set her down on the bed, their hands remaining interlocked. The water still dripped from his hair, wet patches growing on the sheets under him, but neither of them cared. In this moment, their world was contained within the four walls of this room.

As Cameron peered into her eyes, a fire ignited within him. His thumb traced intricate patterns on her delicate hand, his eyes conveying a mixture of emotions that he couldn't fully articulate. Regret for leaving her, desperation to make things right, and a glimmer of hope that this time might be different.

"Harper," he started, his voice rough. "I am sorry ..."

But she cut him off with a finger to his lips. "Shh." The rain drummed against the windowpane behind them, a melancholy rhythm that echoed their heartbeats. "No apologies, Cameron. Not tonight."

His eyes searched hers, still holding onto the spark of hope that he saw reflected back at him. She lifted her other hand to brush the damp strands of hair from his forehead. Gently, she began to remove her clothes, taking off her shirt and bra.

Cameron watched her, his eyes growing darker with each button she unclasped. His gaze never left her as he followed suit, the damp fabric of his shirt falling away.

Their clothing discarded on the floor, they came together again in a heated embrace. Her skin against his was like fire meeting ice, a searing contrast that sent shivers down their spines. Their bodies tangled amidst the sheets, their breaths coming out in heavy gasps. The rain continued to drum against the windowpane, but in the small bubble of their world, the storm outside was nothing more than background noise.

Cameron's hands moved along Harper's curves, tracing lines of fiery caresses that left her gasping for air. The heat in her eyes was enough to make his heart pound against his ribcage, matching the rhythm of the rain outside.

Every inch of Harper's body seemed to yearn for Cameron's touch. Her lips on his neck sent tingles down his spine, each kiss more intoxicating than the last. Her hands roamed his body, every touch igniting a blaze under his skin that made him shiver in anticipation.

Slowly, he moved above her, his body hovering over hers. Her eyes reflected everything he felt—longing, passion, and an undeniable need for the other. Her hands ventured up to his face, gently cupping his cheek. Their lips met again in a fervent kiss that was as necessary as the air they breathed.

In the darkness, their bodies moved in perfect harmony with each thunderous stroke of desire. A sense of *déjà vu* washed over him, a memory of past encounters seared into his mind. But this was different. The intensity, the passion, it was heightened by the raw emotion coursing between them.

In soft whispers of pleasure and wordless affirmations, they reached out for each other, their bodies intertwined in a dance as old as time itself. Their breaths hitched, hearts pounded, and senses heightened to an almost unbearable degree. The beautiful ache of need growing with each passing second until it became an all-encompassing crescendo of ecstasy.

As the waves of pleasure slowly subsided, they clung to each other, spent and quivering, their racing hearts beating in sync. The rain had softened to a gentle patter against the window, the sound drowned out by their heavy breathing. Harper's fingers traced lazy patterns on Cameron's damp skin, her eyes closed as she relished the feel of him.

"Harper," Cameron murmured, his voice low and husky in the quiet. His hand reached up to tuck a loose strand of hair behind her ear, his touch as soft as a whisper against her skin.

"Mmm?" Her eyes fluttered open, her heart still pounding from their intimate connection.

"I love you." His declaration was mirrored in his gaze— vulnerable, genuine, filled with an intensity that stole her breath.

"I love you too."

When they woke the next morning, the rain was gone, replaced by rays of sunlight that streamed in through the cracks in the curtains. The golden light bathed them both in a soft glow, tracing delicate patterns over their bodies.

Cameron was the first to stir, his eyes blinking open to the sight of Harper sleeping peacefully on his chest. He took in the beauty of every line and curve of her serene features, then reached up to gently brush errant strands of hair from her forehead, a tender smile playing on his lips.

Harper stirred under his touch, finding herself cocooned in the warmth of Cameron's arms. She looked up to see his eyes, blue as the morning sky, watching her. She reached up, tracing the lines of his face with her fingers, still marveling at the reality of him being hers.

"Good morning," she murmured softly.

"Good morning to you too." His hand slipped down to rest on the small of her back as they continued to bask in the peace of the morning.

"I could stay like this forever," Harper mumbled, tracing patterns over Cameron's chest with her fingers. Her words were more to herself than him, a whisper through the open window into her soul.

Cameron responded by pulling her closer, his arms wrapping around her in a protective embrace. "So could I," he said.

"Do you really have to go?" Harper asked, her fingers tracing patterns on the back of Cameron's hand. "Or was it all just a bad dream?"

"It wasn't just a dream," he said, finally tearing his gaze away from her angelic face.

Harper nodded, slowly withdrawing her hand from under his. She didn't immediately respond, instead choosing to stare blankly at their interlocked fingers. "I understand," she murmured at last, her voice quivering. She looked up at Cameron, desperately trying to memorize every detail of his face. Every laughter line surrounding his ocean blue eyes, every freckle that adorned his tanned skin, and every strand of his chestnut hair that fell carelessly onto his forehead.

Cameron couldn't suppress the sigh that escaped his lips. It carried all the weight of his unvoiced concerns, his silent promises, and his whispered farewells. He gently cupped Harper's face, brushing away a single tear that had made its way down her cheek with his thumb. "I will come back to you," he assured her, trying to sound more confident than he felt. Yet he was all too aware of the dangerous mission that lay ahead of him, of the possibility that it might not be a promise he could keep.

Harper bit her lower lip in an attempt to stop it from quivering. She leaned into Cameron's touch, closing her eyes as the familiar warmth seeped into her skin. She fought the urge to hold him back, to beg him to stay just a little bit longer. But she knew it wouldn't make a difference. The call of duty was never negotiable and had always been a constant in Cameron's life.

And it was at that moment Harper remembered the reason she and Cameron had broken up in the first place—the distance between them and the constant worry of whether he would return safely. She couldn't help but think that history, as unkind as it had been to them, was repeating itself. And she wondered if there would be a time when all of these struggles would come to an end, and they could finally move forward with the rest of their lives.

***

When it was time for Cameron to go, Harper struggled with the inevitable goodbye. Their weekend together had run her through the gamut of emotions, from bitter sadness to longing and passion to quiet contentment. It had been a rollercoaster ride—moments under the covers, long walks under the star-studded sky, and whispered confessions. All that was left now was the sobering reality of his departure.

Cameron, sensing her distress, held her closer. His hand

traced soothing circles on her back as her head rested on his chest. They stood at the airport security checkpoint, their fingers lacing together in an attempt to hold onto what little time they had left.

"Please be careful," Harper blurted out amidst the hum of activity around them.

"I promise," said Cameron. And there was an almost imperceptible tremor in his voice, giving away his feelings. "Thank you for understanding. I don't think I could make it through this without you."

Harper lifted her head, their eyes locking. "You don't ever need to thank me, Cam. I'll always be here for you."

When the last boarding call echoed over the loudspeaker, Harper and Cameron shared one final kiss before he grabbed his bags and walked away. As Cameron disappeared from view, Harper held onto the hope that he would keep his promise and come back to her once again.

CHAPTER 23

As the November sun began to rise, Harper tossed and turned in her bed, unable to find a comfortable position. The night had been long and difficult, filled with thoughts and worries for Cameron's safety. He hadn't revealed much during their last conversation, but he hinted at an upcoming mission that seemed to be weighing heavily on him.

The moment her eyes fluttered open, Harper sensed that something was wrong. Instinctively, she checked her phone, where she saw a text and two missed calls from Cameron. She scrambled to open the message.

CALL ME ASAP.

Dread curdled in the pit of her stomach. She swiftly dialed Cameron's number, her heart pounding against her rib cage as each ring seemed to echo into oblivion.

The line finally connected, and she barely had time to blurt out a panicked "Hello?" before Cameron's voice came through, rough and strained. "Harper, it's me. Trevor's ... gone."

The words hit Harper like a freight train. She gripped the edge of the bed, searching for words that seemed impossible to find. "Gone? What do you mean, gone? How?"

"It ... it doesn't seem real," Cameron answered, hardly able to get the words out. "I still can't believe it. One minute he was here, and the next ... His plane was shot down this morning as we were leaving the combat zone. There were no survivors."

Harper's mind spun, unable to process the magnitude of what Cameron had just revealed. Trevor, the once vibrant and happy-go-lucky young man who had recently gotten married and was expecting his first child, the person Cameron had vowed to protect, was now gone.

Tears welled up in Harper's eyes, clouding her vision as she tried to steady her trembling voice. "Cameron, I'm so sorry. I can't even begin to imagine what you're going through right now."

Cameron let out a shaky sigh. "I don't know how to get through this, Harper. Trevor was like my brother."

Harper's heart ached as she listened to Cameron's voice break with sorrow. She wished she could reach through the phone and hold him, comfort him in any way possible. But all she could offer were words.

"What can I do?"

Cameron drew a breath. "I know it's a lot to ask, but I was wondering if you could be at the funeral. I'm flying home tomorrow, and the service is on Friday. It would really mean a lot."

"Of course," she said without hesitation. "Whatever you need. I'm here for you."

"Thanks," he said, then paused, trying to steady his voice. "Listen, I know things have been tense between us lately, but I—"

"Don't worry about that now," she said gently cutting him off. "Just focus on getting home safely, okay? We'll talk about everything else later."

Cameron paused, his breath hitching slightly. "Thank you,

Harper. I ... I appreciate it."

She hung up the phone and immediately called Sidney, breaking the news to her. Afterward, she took a seat on the barstool in her kitchen, her thoughts a jumbled mess.

Over the years, the four of them had become good friends, their lives entwined like the roots of an old tree. They had shared laughter, tears, triumphs, and disappointments, and now this.

Harper stared at a picture that sat on her kitchen counter, a memory captured in time. It was from that night on the beach when Trevor had played his guitar. There they were, the four of them, arms slung over each other's shoulders, standing tall in the glow of a roaring bonfire.

Harper traced a finger over the glossy surface, pausing over each of their laughing faces. She stopped when she came to Trevor, her finger lingering over the contours of his eternally frozen smile. For a moment, Harper thought she could hear his laughter, could feel the warmth of his arm around her shoulder.

With effort, Harper pulled herself out of her memories and focused on the past six months Cameron had been away. Their relationship had grown strained to the point of breaking. Old arguments, misunderstandings, and distance had taken their toll, leaving them both bruised and guarded. Yet, beneath the layers of hurt and frustration, their bond remained. But in this moment, none of that mattered. All that mattered was Cameron's loss, his pain, and the gaping hole left in their lives with Trevor's sudden death.

***

Forty-eight hours later, Harper found herself in a cemetery

surrounded by a sea of mourning faces. From a distance, she watched Cameron, his eyes swollen and red, trying to put on a brave face as he gave the eulogy. His voice trembled with every word, each sentence etching a deeper sorrow onto the faces of those who had gathered. He recounted stories of Trevor's love of music, his generosity, his infectious laughter that could light up a room. It was as if he was painting an incomplete masterpiece, trying to encapsulate as much of Trevor's life and spirit within his words as he possibly could.

Harper stood at a distance, anchored by the weight of her own grief, watching Cameron struggle to give Trevor the tribute he deserved. Her fingers clenched the edge of her black dress as she listened, a lump forming in her throat.

When his speech ended, the crowd filed past the casket, offering Cameron a comforting pat on the shoulder. Harper watched as they shuffled by: friends and neighbors, relatives and acquaintances, each one a testament to Trevor's impact on the world.

When it was over, only Cameron and Harper remained. Cameron stood, his figure a silhouette against the gloomy horizon. His shoulders sagged under the unseen weight of his sorrow, and Harper feared he might crumble beneath it. She then took a deep breath and walked over to him, her heels sinking into the soft earth with each step.

"Cameron, what you did today took a lot of strength," she began, grasping both his hands in hers. "I know this wasn't easy. I know how much Trevor meant to you."

Cameron merely nodded, his gaze never leaving the marble headstone bearing Trevor's name.

"It's just not fair," he said as fresh tears spilled from his eyes.

The wind picked up, carrying with it a chill that seeped into their bones. Harper pulled her coat tighter around herself.

"Why don't I give you some time alone," she said gently, releasing his hands and stepping back. "I'll wait in the car. Take as long as you need." Cameron nodded again, his eyes still locked onto the name on the headstone. As Harper turned to leave him alone with his grief, she glanced back one more time. The sight of him, standing alone at the foot of Trevor's grave, pushed at her heart with an incomprehensible sadness.

***

After dinner, Harper and Cameron stood on Cameron's front porch, enjoying a beer as the night settled in around them.

"Today was rough, wasn't it?" Harper asked quietly.

Cameron swallowed a mouthful of beer, his gaze fixed on the dark horizon.

"Yeah," he responded. "You know, I can't help but wonder if Trevor's death is a sign—a warning that I should get out, before it's too late."

Harper let out a slow breath, watching as it crystallized in the cold night air. She tilted her head to look at Cameron, studying him carefully under the cover of darkness.

"What does your gut tell you?" she asked.

Cameron was silent for a long time, his expression unreadable in the muted light. He took another swig from the bottle, his throat working as he swallowed.

"It's screaming at me to run," he admitted, the words heavy with unease.

"Then run."

Cameron turned to stare at her, his eyes wide with surprise.

"What?" he stammered, the bottle of beer nearly slipping from his fingers.

"You heard me," Harper said. "You've devoted the last ten years of your life to this and look where it's gotten you. You're tired, frustrated, and barely keeping your sanity intact. That's no life, Cam."

"But the promise I made ..."

Harper shook her head and set her beer down on the porch rail. She turned to him, her hands resting lightly on his shoulders.

"Promises are words, Cam. They're meant to bind us, yes, but not at the cost of our own peace. You need to do what's best for you, not what you think you owe to your mother or Trevor or anyone else."

Cameron's face was a pained, conflicted mask in the hazy glow of the porch light. "I—I just can't let it go, Harper," he choked out. "I gave my word that I would see this through to the end."

"And what if the end is your death, Cameron?" Harper choked out, her hands gripping his shoulders tighter. "Or the death of us?" she continued. "Is that a price you're willing to pay?"

Cameron took a deep breath, the chilly air filling his lungs as he thought about her question. He pulled away from her grip and paced away a few steps before turning back to her, his eyes ablaze with conflict. "It's not that simple, Harper." His voice was strained, tension threading through every word. "I wish it was, but it's not." He raked a hand through his disheveled hair, the normally smooth strands standing in wild rebellion against his scalp.

"Then I'll make it simple for you." Harper's voice was

steady despite the tremor that had taken hold of her hands. She clenched them into fists at her side, regaining control. "Choose us, Cameron. Leave that life behind and we can start over, somewhere far away from here, if that's what it takes."

Cameron looked at her incredulously, her offer lingering in the air between them. "Start over?" he echoed, his eyes wide with disbelief. "Listen to yourself. You know I can't just abandon my—"

"Stop!" Harper cut him off sharply, her hands flying up in exasperation. "Stop using your promise as an excuse, Cam! This isn't about your mother anymore. This is about you. You're a grown man, capable of making your own choices!" She grabbed his face, forcing him to look into her eyes. "Please, Cameron. It's your life we're talking about here. It's our life."

Cameron's eyes met hers, blue depths plagued with regret and determination. He reached up, gently prying her fingers from his face. "Harper," he began softly, "Don't you think I want that? A fresh start ... with you?" His voice was filled with a raw longing that was almost painful to hear. "But I have a responsibility, an obligation."

"But to whom, Cameron?" Harper's voice had softened, and her hands dropped to her sides. "To a memory?"

"To myself ... my country and ...," Cameron said, his voice heavy. His gaze remained locked on hers, baring the raw truth they both knew. He stepped away, turning his back to Harper and looking out into the deepening night. "To Trevor. I promised to take care of him. I promised ..."

"You also made a promise to me," Harper pleaded. "To do whatever it took to make this work. And this may not be the best time or place, but you've left me no choice. Trevor is gone, Cameron. But we're still here. And if we are to survive the next three-and-a-half-years, we need to have this conversation."

He sighed heavily, the weight of her words sinking deep into his core. "All right." He shifted uncomfortably, seeking the right words to express his thoughts. "Do you remember when we first met? No false pretenses, no hidden agendas ... Just two people who felt an inexplicable connection."

She nodded, remembering the electric spark that had flashed between them as he pulled her from the surf. "Yes, I remember it well."

A slow smile spread across his face, an echo of past happiness. "You wouldn't admit it, but you were so scared. I could see the fear in your eyes, but there was something else— sadness, longing, the desire to be loved—it was all there in that single glance. And it was like I could see the rest of my life in your eyes."

She frowned slightly, her pulse quickening in response to his words. "And I saw the same in you," she replied. "That day at the jetty. I saw a young man carrying the weight of the world on his shoulders, looking for someone to share that burden with."

He nodded, acknowledging the truth in her words. His eyes found hers again, the intensity of his gaze making her feel like she was the only person in the world.

"But things have changed since then," he confessed, his voice heavy with regret. "They've gotten complicated."

She moved closer, her hand instinctively reaching out to grasp his. "Of course they have. That's life. But that doesn't mean we should forget what brought us together in the first place."

He looked at her, lost in her honesty. "I'm not forgetting, I promise you that. But I am ... afraid," he admitted and swallowed hard, as if the confession wounded him.

"Afraid of what?"

He struggled briefly before responding, his fingers tightening around hers in a desperate grip. "Of losing you ... Of not being able to protect you from this shadow that seems to follow me wherever I go."

His confession hung heavily in the air between them, a truth that neither of them could deny or evade. She felt his fear, saw it in his eyes, but she also knew her own resolve.

"You don't have to protect me," she said gently, pressing further into his grasp. "I'm not the same girl you pulled from the undertow. I'm a woman now, independent, successful, strong."

"You're right," he admitted with a lopsided grin. "I just ... I love you too much to watch you suffer the same fate as my mother, as Trevor ..."

She squeezed his hand, a tear slipping past her defenses. His pain, his fears ... They were hers too. "I love you too," she said. "Which is why we can't live our lives in fear. Bad things happen, Cam, even to good people. There's nothing we can do about that. But we can't let that reality cripple us."

Cameron looked at her, his eyes clouded with worry. He wanted to stay strong for her, wanted to be her rock as she always was for him. But the world was shadowed for him now, every corner filled with terrible possibilities. Finally, he turned away, his face pained. "But what if I'm cursed? What if everyone I get close to is destined to meet the same end?"

"Do you really believe that?"

"Sometimes," he answered, dropping his head.

She looked at him, his shame palpable in the uneasy silence, and put her arms around him. "Cam," she whispered against his ear, "I can't bear to see you like this."

He was quiet before his body sagged, leaning into hers.

"I'm sorry, Harper," he muttered, his voice muffled by her shoulder. "I just can't afford to lose you. You're the only good thing I have left in this world."

Harper held him tighter, wishing somehow she could absorb his pain. She knew Cameron was a strong man, physically and emotionally, but these tragedies—first his mother, then Trevor—had taken their toll on him, had left scars that would never heal.

"It's not your responsibility to protect me, Cam," she murmured into his hair, stroking the back of his head gently. "You've carried enough burdens on your shoulders. Now it's time to let them go."

"But what if—"

She interrupted him by placing her fingers gently on his lips. "No more what-ifs. We have to live in the present, not in some dark future filled with imaginary horrors."

"But if anything happened to you because of me—"

She cut him off again, this time pressing her lips softly against his. When she pulled back, her eyes were resolute. "Then know that it was my choice, my decision to stay with you. I am not blind to the possibility of danger, Cam. But love isn't safe or predictable. It's risky and it's wild, and it's worth fighting for."

With a sigh, Cameron rested his forehead against hers. His breath hitched as he tried to grasp her words. "I want to believe you, Harper," he whispered. "But the fear ... it's always there, lurking just beneath the surface."

She looked deep into his eyes. "I know," she replied, her voice steady. "I have the same fears. But fear is a part of life. It's what makes us human. It's what keeps us on our toes and forces us to keep fighting, even when the odds are stacked against us."

"I'm tired of fighting, Harper," said Cameron, the look of

defeat in his eyes. "I just don't think I have it in me anymore."

Harper leaned away, realizing that Cameron wasn't the same man she once knew. She looked into his eyes, searching for the spark of resilience that she knew he once possessed. But all she saw was a man who had been worn down by life, a man defeated by circumstances beyond his control.

"Cameron," she said softly, taking his hands in hers. "I understand. I really do. But you can't give up, not now. We've come so far together, cleared too many hurdles ..."

But Cameron said nothing, lost in thoughts she could only guess. His hand was limp in hers, a sharp contrast to the strong grip he always maintained. At this, Harper felt a lump form in her throat; this vulnerable side of Cameron was something she hadn't seen often, and it frightened her.

She squeezed his hands, trying to reignite that spark within him, but the flicker seemed to have vanished, replaced by an all-encompassing darkness. Harper knew she had to tread carefully now, the wrong word could break him. Taking a deep breath, she drew closer to him.

"Cam," she whispered, "I won't pretend to understand everything you're going through. But I promise you, you aren't alone in this fight. You have people who love you, who care for you. You have me." Her voice cracked slightly, and she cleared her throat before continuing. "And if you need time to sort things out, or space ... Whatever you need, I'll give it to you. But you have to promise me you won't give up ... on life, or on us."

Cameron stared at her for a long time before saying, "I'm sorry, Harper, but I can't promise you that. Not now. I just can't."

Harper felt a sharp pain in her chest, as if a cold dagger had sliced through her. This was the moment she'd been hoping to avoid, the moment she'd dreaded since their paths crossed in that airport terminal nine months earlier. She nodded, swallowing the lump in her throat, then stood up slowly, releasing his hands and taking a step back. "If that's the way you feel, then maybe I should go." With that, Harper stepped off the porch and into the night.

"No," he pleaded, stopping her in her tracks. "Harper, please don't leave! Stay with me tonight."

"I'm sorry, Cam," she said, "but I can't. I'm tired of doing this with you."

"Doing what?"

She turned on her heel. "Going round and round, always ending up in the same place. It's exhausting. Look," she said after composing herself. "I love you, Cameron. I always have, and always will. But you have some things you need to sort out, and until you do, I don't think we need to see each other again." With that, she turned and continued toward her car.

"No, Harper. Please!"

But this time she didn't turn back. She continued on, her strides steady and strong until she reached the safety of her car. With her heart in her throat, she started the engine and pulled away, leaving Cameron standing alone on the porch.

CHAPTER 24

"I'll never forget the day you called to tell me about your diagnosis," said Sidney over dessert, her voice heavy. "I was devastated for you. And then when I heard about Trevor's passing and your breakup with Cameron ... I was in utter shock." Sidney took a deep breath, looking as if she might cry. "That year was a tough one for all of us."

"I think that's why, when I met Grant a few months later, I quickly threw myself into a relationship with him. At that point, I just needed something—anything—to take my mind off the pain," she continued, playing idly with the remains of her crème brûlée. "But if I'd known what I know now ..."

"Don't beat yourself up, Harp. Hindsight is always twenty-twenty. On a different note, what have your doctors said about your chances of having a child?"

Harper put down the spoon and stared into Sidney's warm brown eyes, deeply appreciating the empathy she found there. "The doctors ... They say it's possible, but highly improbable." She bit her lower lip, tears stinging behind her eyes.

"And what about adoption?" Sidney ventured gently.

Harper shrugged. "I've thought about it, but the process is so long and bureaucratic. Plus, I don't want to do it alone. Raising a child is a two-person job, especially with the demands of my career. I can't imagine going through all those sleepless nights and diaper changes alone."

Sidney reached across the table, covering Harper's hand with her own. "You're not alone, Harper," she said earnestly. "You've got a whole network of people who care about you. More importantly, you've got me. And as long as I'm around, you'll never have to go it alone."

After dinner, Harper and Sidney strolled back toward the hotel under the cover of darkness, their arms linked, their steps synced to the rhythm of the ocean.

"Not to belabor the point, but you know what I always admired most about Cameron?" Sidney asked as they eased along the lighted path, letting the wind play with their hair. "For better or worse, he always kept his word, no matter what. Jason is the same way. There aren't that many people out there that do that anymore."

"You're right," said Harper, eyes on the stars above. "Well, mostly. In all the time I've known Cameron, there's only one promise he never delivered on."

Six years earlier

The scene unfolded before Harper like an old movie playing on a projector. It was the final day of her spontaneous weekend trip to see Cameron. Destin's warm beaches stretched out for miles, the pristine white sand almost blinding in the bright sunlight. The salty sea breeze carried the scent of sunscreen, mingling with the aroma of fresh seafood from nearby restaurants. Seagulls cawed overhead, their cries competing with the laughter of children splashing in the shallows. In the distance, the turquoise waves crashed against the shore, leaving behind foamy tendrils that reached out for her bare feet before retreating back into the ocean.

Harper and Cameron stood side by side, their toes sinking into the warm sand as they watched the sun dip below the horizon.

"Isn't it beautiful?" Harper said over the sound of the crashing waves. She didn't need to specify what she was referring to; Cameron knew she meant more than just the sunset. Their time together in this idyllic beach town had been nothing short of magical, each day filled with laughter, adventure, and stolen kisses, just as it had been six years earlier, when they first fell in love.

Cameron nodded, his eyes never leaving the horizon. "It is," he agreed, his voice tinged with sadness. He knew, as she did, that their time together was drawing to a close. Soon, they would go their separate ways again—she to the hustle and bustle of the city, he to destinations unknown.

But for now, they stood there on the beach, the sun sinking lower and lower in the sky, as if reluctant to end the day. Harper sighed, a mixture of contentment and melancholy filling her chest. She didn't know what the future held for them, but in that moment, she knew that she would cherish this memory forever.

As night closed in around them, they remained standing, their bodies silhouetted against the glow of the disappearing sun. A brilliant tapestry of stars slowly unfurled above them, casting a shimmering light over the tranquil waters. Cameron tightened his grip around Harper, pulling her close in a warm embrace.

"I have something for you," Cameron said as he reached into his pocket. His hand reappeared, cradling a small object that sparkled softly under the light of the stars. It was a promise ring, as delicate as it was beautiful, encrusted with tiny diamonds that mirrored the stars above them.

"Cameron, is this …?"

"It's not an engagement ring," he said, allaying her fears. "But it is a promise that someday, when I've fulfilled my commitment to my country, I will ask you to marry me."

Harper looked down at the ring, her heart pounding. "It's beautiful," she stuttered a little, tears blurring her vision.

Cameron took her hand, slipping the ring onto her ring finger. "A perfect fit for a perfect woman."

"Can you really see me as your wife?" she asked after she had composed herself.

He stared longingly into her eyes. "Oh yes. I see it every time I look at you, feel it every time I touch you. No matter where I am or what I'm doing, my thoughts always come back to you. You're my compass, Harper, my true north. You are both the journey and the destination. And when I close my eyes, there's no one else I see as my wife."

His words caught her off guard, and it took her a minute to gather her thoughts. "All right, Mr. Spears," she finally acquiesced. "You've got yourself a deal," she'd agreed, never thinking that the moment would come to define the rest of her life.

Present day

Sidney was quiet for a long time before speaking, seemingly swept up in yet another detail of Harper and Cameron's romance. "I remember that ring," she said as they sat settled into chairs on the terrace. "Whatever happened to it?"

Harper looked away, fighting tears. "I gave it back to

Cameron the day after Grant proposed. I didn't see the point in keeping it when I had already agreed to marry another man."

Two years earlier

"What are you doing here, Harper?" Cameron asked as he stood in the doorway of his hotel room.

Harper paused before answering, her eyes darting around the room before settling back on Cameron. "I ... I came to give you this," she replied, slowly bringing out a small, velvet box from her pocket.

Cameron stared at the box, his words trapped in his throat. "Harper ... you don't have to do this."

A pang of regret swept over her. "I know, but I need to." She reached out, placing the box in Cameron's hand.

His eyes flickered from the box to Harper, questions dancing in the depths of his azure irises. "Why?"

"Because," Harper said with a slight tremble. "It's the only way I know how to move on."

Cameron seemed to absorb her words, his face going pale as he turned the box around in his hands. "I understand," he finally said, looking as if he had swallowed a bitter pill. "Do you want to come in?" he asked, stepping aside to make room for her.

"Um ... maybe for just a minute. But I can't stay long."

Cameron nodded, understanding flickering in his steely eyes. "I'm sorry," he said as he backed away from the door. "For the way things have turned out. I never wanted it to be this way."

"I know," she whispered, her gaze lingering over him—his chiseled jaw, the strength in his eyes, the curve of his mouth that she had once loved so much. "But it is what it is," she added after stepping inside and closing the door. Her voice broke on the last word, a hint of regret seeping through. "So what will you do now? Are you going home soon?"

He eased into the living room and lowered himself onto the sofa. "Later this afternoon," he said as he put away the velvet box. "I'll see my dad for a few days, then it's off to destinations unknown."

"What do you mean?"

He was quiet before he answered. "I just accepted a new assignment with the Navy this morning, so I'll be shipping out soon and won't be home for a while."

Harper swallowed hard, her heart pounding. "Oh no. This isn't because of me, is it? Because of what happened last night?"

"Does it matter? Either way, why do you care?" His question hung between them, a tangible reminder of the chasm that had grown in their relationship.

Harper's eyes welled up with tears, but she held them back, refusing to let her emotions break through. "I care because you're not just anyone, Cameron. You're somebody important to me. Someone I ... Regardless of how things ended between us, I still ... care about you."

Cameron stared at his hands instead of looking at her. "And while I appreciate your concern, Harper, I'm a grown man, and I know what's best for me."

Harper bit her lip, fighting the urge to reach out and take his hand. "I know that, Cam. But you're not invincible. You can't just keep pushing yourself to the brink without consequences."

Cameron clenched his jaw at her words. "I know my limits," he said quietly. "And I know what I'm doing. I'm a pilot. The skies are my domain, my life. They always have been."

Harper sighed, looking at him with a sad smile. "I know they are, Cam. And I've never tried to change that about you. I just ... I worry, you know?"

"I know you do. Which is why I'm glad you showed up today. Because if anything were to happen to me, at least I got to see you one last time."

Harper's breath hitched in her throat at his words, a cold dread seeping through her spine. "Don't say that," she said hoarsely. "You're talking like you're not coming back."

There was an extended pause before Cameron shrugged his shoulders weakly. "You said it yourself—life is unpredictable. We can plan and prepare all we want, but life has a way of throwing curveballs."

"I know what I said, but ..." She shook her head. "You'll be fine. I know you will. Just like I have no doubt that we'll see each other again."

"You're probably right," he said, a hint of a smile pulling at the corners of his mouth. "What am I saying? Of course, you're right." But his eyes didn't meet hers when he said it, and the smile didn't quite reach them. It was as if a shadow had fallen over him, a darkness that Harper could almost touch. She wanted to reach out, wanted to pull him back into the light, into the land of the living, but she knew she couldn't. It wasn't her battle to fight, not anymore.

He stood up, dusting off his pants, the smile still clinging to his lips. "I should finish packing," he said, not looking at her. "But thanks for stopping by."

Harper nodded silently, her throat too tight to speak.

"I'll be seeing you," he said as he pulled her into a hug. "And if we don't get a chance to talk again before your big day, I hope it's everything you've dreamed of."

Present day

"No wonder he won't return your texts," Sidney said, shaking her head in disbelief. "Was there ever a time during your engagement with Grant when you questioned your decision?"

Harper nodded slowly as she stared at the distant city lights. "Of course," she said. "All the time. I thought that was normal, something everyone experiences. But as time went on, the doubts turned into a constant nagging. By then, I was in too deep to see a way out."

Sidney furrowed her brow in confusion. "Then why were you so upset when you found out the truth about Grant, aside from him nearly destroying your business? After what you just told me, shouldn't you have been relieved that he was out of the picture?"

Harper drew in a long, deep breath, staring into the darkness as if it held the answers to Sidney's question. "A part of me was relieved," she admitted finally. "But at the same time, I was deeply hurt. Not to mention ashamed. In the end, it was more about his betrayal than it was about my freedom. And on top of it all, Cameron stopped talking to me at just the time when I needed him most. So in the end, I lost on both fronts."

"But if you needed Cameron so much, why didn't you just tell him what Grant did to you, and that you made a mistake? Surely, he would have understood."

Harper sighed, a soft, almost invisible shrug lifting her shoulders. "I suppose ... I was afraid," she admitted, her fingers picking at the edges of her dress. "Of what he would think ... That he might think I deserved it for leaving him."

Sidney's face softened, her eyes filled with understanding as she took in Harper's painful confession. "That doesn't sound like the Cameron I know," said Sidney. "He would never think that way."

Harper's fingers stilled. Her eyes, heavy with unshed tears, met Sidney's. "I don't know," she said, her voice shaking. "You didn't see the look on his face, the devastation in his eyes when I gave him back that ring."

"And what about now?" Sidney asked, her expression turning curious. "Now that you've had time to heal, have you considered calling him and clearing the air?"

Harper gave a rueful chuckle. "I think about it every day," she admitted. "Which is why I sent that text. But," she said, glancing at the blank screen, "it's clear he's moved on, happily living his life of service. The last thing I want is to disrupt it with the ghosts of my past."

"But don't you see, Harper?" she said softly. "The ghosts of your past are not just about you. They are also about him."

Harper's brows knitted together in confusion. "What do you mean?"

Sidney leaned forward, her hands folded intently as she prepared to reveal a truth. "Cameron loved you, Harper," she said firmly. "I think he still does. And I bet he's carrying his own ghosts from the past, wondering why you shut him out of your life."

"But ..." Harper began to object, but Sidney held up her hand to stop her.

"No, hear me out. Have you ever considered that your silence might have hurt him as much as Grant's betrayal hurt you?" she asked.

Harper blinked, her mind spiraling at the implication. She had been so absorbed in her own pain and guilt that the notion of Cameron being equally affected hadn't crossed her mind. "I

... I didn't think ..."

"Of course, you didn't," Sidney interjected gently, not in a way that was dismissive or cruel, but understanding. "You were hurting too much."

Harper swallowed, feeling as if a chasm had opened up inside her.

"What should I do?" she asked Sidney, her voice barely above a whisper. "So much time has passed. I can't just walk into his life and drop this on him."

"You're right," she agreed after a pause. "You can't just dump this on him. And you can't solve this problem by sending text messages either. Pick up the phone and call the man, Harper. Tell him everything you just told me."

The dam of tears that Harper had been holding back broke, streaming down her cheeks. "But what if he rejects me? What if—"

"Regardless of the outcome, at least you'll have confronted your fears. At least you'll know where you stand with him. Please, Harper, do everyone a favor and call him."

***

Long after midnight, Harper sat alone in her room, haunted by the memory of the one that got away. She sank into the plush hotel bed, allowing herself, for the first time in years, to truly feel the depth of her emotions.

"Cam," she whispered, "I miss you so much."

She wrapped her arms tightly around her waist, as if trying to hold together the pieces of her battered heart. The pain of past heartbreaks pressed heavily upon her chest, the weight of a thousand unspoken words and shattered dreams.

And yet, there was still that flicker of hope—that stubborn, resilient flame that burned within her. She wondered what might have been if she had chosen differently, if she hadn't accepted Grant's proposal and instead waited for the possibility of a life with Cameron.

As she reflected on her decision, an internal conflict stirred within her. On the one hand, Grant had been everything she thought she wanted in a partner: successful, charming, and undeniably handsome. But there were cracks in his façade that she should have seen. In contrast, her memories of Cameron felt warm, genuine, and filled with the kind of love that could withstand the test of time.

"Why did I choose the wrong path?" she whispered to herself.

In her mind's eye, she saw herself walking along the shoreline with Cameron, hands entwined, as the waves lapped at their feet. She remembered the way his eyes seemed to see straight into her soul, the way he made her feel truly understood and cherished. The more she thought about it, the more her heart ached with longing for something she couldn't quite name—something that had been missing in her life with Grant.

"Maybe it's just sentimentality," she tried to reassure herself, but the quiet voice of doubt whispered in the back of her mind. It was impossible to ignore the feeling that there was a deeper truth hidden within those memories, a truth about what love should feel like and the kind of partnership she truly desired.

As Harper wrestled with her thoughts, she knew that she couldn't turn back time or change the choices she had made. But as the rain started to fall outside her window, she held onto the hope that, somehow, she might still find her way back to the love she had once known with Cameron.

She needed time to think, to come to terms with the fact that the path she'd chosen had led her away from the love she'd once known—and perhaps could have known again.

As she shut her eyes, the sound of rain lashing against the window, a single tear slipped down her cheek. The taste of salt lingered on her lips, as bitter and haunting as the question that echoed through her mind: What if?

CHAPTER 25

In the early hours before dawn, Harper was jolted awake by the ringing of her phone. Still consumed with thoughts of Cameron, she answered without checking the caller ID. "Cameron, is that you?"

"No, dear. It's Eleanor."

Harper sat up abruptly, momentarily confused. She glanced at the clock—5:25. Why would Eleanor be calling at this hour?

"I'm ... sorry, Eleanor, I thought you were someone else," Harper said as she switched on the bedside lamp.

"It's quite all right. Listen, I know I said I wouldn't bother you while you were away, but we've run into a bit of a snafu. It seems that in our haste to complete the collection, we failed to create a final design, one that will tie it all together. I hate to ask, but do you think you could come up with something by tomorrow morning?"

Harper hesitated, her fingers tapping against the nightstand. "I ... I don't know. Tomorrow is Sidney's wedding, and ... Can't someone else on my team handle it?"

"I'm afraid not," Eleanor replied. "It has to be you. I know it's a big ask, but it's crucial."

Knowing she couldn't say no, Harper reluctantly agreed. "Fine. I'll see what I can do. What did you have in mind?"

"Something elegant, of course," said Eleanor, a note of desperation creeping in. "But something unique. Something that screams Chanel but also Harper."

Harper got out of bed and peered through the curtains at the world outside. The pool below beckoned her, shimmering under the morning sunlight. "I'll do my best," she finally said, her voice carrying a hint of resignation. "I promised Sidney I'd have breakfast with her, but perhaps I'll carve out a couple of hours afterward, before the rest of the guests arrive."

"Excellent! Harper, you're a lifesaver." Eleanor exhaled. "And whatever you come up with, I'm sure it will be brilliant."

Harper didn't share Eleanor's confidence, but nonetheless, she ended the call on a promise to deliver. But as she settled back into bed, she wondered if this was all part of Eleanor's plan—to wait until she was enjoying her vacation before throwing her a curveball.

"Of course," Harper said to herself. "She's testing me. Well, I've got news for her. It'll take more than a last-minute challenge to rattle me."

***

"You'll never believe who called me this morning," Harper said over breakfast.

"It wasn't Cameron, was it?" Sidney asked with a hint of hope in her voice.

"I wish," Harper replied with a sigh. "Actually, it was Eleanor."

Sidney's brows knitted together. "What did she want?"

"She needs another design from me ... and it has to be done by tomorrow."

"Oh no." Sidney's mood instantly shifted.

"Don't worry," Harper reassured her. "I've met tighter

deadlines than this. I'll whip up something this afternoon and be done in plenty of time for the rehearsal dinner."

"It's not that," said Sidney, her mood souring. "I was going to wait until after we'd eaten to tell you, but Rachel called this morning to tell me she's out sick today, which means we'll have to finish things on our own."

Harper's fork, which was halfway to her mouth, froze in mid-air. "What?! Doesn't she have a backup? An assistant? Someone who can fill in for her?"

Sidney shook her head grimly, her mouth set in a line. "I've called the girls to see if they could come early, but Amber is stuck in Atlanta. Chelsea is the only one that'll be here in time."

Harper set her fork down abruptly, her eggs and bacon untouched. The excitement of the morning had lost its appeal. "This day just keeps getting better," she murmured, rubbing her temples in an attempt to fend off a budding headache. After downing the rest of her coffee, she said, "Okay. We can do this."

"Can we, though?" Sidney asked, her voice tinged with uncertainty. "There are a lot of things to handle."

"We can and we will," Harper replied firmly, pushing back from the table. "When I agreed to be maid of honor, I assumed something like this might happen. We just have to split the workload between us, that's all. Divide and conquer."

"All right," Sidney responded, swallowing down the last of her bagel. "So we're looking at decorating the arbor and setting up the tables and chairs."

"What about the catering and flowers?"

"The catering is taken care of, but we still need to call the florist. Chelsea can handle that when she gets here. In the meantime,"—she turned to look at Harper—"why don't I work on the arbor while you start on your design? Let's plan to meet on the lawn at noon."

"Sounds like a plan," said Harper, nodding in agreement.

With that, the pair sprang into action, each diving into their respective tasks. While Sidney rounded up an array of colorful ribbons and flowers, Harper took the elevator to her suite, her mind racing with ideas. She studied the sketches on her laptop, full of grand ideas and ambitious designs. Letting out a breath she hadn't realized she was holding, Harper picked up a pencil and began to sketch, the music from the poolside radio in the distance marking the start of her intense work session. Her fingers moved almost of their own accord, years of practice honing what had once been just an innate skill into a masterful craft. The sounds of the morning began to fade away as she surrendered herself to her art, each stroke of the pencil a testament to her talent and dedication.

***

On the lawn below, Sidney began weaving ribbons through the skeletal frame of the arbor, her nimble fingers moving with practiced precision. She hummed softly to herself, a familiar tune that kept pace with her work. Diffused through the clusters of roses and baby's breath she was coiling around delicate ironwork, the morning sunlight infused everything with a soft glow. Slowly, the arbor transformed from a cold metal structure into a lush, vibrant spectacle.

At noon, Harper joined Sidney on the lawn, her sketches tucked under her arm. As she approached, Sidney took a step back to observe her work, sweat lining her brow from the morning's exertions.

"Wow," Harper breathed out as she took in the arbor. It was

like something out of a fairy tale, a doorway into an enchanted forest.

"Impressive, isn't it?" Sidney asked, her eyes sparkling with delight. "It's amazing what a few yards of ribbon and a bunch of flowers can do."

Harper nodded, the corners of her mouth turning up into a small smile. "Yes, it is. You work fast."

Sidney eyed the sketchbook Harper was holding onto. "So do you. Do you have the final sketches?"

Harper nodded, opening the sketchbook to reveal the detailed drawings within. She held it out for Sidney to see, watching as her friend's eyes widened with surprise and admiration.

"Harper, this is stunning," Sidney breathed, tracing her fingers lightly over the paper. The design was ambitious and intricate—a gown composed of elaborate layers and textures that would require both skill and time to bring to fruition. It was a blend of classic elegance and modern sensibility, the very embodiment of Harper's unique design style.

"Thanks. I hope you don't mind but I used your wedding as inspiration." Harper pointed out the details that echoed the floral theme of Sidney's wedding—delicate lace patterns that echoed the design of the arbor, the floral motifs that mirrored the rose and baby's breath arrangements Sidney had so painstakingly crafted.

"Mind?" Sidney repeated. "Harper, this is ... this is beyond anything I could have imagined. It's beautiful."

Realizing there was still much to be done, Harper put away her drawings and focused on the task at hand—completing the tablescapes and lining the chairs for the ceremony.

***

By mid-afternoon, most of the wedding party had arrived, including Chelsea, who Sidney put to work right away.

Brimming with energy, Chelsea said a quick 'hello' to Harper, then threw herself into the hectic preparations. After coordinating with the florist, she helped Sidney and Harper put the finishing touches on the tables inside the ballroom. Each was adorned with a lace runner and a stunning centerpiece of roses that mirrored the arbor's design. The chairs were draped in flowing fabric, tied back with ribbons to match the color scheme Sidney had chosen.

When everything was finished, they stepped back, surveying the grandeur of the ballroom.

"Well, girls," said Sidney, wrapping an arm around each of them, "we did it."

Harper glanced around the room, examining every detail that they had spent hours perfecting. The chandeliers reflected warm light onto the polished wood panels, casting a shimmer across the carefully placed silverware.

"It's gorgeous," said Chelsea. "It's like walking into a fairytale."

"I couldn't agree more," said Harper. "Who knows, maybe we'll have a future in wedding planning if we ever grow tired of our current careers," she joked.

Laughter echoed around the room. The day had been long, yet there was a sense of satisfaction each woman felt that made every minute worthwhile.

"Let's remember this moment," Chelsea proposed, pulling out her phone. "Say cheese!"

***

Exhausted and in dire need of a break, Harper and Sidney made their way to the pool while Chelsea went upstairs to unpack.

As soon as they sat down, Jason appeared, dressed in a crisp white polo shirt and khakis, his dark hair still wet and slicked back from his own recent swim. His blue eyes twinkled with a certain mischievous delight as he approached them with a tray of frozen piña coladas.

"I thought you ladies might appreciate these," he said, handing each of them a frosty drink. "My way of saying thank you for all your hard work."

"Thanks, honey," Sidney said, giving him a kiss on the cheek.

"Yeah, thanks," echoed Harper before adding, "So how are you? It feels like it's been forever since I've seen you. And congratulations on your new book. Sidney tells me it's going to be a huge success."

"Yeah, it's been a while. And thanks, I'm keeping my fingers crossed, but I have a good feeling about this one. How have you been? Last time we talked, you were up to your eyeballs with the Chanel project."

"I still am," Harper replied with a sigh. "But I'm hoping the worst is behind me." Her gaze shifted toward the shimmering pool, a thoughtful smile playing on her lips. "Right now, I'm just enjoying some downtime before the next thing comes along."

Jason nodded, sipping from his piña colada. "I know what you mean. Life seems to come fast and furious these days, doesn't it?"

"Did you happen to see the arbor as you came down?" Sidney interjected.

"Yes," he replied. "And it looks amazing. You two have been working hard this week. Hopefully not too hard."

"Of course not," Harper laughed, rolling her eyes playfully. "We've had our fair share of fun too." She glanced at Sidney, and they shared a secretive giggle. "So where is everyone else? I thought they'd all be out here by now."

"Last I checked they were getting settled in their rooms," he replied. "They wanted some time to relax before tonight's rehearsal dinner."

"That's smart," Harper agreed. "After a long flight, it's always nice to have some downtime."

"You can say that again." Jason raised his empty hand and stifled a yawn. "I could use a nap myself."

"Why don't you rest," Sidney suggested. "Harper and I were only planning to stay for a few more minutes anyway before we go check on the final details for the rehearsal dinner."

"In that case"—Jason finished off his drink—"I'll catch up with you ladies later."

Once Jason had left, Harper turned to Sidney. "He seems genuinely happy, doesn't he?"

"Are you surprised?"

"A little. Weddings make most men nervous."

"Not Jason," replied Sidney. "It's amazing how attentive he's been now that he's not weighed down by his job. Leaving his corporate career was the best decision he's ever made."

Harper hummed in agreement, recalling how miserable Jason used to be, chasing deadlines instead of his dreams. "Yeah, he was really unhappy back then. I'm just glad he had the courage to leave. Not everyone can walk away from a lucrative job to pursue their dreams."

Sidney chuckled, nodding in approval. "So am I.

Thankfully, it all worked out for him. Now, he's happy, healthy, a bestselling author, and about to marry the love of his life. What more could a man ask for?"

***

Later that afternoon, Harper wandered down to the beach, her bare feet sinking into the warm, fine sand. The salty breeze tugged playfully at her sun-streaked hair as she eased along the shoreline, her eyes scanning the horizon.

Finding an open spot between the scattered seashells and weathered driftwood, she delicately spread out a faded, floral-patterned blanket her mother had given her years earlier. With a sigh, she sunk down onto the soft fabric, her fingers brushing over the frayed edges in absent thought.

Seeing Sidney and Jason together earlier—so happy, so in love—made her long for something similar. She yearned for that feeling of companionship, of being completely understood by someone else. She craved the intimacy of shared secrets and stolen glances. The longing was so potent, it made her chest ache.

The chaos of the morning had been a welcome relief to Harper, a distraction from her own inner turmoil. The clamor and excitement had filled the void in her heart, albeit temporarily. But now, as she sat alone on the beach, watching the couples stroll hand in hand, she could hardly bear it. Each laugh they shared haunted her, each loving glance they exchanged, another stab in the back.

She found herself missing Cameron, the comforting weight of his arm draped around her shoulder. She missed the soft warmth radiating from his presence, the sincere laughter they shared, and the way his eyes sparkled with understated affection.

As she traced patterns in the sand with her fingers, Harper was hit with a wave of nostalgia. She remembered the last time she had spoken to Cameron, the day after her engagement—the things they had said to each other, the things they hadn't said.

If only Grant hadn't proposed, she thought, then Cameron might still be in her life. Or perhaps this whole thing was her fault. Perhaps she had jumped the gun, ended things with Cameron without truly understanding where he was coming from. She had always known him to be a man of honor and integrity. Perhaps she underestimated the weight of those responsibilities.

She picked up a seashell, the smooth cold under her fingers, a stark contrast from the warmth of Cameron's hand she so vividly remembered. She wished she could explain to him how she felt, how she was feeling even now. She wished she could hear his voice one more time. Maybe he would have the right words that she so desperately needed to hear.

Sighing, Harper tucked the shell into her pocket and got up, sand grains clinging to her dress. The sun had started its descent, painting the horizon with hues of pink and orange. And just like the setting sun, her hope for rekindling the flame with Cameron was disappearing.

CHAPTER 26

As the guests arrived for the rehearsal dinner, Harper stood on the sidelines and observed as Jason and Sidney effortlessly played the roles of perfect hosts. Their warm smiles and contagious enthusiasm elevated the entire atmosphere. Harper looked around at the diverse group of friends and family, most of whom were familiar faces to her, and she hoped that someday she could experience something similar.

"And I'd like to propose a toast," said Jason, standing tall at the head of the table. He raised his glass high, waiting for everyone's chatter to simmer down. Eyes twinkling with excitement, he looked around the room and then at Sidney, who beamed back at him. "First, I'd like to thank you all for coming tonight," Jason began. "Your support means the world to both of us. But most importantly, I'd like to thank the woman sitting next to me, my Sidney." A soft sigh passed through the crowd as Jason paused. "Sidney," he said with a gentle but firm voice, "you have been my rock, my constant. You are the one who has faith in me when I doubt myself and my dreams. You, with your boundless love and unwavering support, are the reason why I am standing here today. To Sidney!" he announced, lifting his glass in a toast.

The room reverberated with the clinking of glasses and hearty cheers, their voices echoing off the vaulted ceiling. Jason took a sip of his champagne before placing his arm around Sidney, pulling her close for a tender kiss.

Harper watched from the sidelines, her heart filled with a strange mixture of joy and melancholy. She looked down at her empty champagne glass, lost in thought. Despite the happiness she felt for Jason and Sidney, it was no match for the loneliness that had seeped into her very being.

Suddenly, a voice interrupted her thoughts. "They really are the perfect couple, aren't they?"

"Mom," said Harper, surprised to see her. She pulled her into a hug. "What are you doing here? I wasn't expecting you until tomorrow morning."

"Dad and I changed our minds at the last minute," said Brenda. "I tried calling you, but it went straight to voicemail."

Perplexed, Harper checked her phone. No service. Who else had she missed a call from? Eleanor? Cameron? Setting aside her worry for the moment, she asked, "So where's Dad?"

"Upstairs ordering room service. You know how he feels about crowds." Brenda scanned the room. "This is some place, isn't it?"

"Yes, it is," Harper agreed, her gaze sweeping across the grand ballroom. Then, she had a thought. "Hey Mom, have you ever heard of a man named Todd Pageant?"

"Pageant ... Pageant ..." Brenda's eyebrows furrowed, her eyes thoughtful. "No. Can't say that I have. Why?"

"No reason, just ..." Harper trailed off, deciding not to mention the mysterious phone calls and texts Sidney had received throughout the week. "Just a guy Sidney told me about—someone from back home. I thought he might be an old classmate of mine that I didn't remember."

"Maybe she's thinking of Todd Parker," Brenda suggested, her eyes still squinted in thought. "He was a few years ahead of you in school. Quiet boy, from what I remember."

Harper nodded, chewing on the edge of her lower lip. Truthfully, she had been hoping for more from her mother— some substantial piece of information that could substantiate Sidney's story. Not that she doubted Sidney, especially after the way she'd so passionately defended herself. But she still needed something tangible, something concrete.

After dinner, Harper retreated to her room and slipped out of her dress, happy that the rehearsal was finally over. The day had been a long one, filled with last-minute alterations and stressful decision-making. Enjoying the peace and quiet, she poured herself a small glass of wine and stepped out onto the balcony to admire the moon and stars.

But even as she tried to relax and clear her mind, her thoughts kept circling back to Sidney's odd behavior, absent signal bars on her phone, and the mysterious Todd Pageant. Brenda Emery knew everyone in their small town, so the fact that she had never heard of him was peculiar to Harper, making her feel uneasy.

To satisfy her curiosity, Harper opened her laptop and searched for Todd Pageant on Google, expecting to find a picture of a real estate broker at the top of the results page. Instead, what she found were pages of lawyers in Maine, farmers in Nebraska, doctors in Oregon, but none seemed to match up with the person Sidney had described. With nagging doubt giving way to suspicion, Harper narrowed her search, combining the name 'Todd Pageant' with 'real estate'. This time, she found a single article from a small-town newspaper located deep in Idaho, thousands of miles from Kentucky.

Letting out a sigh, Harper closed her laptop and finished her glass of wine as she thought through the possibilities.

In need of some mental clarity, Harper left the resort and

took a leisurely stroll along the beach. With the moon as her guide, she headed west, feeling the cool sand beneath her bare feet and the gentle waves brushing against her ankles. Lost in thought, she continued to wander along the shore.

Harper realized she had walked more than a mile before she stopped to look back. The resort was now just a small dot in the distance. Turning forward again, she noticed a line of pastel-colored houses with decks facing south toward the ocean. A sense of familiarity overcame her, and she couldn't shake the feeling that she had been here before. She scanned the area and saw a lifeguard tower, a boardwalk leading from the beach to a public parking lot, and then it dawned on her. This was the exact spot—the place she had kept secret from almost everyone in the world. This was the place of her dreams, the place where she had fallen in love and never stopped falling.

It had been years since she had stood on this beach, yet every detail was still vivid in her mind. The scent of rain, the distant rumble of thunder, and the dazzling brightness of lightning streaking across the night sky. And then there was the warmth of his body next to hers, their skin pressed together, and the beat of their hearts.

Amidst the darkness, a light turned on in one of the nearby houses, breaking her train of thought. She looked up and noticed a familiar figure through the window. Counting the years since she had last seen him, she wondered if he was real or a figment of her imagination.

For a moment she stood there, wondering what to do next. With every beat of her heart, she felt the magnetic pull toward the house growing stronger. At last, she slowly approached the house, hesitating at the back door. Taking a deep breath, she raised her hand to knock, the sound echoing across the quiet beach.

Suddenly, the door swung open and there he was.

"Mr. Hanover," she said when he came to the door. "Kenneth Hanover?"

The old man, whose silver hair blazed in the moonlight, tilted his head slightly. "Yes?"

"It's me ... It's Harper Emery." She paused, searching his eyes for a flicker of recognition. "You probably don't remember me, but—"

A smile broke across his face. "Harper?" His voice carried a tone of surprise and delight. "Is it really you?"

She nodded, her heart pounding in her chest. "Yes, Mr. Hanover, it's me. I'm sorry to bother you, it's just ... I was on the beach, and I saw your light come on, and ..."

"It's quite all right, my dear." A whistle sounded from inside the house. "That's the water for my tea. Would you care to join me?"

"Thank you, but I wouldn't want to impose."

"Nonsense. I have enough for both of us."

Harper hesitated, glancing back at the distant glow of the resort.

"Okay, but I can't stay long."

While Kenneth got the tea ready, Harper sat in the living room, admiring the photos scattered around the place. Some were familiar, while others she had never seen before. Among them were pictures of Kenneth and Cynthia taken on a cruise ship, and another of them standing at the edge of the Grand Canyon. There was also one of Trevor on his wedding day. Harper felt a pang in her heart at the sight of his familiar face, so young and vibrant.

Then, there was a picture that caught Harper off guard. It

was of Cameron, a bright smile lighting up his face as he held up what appeared to be a hefty fish. His eyes sparkled with joy, the image so vivid it seemed as if he might jump out of the picture at any moment. Her fingers lightly traced the frame, her mind going back to the time when she first met Cameron. How young and innocent they both were.

Her reverie was broken by the soft clinking of porcelain as Kenneth carried a tray into the room, setting it down on the wooden coffee table.

"Here we are," he said, handing one of the steaming cups to Harper.

They settled into the seats and began to drink the tea, listening to the soft hum of the distant waves.

Kenneth leaned back in his chair, his eyes crinkling with age and wisdom. "So, tell me. What brings you to this part of the world?"

"I'm on vacation," Harper answered with a smile. "Actually, I'm here for a wedding—my best friend is getting married tomorrow. We're staying at the Henderson, just down the beach."

"I see." He nodded. "And is there any particular reason why you chose to take a walk alone on the beach in the middle of the night?"

Harper gathered her thoughts, her suspicions of Sidney resurfacing. "I suppose I just needed some time alone."

"Ah," Kenneth said, sipping his tea. "I can understand that. So how's life been treating you? Last I heard you were a big-shot fashion designer in New York."

She gave a bashful smile and said, "I can't complain. What about you? You look like you're still in good health."

"I'm the same as always, with a few more wrinkles, of

course." His eyes took on a far-off look as his expression turned wistful. "You probably heard that I lost my Cynthia recently."

Harper's breath caught in her throat. "No, I didn't. I'm so sorry for your loss."

"Thank you. It's been a difficult adjustment without her by my side. We were married for over fifty years, you know. If it hadn't been for Cameron, I don't think I would have survived all of this."

Harper's heart gave a lurch at the mention of Cameron's name. "What do you mean?"

Kenneth set his teacup down, his eyes dropping to his folded hands. "When Cynthia fell ill," he began, his voice shaky, "Cameron came to stay with us. He took care of everything ... the doctors, the insurance, even the housework. He was our rock."

Harper's mind spun with confusion. "I—I don't understand. Cameron was here?"

Kenneth nodded solemnly, "For several months."

"How is that possible? I thought he was on a ship somewhere on the other side of the globe."

Kenneth shook his head slowly. "When he found out that Cynthia was dying, he requested an early discharge from the Navy. In light of Trevor's death and the fact that he was within a year of fulfilling his service commitment, they made a special exception. So he came home to be with her, to be with us. He didn't tell you?"

His words threw Harper for a loop. "No." She sat there, frozen, struggling to process everything that Kenneth had shared. "No," she repeated, running a shaky hand through her hair. "He never mentioned it." She took a sip of tea, steadying her nerves. "But I'm not surprised. We lost touch a while back and haven't spoken recently."

"I'm sorry to hear that," said Kenneth, giving her a sympathetic smile. "Was that about the same time you got engaged?"

Harper looked up from her tea. "Yeah. How'd you know?"

Kenneth sighed and set his cup on the table. "Cameron came to see me a few days after that ... Said he needed some time to clear his head before he shipped out again. I don't know if you're aware, but he was pretty upset about how things turned out. Believe it or not, I was the one who gave him the idea."

Harper's mind whirled as she tried to make sense of what he was saying. "I don't understand. You gave him the idea for *what*?"

"To propose to you," he revealed. "After Trevor died, Cameron became depressed, withdrawn ... blamed himself for what happened. I tried to tell him that it wasn't his fault. It wasn't anyone's fault, but ... Anyway, he started talking about the future and what his life could be like after his military service was over. That's when he told me about the fight you had and how things had ended. But he insisted that there was still something there, and he was willing to do whatever it took to win you back." He paused and took a breath. "I told him that if he was serious about being with you, then he needed to lay it all on the line ... tell you exactly how he felt about you and leave nothing open to interpretation."

"What are you saying?"

"I told him if he had any sense at all, he'd stop beating around the bush and ask you to marry him."

Harper's eyes widened, her mind spinning with the memory of that night. She had often wondered if Cameron had planned to reveal something important. But a proposal?

"That's why he was acting so strange that night," Harper mused.

Kenneth chuckled in response. "It's remarkable how nervous you get when you're about to ask the woman you love to marry you. Suddenly, all those elaborate plans and ideas you had just turn into a jumbled mess. It was the same way for me when I proposed to Cynthia." A small laugh escaped his lips. "I could barely get the words out."

"But why didn't he say something? Why didn't he tell me?"

Kenneth lifted a shoulder. "Someone beat him to the punch. After that, he didn't want to do anything that might have ruined your special night. Even though his heart was breaking, he would never have put that burden on you."

Harper took a moment to process. Regret, disappointment, and a glimmer of hope all warred within her. She had spent countless nights replaying that evening in her mind. Now, she wondered what could have been if she had only known.

"So that's why he wouldn't return any of my calls, isn't it?"

Kenneth let out a deep breath. "I wish I had a simple answer for you, dear, but Cameron is a complicated person. He's a lot like his mother in that respect. After you had accepted another proposal, I think he finally realized that any chance he had with you was gone forever, and he knew that in order to get over you, he had to try and move on."

Harper's heart sank, the weight of missed opportunities and unspoken feelings pressing down on her. "But so many things have changed since then. Why won't he speak to me now?"

A pained look marred Kenneth's face as he appeared to be wrestling with something.

"What is it?" Harper asked, realizing that he was holding

something back.

"I don't know if I should be telling you this," he said. "But ... a few weeks ago, Cameron showed up out of the blue one morning and told me that he had recently reconnected with an old friend, that he'd finally found the one he wanted to spend the rest of his life with, and that for the first time in a long time, he was hopeful for the future."

The air left Harper's lungs. To hear that Cameron had found someone else left her weak and vulnerable. She had hoped that there was still a chance for them, but now it was clear that those hopes were slowly slipping away.

"What do you mean, he found someone else?" Harper's voice trembled.

Kenneth paused, his eyes full of sympathy. "I'm sorry, Harper. Truly, I am."

Tears pricked at Harper's eyes, but she blinked them away. She couldn't let herself break down, not in front of Kenneth, not when her heart was already shattered into a thousand irreparable pieces.

***

As soon as Harper burst through the front door of the hotel, she spotted Sidney sitting on one of the comfy couches. Pushing past the concierge she yelled, "He was going to propose!"

Sidney's brow furrowed in confusion as she tried to make sense of Harper's words. "What are you talking about? And where have you been? I've been looking all over for you."

"I took a walk," Harper replied, still reeling from what Kenneth had told her. "And then I ran into Cameron's grandfather, and ..."

Sydney's eyes widened in surprise.

"That's when he told me everything," Harper continued, shaking her head in disbelief. "About how Cameron came to the show that night to propose."

Sidney led Harper out onto the patio, where they could continue their conversation in private. "Are you okay?"

Harper nodded, her hands trembling. "Yes. No. I don't know. I never saw it coming, Sid. I thought Cameron had moved on. I thought ..."

"At least now you know he still cares about you," Sidney pointed out while trying to console her. "Did you ask his grandfather why he never returned your calls?"

Harper nodded sadly. "He's with someone else," she revealed. "Someone new. And that's not even the worst part." She took a breath, trying to compose herself. "He's planning to ask her to marry him."

Sidney took Harper's hand and squeezed it. "That doesn't mean he's forgotten about you, Harper. People don't forget about those they've truly loved. But I think it's time you called him. He needs to hear your voice, to know how you feel about him, before it's too late."

Harper thought about it before shaking her head. "No. It's already too late," she said, on the verge of tears. "Our time is over. He's moved on, and as much as I hate to admit it, I have to do the same."

"But Harper, do you really mean that?"

"Yes," she replied firmly. "I thought that I could do it, Sid—that I could come back here, and everything would be okay. But it isn't. Being back here has only made things worse." She turned away, blinking back tears. "I just need to make it through tomorrow and then I can go back to New York where everything is familiar and makes sense."

***

As the hours slipped away, Harper felt the gentle tug of sleep pulling her under. She welcomed its embrace, letting her thoughts drift back to those peaceful days spent by the sea, their laughter and whispered secrets carried away on the breeze.

In the world of her dreams, Cameron was still with her, his strong arms encircling her waist, their bodies swaying in time to the music of the crashing waves. Their love was like a song, a bittersweet symphony of joy and sorrow that echoed through the chambers of her heart.

"Promise me," he murmured into her ear, "that you won't give up on love."

"I promise," she whispered back, her breath catching in her throat as she clung to him, knowing that this moment, too, would soon slip away.

CHAPTER 27

The first light of dawn cast a soft glow over the beach as the ocean waves gently lapped against the pristine shoreline. It was the morning of Sidney's wedding, and the air was filled with the promise of love and celebration.

Just after sunrise, Harper rose from her bed and made her way to the Keurig for some much-needed caffeine. The night before had been emotional, but she was determined not to let it ruin Sidney's day. After chugging down her coffee, she went for a quick run on the beach, returning to her room to take a refreshing shower that washed away her worries and troubles, at least temporarily. Once dressed, she ordered breakfast and enjoyed it on the balcony while the world around her came to life.

On the lawn below and in the ballroom, preparations were already underway for the grand event. Nestled between swaying palm trees and the emerald waters of the Gulf, the venue itself was a testament to elegance and sophistication. White chiffon billowed in the gentle breeze, draped gracefully from the wooden pergola under which the couple would soon exchange their vows. Delicate floral arrangements adorned each row of chairs, their sweet fragrance mingling with the salty sea air, while a string quartet tuned their instruments in readiness to set the tone for the ceremony.

In true Sidney fashion, even the small details of the wedding showcased her impeccable taste and flair for style. The color palette of lilacs, blush pinks, and crisp whites blended effortlessly with the natural beauty of the surroundings, while artful touches—like a vintage mirror framed in gold that displayed the evening's menu—spoke to her love for all things fashionable and elegant.

As guests began to arrive, they were greeted by waitstaff offering glasses of sparkling champagne and trays of hors d'oeuvres. Conversations bubbled with excitement, the laughter of old friends reuniting and family members catching up after months apart. The atmosphere was one of pure joy, an infectious energy that seemed to dance on the breeze.

Before she left the room, Harper checked her phone one last time. Any doubts she may have had about Cameron before were now completely gone. For months, Harper had been struggling against her feelings, trying to convince herself that she didn't need anyone else, that she could make it on her own. But as she stood there, staring at her phone, a flood of emotions washed over her. She couldn't deny the truth any longer—she was in love with Cameron, and perhaps a part of her always had been. The way he made her feel alive, the way his touch ignited a fire within her, it was undeniable. And even though he was in love with someone else, she knew that Sidney was right—she had to tell him. The weight of her unspoken feelings had become too heavy to bear, especially on such a momentous day. With trembling hands, Harper dialed Cameron's number and held her breath as the phone rang.

As each ring echoed in her ears, crippling uncertainty started to creep into her heart. Yet, she refused to let herself hang up the phone. She was past the stage of denial and running away; she had bravely anchored herself on the path of honesty and vulnerability. It was time for Cameron to know.

The third ring seemed to stretch out longer than the others, drawing out Harper's anxiety until it was as taut as a guitar string. Her heart thumped loudly in her chest, each beat pleading with fate to grant her the courage she needed.

As the fourth ring mingled with the silent tension of her surroundings, Harper steeled herself against the imminent conversation. Then, abruptly, the ringing ceased—replaced by Cameron's deep, resonant voice as his voicemail picked up. After the beep, Harper swallowed, her heart pounding so hard that she worried he might hear it. Her voice was a hushed whisper as she began to speak. "Cameron," she said hesitantly, "it's me, Harper."

She took a shaky breath, her mind racing to string the right words together. She wanted to say so much, to pour out all her emotions that had been pent up for far too long. "Cameron, I ... I need you to know something," she began, her voice growing stronger with each word. "I need to tell you ... to tell you that I love you. I always have," she continued, her voice shaky but determined. "I've been scared, I've been foolish, and I've been running away from this ... from us." She paused, trying to gather her scattered thoughts as tears filled her eyes. "But I can't run anymore. Not when my heart calls out for you every waking moment. And I know this isn't fair, because you're in love with someone else ... someone you're ready to propose to, but I couldn't live with myself if I didn't tell you the truth. And the truth is, Cameron ... I need you. More than I've ever needed anyone. More than I thought was ever possible."

The following seconds were deafening, but Harper continued. "And I don't expect anything from you, Cameron. I don't expect you to leave her or to return my feelings." She let out a small sigh. "In fact, I hope you don't. I've caused enough pain already." She paused again, struggling to keep her voice steady as the tears streamed down her face. "I just wanted you to know."

She inhaled sharply, her breath hitching in her throat as the silence stretched out. "I hope you're happy," she finally said. "Truly happy." With a sigh that held the weight of her confession, Harper ended the message with a quiet, "Goodbye, Cameron."

***

While she waited for her turn to put on her bridesmaid's dress, Harper stood on the veranda, peering down at the gathering crowd below. The laughter, the setting, the soft music all came together in a perfect storm.

Needing a moment, she retreated around the corner, out of sight from the crowd. To her surprise, she found Chelsea already there.

"Hey," Harper said as she approached. "What are you doing out here?"

"I needed a breather," Harper confessed. "Weddings always make me a bit emotional."

"You and me both."

"I remember your wedding," Harper said, her gaze still fixated on the slowly descending sun. "You were so nervous, but you looked absolutely beautiful."

Chelsea chuckled at the memory. "I was a mess. I couldn't even recite my vows properly."

"That's not what I remember," Harper replied. "I remember a woman deeply in love, standing there in her mother's vintage lace gown, tears streaming down her face as she looked at the man she was about to marry. That was real, Chels."

"I suppose it was, wasn't it?" she murmured. "God, that feels like another lifetime ago."

Harper nodded, a hint of melancholy in her voice as she added, "Time really flies, doesn't it?"

"Yes, it does," Chelsea replied. "Which is why I'm so thankful for weeks like this one. All of us gathered together, just like old times. It almost makes me forget I have this other life to go back to."

"I know what you mean," said Harper. "It'll take me a week just to catch up on everything I've missed while I've been away."

Chelsea laughed. "Me too."

"At least you've got Todd helping you while you're away," said Harper. "So maybe it won't be that bad."

Chelsea tipped her head to one side. "Todd?"

"Yeah, you know, your boss."

Chelsea's expression turned puzzled. "My boss's name isn't Todd, Harper. It's Tracy."

Harper's face flushed in confusion and embarrassment. "But Sidney said ..." Her voice trailed off as realization hit her. "Damn it," Harper muttered under her breath, running a hand through her hair as she put two and two together. She had been right all along. Sidney had been lying to her the entire time. Filled with a sense of betrayal, Harper backed away, her heart pounding in her chest.

"Is something the matter?" Chelsea asked, worry creasing her brow.

Harper shook her head. "No. I just ... There's something I need to take care of. Excuse me." She turned and walked away, moving with purpose as the truth ignited a fire within her. Sidney had played her for a fool. She felt the hot sting of anger welling up within her as she quickly moved from room to room, searching for her best friend.

"Sidney! Where are you?" Harper's voice echoed through the hallways, filled with frustration and hurt. But there was no response. Only silence. Finally, she found Sidney in the ballroom with her back turned, engrossed in a phone call.

"I know this is hard, but I just need you to be patient," she heard Sidney say. "No, I don't think so ... I know ... I know. But you have to trust me ... I'll see you soon ... Okay. Bye."

When Sidney turned around, Harper stood with her arms crossed, ready to confront her.

"Harper!" Sidney stopped, her eyes as wide as saucers. "What are you doing down here?" she asked before quickly stowing away her phone.

"I could ask you the same question," Harper replied, her voice as sharp as a blade.

"I ... um," Sidney stuttered, her composed facade cracking under Harper's piercing gaze. "I didn't expect you to be ... I mean, it's almost time for the wedding. Shouldn't you be getting dressed right now?"

"Never mind the wedding. Who were you talking to just now?"

Sidney laughed awkwardly, fiddling with her earring. "Would you believe me if I said it was Todd?"

Harper narrowed her eyes. "Look, I don't know what's going on here, but you've been acting strange all week. Between the phone calls and the texts, and the secret conversations ... I know you told me you weren't cheating on Jason, but from where I stand it looks as if you are. Please tell me I'm wrong."

"You are wrong!" Sidney protested. "Like I told you before, I would never cheat on Jason."

"Then tell me what's going on," Harper demanded. "And don't lie ... not to me."

Sidney took a deep breath, her shoulders sagging under Harper's relentless glare. "You're right," she conceded as she sat down at a nearby table. "The truth is I've been lying to you this whole time, about everything."

Harper felt a jolt of triumph, but it was quickly quenched by the sinking feeling in her gut. This wasn't a victory. This was just the beginning of something much darker, she feared.

"But Harper," Sidney's voice echoed through the room, shaking Harper from her thoughts, "before you jump to conclusions, I want you to know this isn't what it seems."

"Then what is it, Sidney? Who have you been talking to?"

"Me."

Harper froze, her heart stuttered and stopped. She turned around slowly, her eyes widening with shock as she laid her gaze upon the man standing before her. Harper's knees weakened and her hands trembled. She had rehearsed this moment a thousand times in her mind, but nothing could have prepared her for the reality of seeing Cameron again. He was still the same handsome man she had loved; the man she thought she'd never see again. His hair was a little longer, his eyes a little sadder, but it was undeniably him.

Sidney stepped forward, her voice breaking through the haze that enveloped Harper's thoughts. "Surprise," she whispered, a mischievous smile playing on her lips. "I hope you don't mind, but I decided to save the best one for last."

Sidney walked over and addressed Cameron. "She's all yours, Todd." She winked. "Just promise me you won't screw it up this time."

"I promise," he said as his smile widened.

When Sidney left, Harper and Cameron stood there, their eyes locked on each other, the weight of their unspoken history hanging heavy in the air.

"I can't believe you're actually here," Harper finally managed to say. "I've been trying to reach you, and ..."

"I know." Cameron took a step closer, his gaze intense and unwavering. "And I'm sorry for not responding, but we wanted it to be a surprise. I hope you're not angry."

Harper felt a rush of confusion, anger, relief, and desire, all tangled up within her chest, making it hard to breathe. Finally, she shook her head, managing a weak smile.

"But all I wanted was to get to you. I couldn't stay away any longer, Harper," he confessed, his voice laced with remorse. "I've tried to forget you, to convince myself that I didn't need you in my life, but I was wrong. I can't live without you ... won't live without you."

Harper's breath caught in her throat, the weight of Cameron's words sinking deep into her soul. She reached out a trembling hand, needing to touch him to believe that he was real. His fingers intertwined with hers, their connection electric and undeniable.

"I've missed you," Harper choked out, tears streaming down her face.

Cameron brushed away her tears with his thumb, his touch gentle and full of tenderness. "I've missed you too, more than words can express. Every day without you felt like an eternity."

Harper felt the warmth of his touch seep into her skin, slowly erasing the aching void that had consumed her since their separation. It was as if his presence breathed life back into her, rekindling the flickering embers of hope that she had long thought extinguished.

"But what about *her*?" she asked, thinking clearly. "The woman you're in love with? The one you're going to propose to?"

"Don't you see?" said Cameron. "There is no other woman. There's never been anyone but you."

Harper's mind reeled as she put the pieces together. "You mean—?" She held her breath, excitement coursing through her veins.

"Harper ..." he whispered. "From the first day I saw you out there on that beach, I knew there was something about you ... something special, and that my life would never be the same. Today, I stand before you a broken man ... a man needing the other half to make him whole." He paused and reached into his pocket. He pulled out a black box and opened it, revealing a stunning diamond ring. "Harper, I've been a fool. I've denied what my heart has known all along. And I don't want to spend another day blind to the truth." He took a deep breath. "Harper Emery," he said, dropping to one knee. "Marry me, and let's spend the rest of our lives completing each other."

Harper gasped, her hand flying to her mouth as tears of joy streamed down her face. Never in her wildest dreams did she imagine this moment would come. Every doubt, every fear that had plagued her during their time apart melted away in that instant. Harper's mind raced, her heart thumped within her chest, and for a fleeting moment, she felt as though time had come to a standstill.

"Cam," she whispered. "You've always had a piece of my heart, and I thought I had lost you. But here you are, kneeling before me, asking for something I never dreamed possible." She hesitated, then took a deep breath, steeling herself for what came next. "Yes," she said, her voice stronger now and filled with conviction. "Yes, Cameron, I want to spend the rest of my life with you."

Cameron's smile illuminated the room, his eyes shining with overwhelming happiness. Slowly, he stood up and slid the diamond ring onto Harper's trembling finger, sealing their promise of forever.

***

Inside the elegant bridal suite, Harper adjusted Sidney's veil as they looked at their reflections in the mirror. Both women were dressed impeccably—Sidney in a breathtaking, custom-designed gown that seemed as though it had been spun from moonlight and dreams, while Harper donned a sophisticated off-the-shoulder lilac dress that hugged her slender frame.

"Harper," Sidney murmured, her voice wavering slightly, "I can't believe this day is finally here."

"Neither can I," Harper admitted. She forced a smile and added, "But it's happening, and you're going to be the most beautiful bride anyone has ever seen."

"Thanks," Sidney said, reaching out to squeeze her hand. "And thanks for being here with me this week. I couldn't have done this without you."

"And I couldn't have done this without you," said Harper, thinking of Cameron and the fact that they were now engaged.

As they embraced, Harper marveled at the way life had brought them to this moment. They had been friends since childhood, supporting each other through thick and thin, and now Harper was about to witness Sidney give her love to the man of her dreams. It was almost too perfect to be real.

"And I'm sorry for doubting you," said Harper. "It was

foolish of me to think you would ever cheat on Jason."

Sidney chuckled. "I didn't leave you much choice," she said. "Honestly, I'm surprised you didn't say something to Jason."

Harper smiled, thankful to have a friend who would go to such lengths to make her happy.

"You know, it's still not too late to have a double wedding," said Sidney.

Despite the temptation, Harper politely declined. "I think today should be all about you and Jason. Besides," she said, glancing at the ring on her finger, "I want to enjoy being engaged for a while."

Sidney gave her a glance through the mirror. "You always were the considerate one."

"All right, ladies," said Chelsea, poking her head into the room. "It's time. Are you ready?"

"Ready!" they declared.

"All right, let's do this," Harper whispered to herself as they began their procession, her heart pounding in her chest like a drum. She glanced over at Sidney one last time, taking in the happiness that radiated from her friend like sunlight.

"Ladies and gentlemen," the preacher began. "We are gathered here today to bear witness to the union of two souls, deeply in love, promising each other a lifetime of companionship and understanding."

As the preacher continued with his customary introduction, Harper looked at Cameron. She stared into his eyes, pools of unwavering love and determination that seemed to reflect her own heart back at her. It was as if she were seeing him for the first time—truly seeing him–and the beauty of his soul was laid bare before her.

When Jason had said "I do," the preacher turned to Sidney.

"And do you, Sidney, take Jason to have and to hold, to love and to cherish, for richer or poorer, in sickness and in health, till death do you part?"

"I do," she whispered, her voice soft yet resolute. It was more than just a simple affirmation; it was an ode to the love they shared, a declaration of commitment to the man who had stolen her heart.

"Then by the power vested in me," the preacher announced, "I now pronounce you husband and wife."

Laughter and applause rose from the guests as the newlyweds shared their first kiss as a married couple.

***

At the reception, Harper sat with Cameron, watching as Sidney and Jason shared their first dance as husband and wife. The way they moved together was magical, each step perfectly choreographed yet, spontaneous. It was a dance not only of bodies but also, it seemed, of souls.

"That'll be us one day," said Cameron, interrupting the silence.

Harper looked at him and smiled. "I can't wait."

Cameron returned her smile, his hand finding hers. Their fingers intertwined naturally, as if they had been designed to be together. "I love you, Harper," he said.

"I love you too," she responded. The simplicity of the statement did no justice to the profound depth of her feelings for him. But she supposed that was the beauty of love—it was an entire universe wrapped in three simple words.

The party continued deep into the night, the laughter and joy filling through the grand ballroom. There were shared kisses, father-daughter dances, and toasts that brought tears of joy to the eyes of many. The night was one of pure happiness, a moment frozen in time that would forever be etched in their hearts.

PART 3

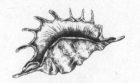

PART 3

CHAPTER 28

After the wedding, Harper and Cameron settled into Harper's penthouse in the city. When she finally returned to work, the rush of city life hit Harper hard. The skyscrapers seemed to tower taller, the streets buzzed with intensity. Her penthouse was a stark contrast to the serene lap of the azure waves that had lulled her into sleep just a few days prior. The difference was jarring, and it felt as if she had been rudely awakened from a dream.

Eventually, Harper slipped back into her old routine—the endless emails, phone calls, and meetings. She swapped her flowy sundresses for sharp blazers and heels, the ocean breeze for cool gusts of city wind. Cameron, too, had difficulty adjusting to the hustle and bustle of Manhattan. After being accustomed to a strict military schedule, his new civilian life felt chaotic and unstructured. With no specific orders or duties to fulfill, he felt lost and aimless. To stay busy, he started waking up early with Harper, cooking breakfast, and sticking to a strict exercise routine. During the day, he brainstormed ideas for potential careers that would allow him to do something he loved, while also supporting Harper in her burgeoning career.

Evenings at the penthouse were a conciliatory reprieve. Harper and Cameron would leave their work behind to indulge in home-cooked meals and moments of intimacy. Their world, filled with the soft hum of jazz music, the scent of simmering herbs, and the cozy warmth of their shared space, became a sanctuary. The skyline's twinkling lights served as a backdrop to their quiet nights, casting long shadows on them as they moved about the spacious rooms.

Weekends were spent exploring the city. Harper showed Cameron her favorite spots. They strolled through Central Park and visited art galleries. They dined at quaint cafes that dotted Greenwich Village and caught Broadway shows every chance they could. Each corner of the city was a piece of Harper's past, and she shared with him her past adventures as they explored the sprawling metropolis.

Slowly, Cameron started to create his own stories within the vast urban jungle. He found solace in the early morning runs along the Hudson River, the vibrant farmers markets with their colorful offerings, and even in the bright yellow cabs that honked their way through the traffic.

As the days turned into months, Harper and Cameron became inseparable. Autumn came, and with it, the city shifted under a canopy of gold and crimson. The air grew crisp and cool, the rhythm of the bustling city slowed, as if giving deference to the changing of seasons.

***

The following spring, Harper and Cameron were married in an intimate ceremony in Harper's hometown. Unlike Sidney, Harper opted for the little white chapel where she had gone to church as a child, and although it was simple, it was beautiful. It also gave Harper the opportunity to put her touch on things, elevating the setting from simple to spectacular.

Of course, Sidney was by Harper's side every step of the way, as her best friend, as her matron of honor, and most importantly, her rock during the chaos of preparations. The two of them were inseparable, planning every detail down to the tiny edible flowers on the wedding cake.

The day of the wedding dawned clear and bright. The air was sweet with a spring bloom fragrance and a spectacular array of colors decorating the church's surroundings.

The guests began to pour in, a sea of familiar faces from all walks of Harper's life—family, childhood friends, colleagues— all dressed in their Sunday best. As everyone found their seats, their murmurs and laughter filled the air. Amid this buzz of anticipation, Sidney held her friend's hand, squeezing it gently as she offered a reassuring smile.

"Did you think this day would ever come?" Sidney asked.

Harper laughed, a trace of nervousness in her voice. "Honestly? No. But then again I never thought I'd meet someone like Cameron."

Sidney cast a glance down the aisle where Cameron stood, looking dashing as ever in his Navy uniform. "But I'm glad you did, because you deserve to be happy. See," she said, turning back to Harper, "happily-ever-after really does still exist."

Harper gave her friend a tearful smile, and with a final squeeze of Sidney's hand, she turned toward the door. As it swung open, it was like time itself held its breath.

Just then, the wedding march began to play. Harper, draped in an elegant A-line white gown with silver-threaded embroidery, stepped forward, shimmering like a diamond under the soft light. The lace veil she wore was intricately woven with a subtle design that trailed down her back and ended in soft ripples around her feet. Her eyes were wide and expectant, carrying within them the beautiful fear and excitement of a woman on the brink of having everything she ever wanted.

Their vows were spoken with genuine love, their hands locked together as if they could never let go. They exchanged rings, a symbol of their eternal bond—and sealed their promises with a kiss while the congregation erupted into applause.

And in that moment of complete surrender and jubilation, Harper felt the last remnants of her fears dissipate like shadows before the sun. As she and Cameron embraced, their hearts beating in unison, they knew that their love had triumphed over all obstacles, giving them a fresh start and a chance at a lifetime of happiness together. As they stood there, locked in each other's arms, Harper reflected on the journey they had taken to reach this moment. The years spent apart, the missed chances, and the heartaches now seemed like stepping stones, leading them to the exact place where they were meant to be.

CHAPTER 29

In the middle of a chilly October night, Harper awoke suddenly, drenched in sweat. She sat up in bed, wondering if the dream she'd had was real or just a figment of her imagination.

"You okay?" Cameron's raspy voice interrupted her thoughts. He had rolled over to face her, concern evident in his sleep-softened features.

"Yeah," she stammered, pushing back the strands of dark hair stuck to her forehead. "Just a bad dream."

Cameron's hand moved through the darkness, finding hers under the covers. "Want to talk about it?"

Harper shook her head, though she knew he couldn't see her. The dream was too fresh, too raw to put into words. She didn't even know where to start. "No," she finally said as she settled back onto her pillow. "I'm fine."

The faint glow of moonlight sneaking through the curtains allowed her to see the outline of his face, to watch as he studied her with those gentle eyes.

"It's okay," Cameron murmured, offering a comforting smile that seemed to glow in the light of their room. "It was only a dream."

Harper nodded, welcoming the silence and the warmth of Cameron's body next to hers. The remnants of the dream were still crawling like shadows through the corners of her mind, but she felt safer now. Eventually, the rhythm of Harper's breathing returned to normal, and she drifted back into a welcomed sleep.

When Harper woke again, it was to the sound of birds chirping in the pre-dawn light. She glanced over at Cameron who was still deeply asleep, his arm sprawled over hers. His chest rose and fell in rhythm with the soft snores that escaped from his slightly parted lips. Harper watched him, finding solace in his steady, peaceful sleep as the tendrils of the dreaded dream penetrated her thoughts.

Careful not to wake him, she slipped from beneath his arm and tiptoed over to the window, drawing back the curtain just enough to peek out. The world outside was gradually coming alive, bathed in a reddish glow that gave Harper the slightest hint of unease.

By noon, any trace of the dream Harper had the night before was gone, replaced by the hustle and bustle of a typical day.

"I was thinking," Harper said as she leaned against the kitchen counter. "Maybe Sidney's right ... maybe we should consider getting a place in Kentucky, so we can be close to her and Jason."

Cameron looked up from his phone. "You mean it?"

Harper nodded, thinking how much simpler her life would be if she were to move back home. Her family was there, her best friend. "I just think it might be a nice change of pace," she said. "For both of us."

Cameron, who had been glancing through emails, set his phone aside and leaned back in his chair. Running a hand over his stubble, he considered her proposition. "Kentucky, huh?" he echoed, a faint smile tugging at the corners of his mouth.

Harper shrugged, twirling a strand of hair around her finger nervously. "Yeah, I mean, I think we'd both be happier than we are here in the city. Don't you?"

Cameron gave her a thoughtful look, his eyes roving over her face as if trying to discern the depth of her proposition. "I'm fine anywhere, as long as I'm with you," he said. "But would it make you happy? I mean, what would you do about work? You're not ready to give all this up, are you?"

Harper paused, biting at her lower lip as she pondered his question. Work had always been a vital part of who she was. It was her ticket to independence, her escape from the boredom that crept in whenever she was left idle.

"I don't know," she admitted. "But maybe I could do both. She pushed off the counter and eased into the living room. "The firm runs like clockwork, whether I'm there or not. Marco sees to that. But what if I turned over the reins a little at a time ... You know, transitioned out? Maybe not completely, at least not at first. But over time. And I could always rent a place to stay when I'm in town. Hell," she allowed her mind to wonder, "I may even open up a place in Kentucky. Boutiques are all the rage these days, and I know I could make it work."

Cameron's smile widened as he watched Harper pace about, her hands animated as her ideas came to life.

"You don't have to convince me," he said. "Besides, I've been thinking of returning to flying."

Harper snapped her head in his direction.

"Not for the Navy," he assured her. "But I was thinking of opening a flight school ... a place to train young aviators."

"That's a wonderful idea." Harper moved toward him, falling into his lap with a soft sigh of contentment. "Just think, we could each be running our own businesses, but we'd be doing it together."

Cameron's arms closed around Harper, drawing her close. "Yes," he murmured, pressing a kiss to her temple. "And the best part is we'd both be doing something we love. It would really be the best of both worlds."

Harper sighed deeply, her thoughts drifting to what their future might hold. It was all coming together so beautifully. Cameron's passion for aviation had always fascinated her, and his idea of a flight school seemed perfect. She could already see him, bathed in the warm Kentucky sun, instructing young pilots, their faces alight with wonder and excitement as they experienced the freedom of flight for the first time.

As for her, she pictured herself in a quaint boutique, surrounded by a myriad of garments and accessories, each telling its own unique story. She would use her wealth of experience to handpick every item, ensuring it reflected her distinctive taste and style. She would get a thrill out of helping others discover the joy of finding the perfect outfit or accessory, something that would give them confidence and make them shine. Or maybe she'd become a mentor to the next young lady who dreamed of designing clothes for the runway. Either way, she'd be back home, in the heart of Kentucky, where her roots were deeply embedded, and her heart longed to return.

***

The next morning, Cameron watched as Harper gathered her belongings, preparing to leave for the day. "Where are you headed today?" he asked curiously.

"To see Eleanor," Harper replied, tucking her phone into her bag. "She called me this morning and said she wanted to talk."

"What do you think she wants?"

Harper shrugged. "With Eleanor, it could be anything."

"Good luck," he said before giving her a kiss on the cheek.

"Thanks. Hey, why don't we meet later for lunch, and I'll tell you all about it?"

"I'd like that," Cameron replied as he sipped his morning coffee. "Did you have someplace in mind?"

Harper shook her head. "Why don't you surprise me?"

***

"Harper," said Eleanor, greeting her with a warm embrace. "How nice to see you." She stepped back, studying Harper in the fading afternoon light. "Being married suits you—you're practically glowing." Eleanor invited Harper into her private office. A fire crackled in the wall-mounted glass fireplace, its warmth contrasting the chill of Manhattan's first bite of autumn. Eleanor suggested they start their conversation over a kettle of her favorite afternoon tea and pastries brought in from a renowned bakery nearby.

"What's all this?" Harper asked, taking in the spread Eleanor had prepared.

"Consider it a celebration," Eleanor replied as she poured a steaming cup of Earl Grey. "Or perhaps a fitting backdrop to our conversation."

The two women settled into plush velvet chairs, the tea-steeped air between them electrifying with anticipation.

Harper curled her fingers around her cup, feeling the heat seep through the delicate china.

"To us," Eleanor toasted, clinking her cup against Harper's. "And to the surprises that life brings." She held the teacup to her lips, her eyes never leaving Harper's face. Then, with a small clearing of the throat, Eleanor set her cup on the table and straightened her back. Her expression was serious. "Harper," she said, her voice dropping to a whisper. "There's something I need to tell you."

Harper felt a shiver of unease creep down her spine. She had never seen Eleanor so solemn, so intense.

"First, I want to thank you for your help last year on the collaboration. As expected, the line was well-received, which is exactly what I had envisioned when I contemplated working with you. You never disappoint."

Harper beamed a smile. "Thank you, Eleanor, from the bottom of my heart. Everyone at the firm thanks you as well."

Eleanor took a sip of tea before speaking again. "I've been doing a fair bit of soul-searching recently, and I've come to the conclusion that it's time for me to retire."

It took Harper a moment to process Eleanor's words. "You? Retire?"

"I know it may be difficult to believe," said Eleanor. "But if I'm to enjoy my golden years, I can't do it from behind a desk. I need to be out there." She motioned toward the world outside. "Living. Breathing. Exploring."

"What will you do to occupy your time?" Harper asked.

"I've always wanted to explore Southeast Asia, so I plan on traveling for a while. After that, who knows? But I want to live a life untethered for once, and this may be my last chance to do it."

Harper considered that. "In that case, congratulations! I think it's wonderful that you've realized there are more important things in life than work. I'm starting to see that too." She paused and stared into her tea. "Does anyone else know about this?"

Eleanor shook her head. "I wanted to talk to you before

announcing it to everyone else because there's something I want to ask you. Harper, when I leave, I want you to take my place as CEO. And before you say no, I want you to know that there is no one more qualified or deserving to lead this company into the future than you. That's the real reason I reached out to you earlier this year. I wanted everyone at Chanel to see just how brilliant you are, so that when—if—you take over, they'll know they're in good hands."

Harper was at a loss for words. Her heart fluttered in her chest as she looked at the woman who had been her mentor, guide, and sometimes pain-in-the-ass throughout her career. Filled with shock and disbelief, Harper mumbled an incoherent response before regaining enough composure to form a proper sentence.

"Eleanor ... I ... I don't know what to say."

"Then don't say anything just yet," Eleanor said, her eyes shining with understanding and compassion. "Take some time to think about it, dear. I won't force this decision upon you."

"Thank you. And just so you know, I'm ... I'm honored," she stammered, her heart pounding in her chest. "This is more than I ever imagined for myself."

Eleanor simply smiled, leaning back in her chair.

"Wait," Harper interjected, her mind racing. "What about my company ... my team? I can't leave them behind."

"Bring them with you," Eleanor replied. "If you decide to take the job, you'll have full autonomy."

Harper blinked in disbelief, letting Eleanor's words sink in. She had always believed in her abilities, but to be entrusted with a company of this scale was beyond her wildest dreams.

"Well," she stuttered, gathering her thoughts. "You've given me a lot to think about. How soon do you need an answer?"

"I'm not in a huge hurry, but I'd like to have an answer by the end of November. That way, I can get to work on my exit strategy."

***

By the time Harper got to Parker & Quinn, her mind was still spinning. She found Cameron sitting at the bar, so she sank onto the bright red chair beside him, her heart a frenzied drum in her chest.

"Is everything all right?" Cameron asked. "Did you talk to Eleanor?"

She nodded, still lost in thought. "She offered me a job," she said.

"A job?" His eyebrows shot up in surprise. "What kind of job?"

"You'll never believe it. She is stepping down as CEO of Chanel, and she wants me to take her place."

Cameron froze, the surprise clearly written on his face. "Wow! That's ... huge!"

"Yeah ... huge!" Harper echoed his words as she rubbed her temples.

"So are you going to take it?"

Harper could only shrug noncommittally, the enormity of the proposition still sinking in. "I ... I don't know," she said, running a hand through her hair. "There's so much to consider."

After ordering a soppressata flatbread and two glasses of wine, Harper let out a long sigh.

"Hey," Cameron whispered, "I know this is a lot. But remember ... we're in this together."

"I know. It's just that this is life-changing ... for both of us."

"You're right. When do you have to let her know of your decision?"

"By Thanksgiving. Which gives us plenty of time to weigh the pros and cons."

"What about your idea of moving back home?" he asked.

Harper let out a deep sigh. "I don't know. If I take this, moving back home won't be an option. At least not for a while."

"Well, whatever you decide, I'm with you one hundred percent."

"That's what I love about you," she said, beaming at him. "Your ability to go with the flow."

Their food arrived then, and the conversation continued.

"So I was thinking," Harper said around a bite of crust. "About a conversation I had with my mom last year. It didn't seem important at the time, but now everything has changed.

Cameron looked up from his plate. "What was it about?"

"Having kids," Harper replied. "You still want to have kids, don't you?"

"Of course I do," said Cameron. "But what about—?"

"I was thinking of adopting," she said. "It's been on my mind for a while, and it's something I feel strongly about."

"You won't get any objection from me," said Cameron. "But," he continued after a few seconds, "you're worried about where we would raise a child, right?" he guessed.

Harper nodded. "I know people do it all the time, but I don't know if this is the environment I want to bring a child into. I always imagined raising kids in a town similar to the one I grew up in; it holds so many happy memories for me. In fact, I would go as far as to say that it is those memories that have shaped me into who I am today."

"I know what you mean," said Cameron as he slid another

slice of flatbread onto his plate. "I have similar fond memories of growing up in East Tennessee—the lakes, the mountains, the colors in fall. But we could make it work here too."

"I suppose you're right," said Harper, letting out a sigh. "But what about the noise, the hustle and bustle? It all seems too chaotic for a child ... for our child."

Cameron scooted closer and wrapped his arm around her shoulders. "We don't have to decide this today," he said lovingly. "Adoption is a long process. Why don't you take Eleanor's advice and give it time to sink in?"

***

As the weeks passed, Harper and Cameron had numerous conversations about whether she should accept the job offer. On one hand, the idea of being the CEO of her favorite brand was alluring, with its power, prestige, and financial benefits. However, another part of Harper yearned for a more tranquil and uncomplicated lifestyle—leisurely strolls in nature, and peaceful evenings spent gazing at the stars from the comfort of a front porch.

Still undecided, she called Sidney to get her opinion.

"Sid, I need your advice," Harper started, words tumbling out in a rush. Sidney's calming presence on the other end of the line settled her nerves.

"Harp, you know my answer is always the same. Follow your heart."

"But what if my heart is sending me mixed messages?"

Sidney chuckled. "There's no one in the world who wants you to come home more than me, but I also recognize the enormity of this opportunity. It's not every day that someone has the chance to live out their wildest dream, to run an iconic brand, and be at the top of their industry. Not to add more pressure to the situation, but taking this job will mean more than just a change in your career; it will set the stage for the rest of your life. On the other hand, leaving behind the city and all its allure for a quieter life isn't a decision to take lightly either. Whatever choice you make will impact not only you but Cameron as well, and any future family you may have."

"But that's what concerns me most," said Harper. "I don't know if I want to raise children in the city."

"So get a place outside the city, maybe on Long Island. With the money you'll be making, you can afford whatever you want. But whatever you decide, just remember, a place does not define the type of parent you become nor the happiness of a child. It's the love and care you provide."

Harper absorbed Sidney's words. She knew Sidney was right, but it didn't make the decision any easier.

"Thanks, Sid. You've given me a lot to think about."

"You're welcome. Hey," she said after a brief pause, "not to take away from your big opportunity, but I have some news of my own. We were going to wait until Thanksgiving to make the announcement, but since I've got you on the phone ... Jason and I are pregnant."

"Oh my God! Are you serious? Sid, that's wonderful news! It's like everything is falling into place. I'm so happy for you two."

"I know, it's crazy," Sidney said, her voice vibrating with excitement. "And the timing couldn't be better. Jason's book is climbing the charts, and we're almost finished unpacking in our new place."

Harper could practically see Sidney's glowing face through

the phone. "This calls for a celebration," Harper suggested. "Cameron and I were just discussing coming home for a few days. Maybe the four of us could have dinner together while we're there?"

"I think we can do better than that," said Sidney. "Why don't you stay with us while you're here? We've got plenty of room, and I need an excuse to get the guest room ready. Plus, Jason and I could use a break from all the unpacking."

"All right," said Harper. "That will give us an opportunity to catch up."

After agreeing on a date and time, Harper finally ended the call, her mind abuzz with excitement over Sidney's pregnancy.

CHAPTER 30

After catching an Uber from the airport, Harper and Cameron arrived at Sidney and Jason's sprawling Victorian home and settled in for the weekend. They unpacked their belongings in the guest room under the sloping eaves, where lace curtains billowed gently with the late autumn breeze.

At dinner, they filled their plates and gathered around the worn oak dining table, the golden glow from the chandelier overhead casting long, flickering shadows against the freshly painted walls. Sidney served a hearty stew, complete with herbs and root vegetables, its steam coiling upwards like specters in the dim light.

Over dinner, the conversation flowed like a gentle brook, highlighted by bursts of laughter and quiet moments of contemplation. Cameron and Jason listened quietly as Harper and Sidney traded tales from their past. The stories painted pictures of youthful exploits and old friendships, of summers spent chasing the sun and winters huddled around a fireplace, warming their bones.

As the evening waned, they retired to the living room, sinking into plush armchairs. A ceramic mug of steaming tea lingered in Harper's hand as she listened to the soft crackle of the fireplace.

"Thanks for letting us stay with you," said Harper. "We hope our being here isn't too much of an imposition."

"Of course not," Sidney replied, waving her hand

dismissively. "This old house is too quiet with just the two of us in it. It's nice to have company for a change."

"She's right," said Jason. "It's good to hear laughter and conversation filling these old rooms. Makes the place feel alive."

"You've both done a great job of fixing this place up," said Cameron, his eyes roaming the spacious living room, taking in every detail.

"Thanks," said Jason. "But I can't take all the credit. Sid found a team that specializes in restoring old homes. They did most of the hard work. I just added a few touches here and there."

With night settling in, the house descended into a comfortable silence. Outside, the wind rustled the oak trees that stood sentinel over the house, while inside, the flames in the fireplace cast a warm glow over the room.

"I still can't get over your baby bump," Harper said, admiring Sidney's belly.

Sidney patted her rounded stomach, a soft smile playing on her lips. "Yes, it's quite a sight, isn't it? The first three months have gone by like that," she said, snapping her fingers. "And the best part—I've had very little morning sickness. Fingers crossed that the next six months are just as smooth."

"I'm sure they will be," Harper replied, returning the smile. She took a sip of her tea and then placed her mug on the coffee table, picking up a small, hand-knitted blanket in faded pastel colors. "Is this for the baby?"

Sidney nodded, her eyes gleaming under the dull flicker of the fireplace light. "Yes, it was mine, once upon a time. It's been passed down in our family for generations. I started washing and mending it as soon as I knew I was pregnant."

Harper traced the tiny, intricate stitches with her fingers.

"Such delicate work," she murmured. "It's beautiful."

Sidney chuckled, her eyes lighting up with maternal pride. "Wait till you see the crib." While the men went to pour a nightcap, Sidney led Harper to the second-floor nursery, where the scent of freshly painted walls and new linens lingered in the air. The room was a shade of soft blue, invoking images of cloudless summer skies. A charming crib made of rich mahogany stood by the window, its bars polished to a warm glow. A mobile of hand-carved wooden animals suspended above it, twirling gently in the tranquil air.

Sidney beamed as she watched Harper's eyes dart about the room full of wonder, taking in every meticulous detail. "Our little piece of heaven," she said, her voice barely above a whisper.

Harper turned to Sidney, her eyes welling up with tears. "It's truly beautiful, Sid. So well thought out." She ran a hand over the polished wood of the crib, then reached out to touch the mobile, setting it spinning gently. The wooden creatures danced in the soft light filtering through the window.

"Let me guess—you're thinking about what your nursery will look like, aren't you?" Sidney asked.

"How'd you know?"

"Because I did the same thing before I got pregnant. I think it's in our nature as women."

Harper smiled, imagining a room filled with soft pinks and lavenders, a corner filled with stuffed animals waiting to be claimed by tiny hands. "I do wonder sometimes," she admitted, her voice brimming with wistful anticipation. She imagined the walls adorned with whimsical artwork, a comfortable rocking chair for late-night feedings and lullabies, and a chest of drawers heavy with tiny clothes, diapers, and blankets, each article meticulously folded and sorted. She imagined the windowsill decorated with potted plants, their scent subtly perfuming the room and bringing a touch of nature indoors.

Sidney smiled, a knowing glint in her eyes as she watched Harper paint imaginary pictures in her mind. "What does Cameron think of your plan to adopt?"

"He's just as excited as I am," Harper replied. "Just knowing we can give a home and family to a child who needs it is deeply fulfilling for both of us."

"What about this opportunity at Chanel—have you all thought any more about what you're going to do?"

It took Harper a few seconds to find the right words. "As you might imagine, we've discussed it ad nauseam. My first inclination was to turn it down, but after giving it more thought, I decided to take it. I just think if I don't do this now, I'll always have regrets."

A hint of disappointment flashed across Sidney's face. "I kind of figured you would. I know you've always had bigger dreams than what this small town has to offer." She placed her hands calmly in her lap, glancing down at them. "But what about starting a family? Is that off the table?"

"For now," Harper replied. "We want to see how things go with me in this new position. I want to give it all I've got for at least a year or two. Then, we can reevaluate. Besides, what's the hurry, right? I mean, everything happened so quickly with the engagement and the wedding that we want to enjoy it being just the two of us for a while."

"I can understand that," said Sidney. "It does have its advantages—traveling together, long weekends spent in bed, no worries ... Cherish these days, Harper"—she placed a hand on her stomach—"because they won't last forever."

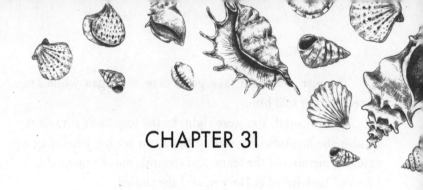

CHAPTER 31

"You're going to be late."

From her desk at the Chanel headquarters, Harper looked up from her laptop at her assistant. "Planes can wait, Kim. Vogue can't," she replied coolly. After checking her carefully worded email, Harper pressed SEND, then leaned back in her chair and breathed a sigh of relief. "There. All done."

While Harper gathered her belongings, Kim went to get the car.

"Aren't you forgetting something?" Marco asked as Harper breezed past him. He held up Harper's rose gold iPhone.

She let out another sigh. "Thanks, Marco. What would I do without you?"

"I shudder to think." Marco followed her out of the office, and they rode the elevator down to the lobby together. "So you'll be back on Tuesday, right?"

"That's the plan."

"And you remembered to pack the gifts we bought at Bloomingdales?"

"Yes. I put Cam in charge of that, so I wouldn't forget."

Marco raised his eyes to the heavens. "God bless that man!"

When the car pulled up to the curb, Marco helped Harper load her bags into the trunk.

"Promise me you'll take good care of Megan while I'm gone," Harper told him.

"Already on it. You were right, by the way. She's got talent. I know she just officially started but I can see her becoming a valuable member of the team. She reminds me of someone else I know." He winked at Harper, and she smiled.

"Why do you think I hired her?"

***

Thanks to a smooth flight, and very little traffic, Harper and Cameron arrived at the hospital before Sidney gave birth.

"I can't believe you're going to be a mom," Harper said, taking a seat in the chair beside the bed.

Sidney beamed. "I know. I can hardly wait." A sharp pain hit her, causing her to flinch.

"Based on your contractions, you won't have to wait long." After the contraction passed, Harper asked, "Have you and Jason settled on a name for the baby?"

Sidney shook her head. "I want to see her face first before deciding."

Harper laughed softly at that. "That's so like you, Sid." She gave Sidney's hand a gentle squeeze before letting go, then glanced over at the clock on the wall, the hands ticking steadily as if marking each passing moment before the big event. "Are you nervous?"

Sidney looked down at her swollen belly, instinctively smoothing it over with her hand. "Terrified," she admitted. "But also ... excited?"

Harper chuckled softly at that. "By the way, where's Jason? I didn't see him when I came in."

"He was making me a nervous wreck," Sidney replied. "So I sent him to the cafeteria to calm down."

Harper smiled and remarked, "He loves you so much, Sid. He'll make an amazing father."

Suddenly, Sidney clutched her belly and gritted her teeth.

"It's time," said the nurse who had been quietly observing from the corner of the room.

Harper stood up from her chair and gave Sidney's hand a reassuring squeeze before stepping back. The nurse began preparing Sidney for delivery while Harper watched from a distance, filled with anticipation. She knew that when Sidney emerged from this room, she would be holding a new life in her arms. It was an awe-inspiring thought. Before leaving the room, Harper wished Sidney good luck.

***

Less than an hour later, Jason delivered the news that Sidney had given birth to a healthy baby girl. The entire waiting room let out a collective sigh of relief and then proceeded to celebrate the arrival.

Amidst the celebration, Cameron turned to Harper. "Our turn will come soon enough," he said, perhaps sensing the sadness that had crept into her countenance.

Harper nodded, offering him a small smile. "But it won't be the same, will it? We won't get to experience any of this."

"No," Cameron agreed quietly, taking her hand in his and giving it a gentle squeeze. "But that doesn't mean it won't be special. It'll just be different, that's all—it will be uniquely ours."

Harper smiled, the image of her children's faces still fresh in her mind.

"You okay?" he asked, pulling her to his side.

"Fine," she said, blinking back tears. "I'm just so happy ... for Sid."

Cameron's gaze softened as he regarded Harper. He knew her longings well, the unspoken desires that hovered at the corners of her smiles and in the silence of their nights together. "So am I. She's going to be a great mother. And so will you, someday."

Harper's heart fluttered at his words, a blush spreading across her cheeks. "You really think so?"

"I know so," he whispered in her ear.

PART 4

PART 4

CHAPTER 32

Three-and-a-half years later

The call came in just after one, and like a thief in the night, it struck without warning or provocation. The scream that followed pierced the tranquility of Harper's life. After that, everything was a blur.

The next moments were a cyclone of chaos. Cameron rushed to her side, grabbing her just as her knees buckled. The phone fell from Harper's hands, a harsh clatter against the wooden floor as the voice on the other end continued to speak.

Cameron grabbed at it, and stuttered into the receiver. "Who is this?"

Brenda told Cameron what she had already told Harper—that Sidney and Jason were gone.

Gone? The harsh reality of Brenda's words echoed in Cameron's ears, triggering the memory of his mother's death, and of Trevor's. The ground beneath him felt like it was giving way, but he had to be strong for Harper. He could barely comprehend it, let alone begin to comfort Harper who had sunk into a wail of profound agony. He ended the call with Brenda, his mind racing with a million thoughts and a single focus—Harper. Her cries echoed within the confines of their apartment, jarring him more than the grim news. He dropped to his knees beside her, wrapping his arms around her wracked form. His voice felt like a parched riverbed, devoid of the comforting words she needed to hear.

"Harper," he said, as if the sound of his voice could provide some solace. He drew her closer still, his heart aching with every sob that wracked her body. "Harper," he whispered again, holding onto her name like a life preserver in the dark ocean of despair that threatened to drown them both. "I'm here. I'm here."

Harper's tears felt hot against his bare chest, searing through the pale fabric of his shirt. Her sobs were violent, desperate, and he could feel each of them like a brutal punch to the gut. Her world had just shattered, and he was helpless in the face of her torment.

"Cameron," she sobbed, her voice barely a whisper in between her choking cries. "Sidney ... Jason ... they're ..."

"I know," Cameron cut her off gently, his own voice thick with pain. He squeezed his eyes shut, letting the bitter sting of unshed tears engulf him momentarily. "I know."

He held her even tighter, his arms a fortress against the pain that was threatening to tear her apart.

But in the midst of the seemingly endless darkness, there was a small glimmer of hope: Abigail. According to Brenda, she had been in the car with Sidney and Jason when it crashed, her tiny body battered and broken. But somehow, she had survived. Now, she lay in a hospital bed seven hundred miles away, fighting for her life.

"We have to go," Harper insisted, pushing aside her grief for now. "Abigail needs us."

***

The day seemed to drag on interminably. Harper lay motionless in their bed for most of it, the only sound escaping her was the occasional tender whimper or a soft sigh of desolation. She was there physically, but in another sense, she was elsewhere entirely—in a world painted with grief and disbelief.

Meanwhile, Cameron did what was necessary—arranging travel to Lexington, making calls to extended family, handling the logistical nightmares that seemed trivial and overwhelming at the same time. He kept himself busy, his actions driven by a sense of duty.

***

Cameron and Harper arrived at the hospital later that evening, the same one where Sidney had given birth to Abigail three years earlier. The atmosphere was heavy with a bitter taste of *déjà vu*—a haunting echo from a joyous past, swallowed whole by the gaping void of their present predicament. When they finally reached the ICU where Abigail was, they found Sidney and Jason's parents sitting in the stiff, uncomfortable waiting area chairs. Their faces were etched with grief, their eyes drawn and highlighted with dark circles.

Harper rushed to Lucinda Westwood, Sidney's mother, who looked up at her with a weariness that seemed to age her beyond her years.

"I'm so sorry," Harper began, but her voice cracked. She cleared her throat, blinking rapidly to keep the tears at bay. "I'm so sorry, Lucinda."

Lucinda gathered Harper into her arms gently, patting her back with a tired hand.

When Harper pulled back, she wiped away her tears as

she gave condolences to Sidney's father and Jason's parents. When she finally made her way to Cameron, who stood apart from the group, his back rigid and his face a mask of controlled composure, she could see the deep pain in his eyes. It took all her strength to stifle a gasp at the sight of it.

He mustered a weak smile, but it quickly faded as he glanced back toward the ICU doors. "I just ... I can't believe it," he muttered.

"I know," Harper replied as she sank into a seat and closed her eyes. She pleaded with God to protect and heal Abigail, unable to bear the thought of losing her too.

Hours passed with no word. Then, a doctor approached them sometime after midnight. His face was drawn, a mask of sympathetic neutrality. He hesitated before he spoke, and in that pause, the world seemed to hold its breath.

"She is stable for now," he said, his voice laced with fatigue. "But she's very weak. The next twenty-four hours are crucial."

His words hung in the air like a knife dangling by a thread.

Harper gripped Cameron's hand tightly, her knuckles turning white. Cameron squeezed back, a silent promise that he was there, right beside her, no matter what.

"Can we see her?" Harper asked.

The doctor nodded, leading them to the room where Abigail was.

The sight of her was a shock. The once vibrant and playful little girl was now barely recognizable, her small frame swallowed by the large, sterile hospital bed. Wires and tubes were scattered across her body, feeding into machines that beeped and hummed—artificial reminders of life. Her injuries were extensive, including a broken collar bone and multiple cracked ribs. However, it was the internal damage that concerned the doctors most. To alleviate her pain and stabilize her condition, they had placed her in a medically induced coma.

Harper approached the bed, her trembling hand reaching out to brush away a loose strand of hair from Abigail's forehead, her fingers lightly touching the cool skin. It was almost too much for her wounded heart to take. Abigail was just a child, barely three. It wasn't fair.

Cameron moved to the far side of the bed, his own hand reaching out to gently hold Abigail's. Harper could see the ache in his eyes. But there was something else—resolve—a determination that was characteristic of him. His jaw was clenched, the lines around his mouth hardened. "Abby," he whispered, "you're going to fight this, okay? And we're going to be right here with you every step of the way."

***

When morning came, Harper woke with her head resting on Cameron's chest. She couldn't remember when, but sometime during the night she had cried herself to sleep. She lifted her head, her eyes dry and sore from crying, her body aching from the uncomfortable hospital chair she had spent hours in. Cameron was already awake, his eyes fixed on Abigail. It was as if he hadn't moved all night.

"Cam," Harper said, her voice hoarse. "Did you sleep at all?"

He turned to look at her, his tired eyes reflecting all the worry and inner turmoil he was going through. "Very little. She's stable though, and that's all that matters." Cameron brushed away a few loose strands from Harper's tear-streaked face gently before pressing a soft kiss on her forehead. "How are you holding up?"

She smiled sadly. "Not as well as you," she answered, her gaze drifting to the little girl on the bed.

"It's going to be okay," Cameron said. "She's going to be okay."

"How can you say that? How can you know?"

"Because we have to believe that, Harper," he said. "And we have to believe that we'll make it through this, the three of us, no matter what."

As they sat together in silence, an unspoken understanding bridged the gap between them. Life had dealt them an unimaginable blow, and nothing would ever be the same again. Yet here they were, holding each other as they faced this new chapter—more uncertain and terrifying than anything they'd ever known.

***

What came next was a mix of restless nights and dreary mornings, each day blending seamlessly into the next. For two straight weeks, Harper sat at the edge of Abigail's hospital bed, holding the child's small hand in hers. Her heart ached as she watched the steady rise and fall of the girl's little chest, a reminder of the life that was still at stake.

Then, on the fifteenth day, Abigail opened her eyes.

The sight of the fragile little girl looking back at her, eyes glazed and confused, made Harper gasp. She was a hollowed-out shell of the vivacious girl she used to be, but it was Abigail, nonetheless. Alive.

"Hey, sweetie," Harper croaked, trying to smile through her tears. She squeezed Abigail's hand, relief and hope washing over her. "You gave us quite a scare."

At the sound of Harper's voice, a spark flickered in Abigail's eyes. Though weak, she attempted a small nod and squeezed Harper's hand in return. It was a minute gesture, but for Harper, it was monumental. Abigail was responding. She was fighting.

She turned to Cameron who had been silently observing from the corner of the room. Her eyes met his, and she knew they shared the same thought—they had been granted a much-needed lifeline.

But then came the moment Harper had been dreading.

"Where are they?" Abigail asked. "Where are Mommy and Daddy?"

Harper froze, her heart pounding in her chest as the innocent question hung in the air. She glanced helplessly at Cameron, who seemed incapable of words. They both knew this moment would come, but knowing did little to prepare them for the reality of it.

"Sweetheart," Harper said gently, holding Abigail's hand tightly. "Your mommy and daddy had to go on a very long trip." Tears blurred her vision. "They wanted to stay here with you, but ..."

Abigail's youthful eyes widened in confusion, then her small forehead creased in thought. "But why didn't they take me with them?"

"They ..." Harper swallowed hard, the lump in her throat threatening to choke her.

Cameron chimed in then. "Listen," he said, kneeling beside the young girl's bed. "Do you remember that story your parents used to tell you, the one about the stars in the sky?"

Abigail nodded. "About how everyone has a special star?"

"Exactly. Well, you're a lucky little girl because not only do you have one special star, but you have two."

At this, Harper turned away, and let the tears fall freely down her face. She quickly left the room and found solace in the hallway, leaning heavily against the cool wall. A gentle sob wracked her body as she slid down to the floor, cradling her head in her hands. She knew Cameron would explain things to Abigail, would make her believe that her parents were on some fantastical journey. But Harper knew the brutal truth, and someday there would be no escaping it. Someday, Abigail would ask again, would demand the truth, and Harper wondered where she would find the strength to tell a child that her parents were gone forever.

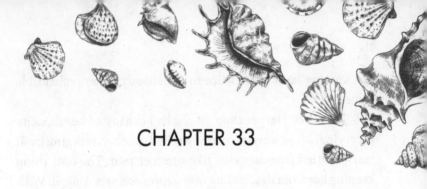

CHAPTER 33

As the days turned into weeks, Abigail started to regain her strength. The hollow look in her eyes was starting to recede, replaced by the familiar sparkle Harper and Cameron had been so desperate to see. Her cheeks, once pale and sunken, filled out and adopted a rosy hue. Every little bit of progress she made was a cause for celebration, a step toward reclaiming normalcy.

The hospital room, once filled with the sterile smell of antiseptics and echoes of beeping machines, started to fill with laughter and stories, balloons and stuffed animals. Harper brought in Abigail's favorite books and toys, anything that could make her feel more at home. Some days, they would pile into her bed and listen to Cameron's animated storytelling, smiles tugging at their lips as he brought classic fairy tales to life.

Every day, they saw Abigail's spirit emerging like a butterfly from its cocoon. She started talking again at first in hushed whispers, and eventually in the lively chatter that had once been her trademark. Conversations with her were no longer one-sided, filled with Harper's desperate pleas, but rather a delightful exchange marked by giggles and a curious inquisition about everything around her.

At the same time, details emerged about the accident that had taken Sidney and Jason. According to the detective assigned to the case, a drunk driver had veered into their lane and hit them head-on. The driver had walked away unscathed, adding just another layer of injustice to the already incomprehensible tragedy.

Just when Harper thought she had exhausted her capacity for crying, a new wave of sorrow washed over her, bringing fresh tears that fell from her eyes like summer rain. The only thing keeping her from descending into depression was Abigail. With each passing day, the little girl grew stronger, her innocence and resilience a buoy for Harper to cling onto. Abigail had always held a special place in Harper's heart. More than just her best friend's daughter, she was her goddaughter, the child she and Cameron had sworn to protect. And as Harper sat there, processing everything that had happened, she recalled the promise she'd made Sidney four years earlier, a promise that now seemed to hold a weight heavier than the mountains.

***

The nursery was quiet, filled only with the soft hum from outside, a symphony of nature's lullabies. Harper looked down at her hands, toying with her wedding ring.

"I was going to wait until later to bring this up, but now seems like the right time." Sidney paused, taking a deep breath and exhaling. "When the baby's born, Jason and I want you and Cameron to be the godparents."

Harper blinked, totally taken aback. "Us? Really?"

Sidney nodded. "You and I are like sisters, Harper, and although I probably don't say it enough, your support has been invaluable to me over the years. Jason and I discussed it, and we can't think of anyone better."

"I ... I don't know what to say," Harper stammered. "Yes," she blurted. "I mean, I'll need to get Cameron's buy-in, but yes."

Sidney laughed, her smile filling the room. "That's wonderful. I'm so happy to hear it."

They shared a warm embrace, their bond deepening with this new layer of responsibility.

Later that evening, Cameron was sitting in bed, absorbed in a book, when Harper walked into the room. Sitting on the edge of the bed, Harper took in a deep breath, trying to compose herself before she spoke.

"Sidney ... She asked me something today," Harper began hesitantly, clutching and unclutching the fabric of the duvet as she tried to put her thoughts into words.

Cameron bookmarked his page and set the book aside. "What did she ask?"

Harper swallowed hard. "She and Jason want us to be their child's godparents. Can you believe it?"

Cameron leaned back against the headboard, his gaze turning thoughtful. "That's huge," he said, running a hand through his messy hair. "Why didn't Jason mention it to me earlier when we were having drinks?"

"I think they wanted to wait for the right moment," said Harper. "She brought it up when I told Sidney about my decision to take the job."

"Did you tell her yes?"

"I told her I needed to talk to you first."

"Harper, when it comes to things like this, I'll always support your decision. Being a godparent is one of the highest honors one can receive. It shows the trust they have in us, the bond we've formed over the years."

"So you're on board?" She pressed after a brief pause.

Cameron nodded resolutely. "Absolutely."

The next morning, while the men slept, Harper and Sidney

sat in the kitchen, chatting over steaming cups of freshly brewed coffee.

Outside, a soft mist clung to the quiet countryside. Inside, the crackling fire in the hearth spread a sense of warmth and comfort throughout the kitchen. The women's voices wove together in hushed tones, intimate and secretive, their conversation punctuated by soft laughter.

"I'm sorry for springing the whole godparent thing on you last night," said Sidney, a small frown furrowing her brow. "I should have at least let you guys get settled first."

Harper leaned back in her chair, absently fiddling with the cream-colored porcelain handle of her coffee cup. "You have nothing to apologize for," she said.

Sidney looked down at her cup of coffee. "I just don't want what I said to put a damper on the weekend. I've been so looking forward to this. Both of us have."

"Hey," said Harper, reaching out and placing a hand gently on Sidney's arm. "You haven't ruined anything. In fact ..." She set down her coffee cup. "Cameron and I discussed it last night before we went to bed, and we've decided to accept your and Jason's offer."

Sidney's eyes widened, her cup of coffee halted midway to her mouth. "Really?" She barely breathed out the word, as if she feared saying it any louder and it would shatter the moment. "Oh my God, this is wonderful! I can't wait to tell Jason."

A comfortable silence enveloped them, and they both reveled in the moment. "Can I ask what made you decide to do it?"

"You're my best friend, Sidney. You know I'd do anything for you."

Sidney's eyes welled up with tears, her hands trembling as she clutched her cup. "Harper," she whispered. "You have no idea how much this means to us."

***

Inhaling deeply, Harper contemplated the weight of the promise she and Cameron had made back then. They had vowed to take on the responsibility of raising Abigail if anything were to ever happen to Sidney and Jason. And something had happened to them ... the unthinkable ... like a bolt of lightning on a clear day. As the reality of their agreement sank in, Harper felt something new—a surge of determination coursing through her veins.

The following Tuesday, Abigail was discharged from the hospital. Despite the cast on her left arm, she had healed nicely, and the doctors were confident she would make a full recovery. Harper filled the car with balloons, stuffed animals, and Abigail's favorite flowers—daisies. She wanted desperately to make the ride home as cheerful as possible.

In the weeks since the accident, Harper and Cameron had secured a rental on the edge of town. As the hospital counselor had told them, familiarity was the key to a smooth transition. So Cameron picked a spot with a backyard, with a view of the forest and a creek. He had also made several trips to Sidney and Jason's house, retrieved most of Abigail's belongings, and done his best to recreate her room in their new house.

The first time they crossed the threshold of their new home, Harper held Abigail in her arms. The child's wide-eyed wonder at the sight of her room—mindfully arranged to mirror the one she had lost—gave Harper a sense of peace and comfort. Every stuffed animal was in its place, every book on the bookshelf, just as it had been before.

In no time, a routine began to take shape. Mornings were

filled with breakfasts of pancakes and berries, Abigail's favorite. They'd then venture into the backyard where Abigail would play in the sandbox while Harper worked on her laptop under the shade of a large sycamore. Afternoons were for learning and exploration, with frequent trips to the nearby creek and forest, where they would search for interesting rocks or crawdads, just as Harper had done when she was a child. And in the evenings, Cameron stepped in and told stories, while Abigail drifted off to sleep.

Days turned into weeks, each one indistinguishable from the last. Winter arrived, and the world outside seemed to hold its breath, as if it too mourned Sidney and Jason. Bare trees stood sentinel against a backdrop of gray skies—a melancholic canvas that mirrored Harper and Cameron's sorrowful existence.

Perhaps it was the cruelty of time that it did not pause—did not even stutter—for their grief. Each day brought them closer to confronting the daunting reality they wished they could avoid. Harper, always resilient, did her best to be there for everyone and handle everything. She split her time between New York and Kentucky, juggling the demands of her burgeoning career, and the desperate need to be close to Abigail.

But even when she was home, Harper spent most of her waking hours staring blankly at distant nooks. Cameron, on the other hand, threw himself into handling the aftermath—insurance claims and countless phone calls that were as draining as they were necessary. He hid his pain well, his grief manifesting in the furrow of his brow and a clenched jaw that spoke volumes, more than words ever could.

They were going through the motions of life without truly living. Harper felt herself becoming a stranger to her own reflection—a hollow shell mimicking the rhythm of life but without its essential beat. The only constants were Cameron and Abigail, their presence an anchoring force amidst the chaos of her melancholy. Cameron's arms remained a haven, his words a relief for her fractured soul. He was the one who held her when the tears came, his warmth seeping into her coldness, filling the cracks in her heart even if it wasn't enough to heal it completely.

As the weeks passed, so did their despair begin to ebb into a numb acceptance. The first sign of change was the crocuses, their purple heads stubbornly piercing through the cold earth. It was a color Cameron hadn't seen in months, the vibrancy of it shocking him out of his haze.

Harper saw it too, their appearance drawing her outside for the first time in weeks. She knelt beside the tiny blooms, the chill of the ground seeping through her jeans as she gently traced a petal with her finger.

"What should we do?" she asked Cameron as she stood and brushed the damp earth from her knees.

Cameron looked at her, his eyes mirroring the tired resolve in her own. They were both marred by the harsh winter, their spirits and bodies, numbed by the biting cold. He took a step toward her, closing the silent gap that had stretched between them for months.

"I think," he began hesitantly, "that we should stay. As much as you love your job, I can't imagine us returning to New York. Not now."

"I agree," said Harper, realizing that, whether she wanted it or not, that chapter of her life was closed. "Abigail is what matters now."

CHAPTER 34

At dawn, while the rest of the world slept, Harper stepped out into the cold, making that all-too-familiar journey from her childhood home to Sidney's. The path she had walked countless times before—those two hundred steps she knew so well—now felt endless and impossible.

Harper bundled herself in a coat, the stars twinkling like icy jewels in the velvet sky above. Her breath formed vapors in the air as she trod the lonely path. Late-season snowflakes swirled around her, dancing with the wind before meeting their end on the ground. The houses stood out against the winter landscape, silhouetted by the soft glow from the streetlamps.

As she moved further away, her own home fell into the background, a distant shadow swallowed by the frosty darkness. Each footstep brought a crunch of snow underfoot, a muffled echo resonating in the stillness of the night. Harper glanced back at her own home, lit by the solitary streetlamp on her side of the road.

As she neared Sidney's childhood home, which now stood vacant, Harper noticed the solitary light in the attic. It pierced the gloom, serving as a beacon of familiarity in the otherwise lonely morning. Drawing a deep breath, she continued her path toward it, the cold air biting at her cheeks as she walked. The unending expanse of snow around her seemed to reflect the loneliness she felt in her heart, the seemingly endless void left in the wake of Sidney's death.

Taking a deep breath, she stepped up onto the porch and paused to catch her breath. The old wooden boards groaned under her boots, adding to the eerie silence surrounding her. Snowflakes settled on her coat as she made her way to the door, the brass doorknob shining in the porch light. Her hand brushed over a spot on the door where some paint still remained, evoking memories that were too painful to relive, but also too precious to forget. And she remembered the conversation she had years ago with the previous owner, about how this house held more than just memories, but a piece of her soul. Now, a piece of Harper's soul resided in that abandoned house as well. With a heavy heart, she knocked in their secret rhythm that only she and Sidney knew. But this time, there would be no answer.

As the sun appeared on the horizon, Harper set off on her journey back home. Along the way, she paused in the park to admire the resilience of the resurrection lily. Years had passed, but it still stood tall, patiently awaiting the arrival of spring to bring forth new growth once again. "Good to see you too, Sid," she whispered before continuing on.

Instead of heading straight home, Harper ventured down a gravel path that led to the cemetery where Sidney and Jason were buried.

Passing beneath the wrought iron arch that marked the entrance, Harper's heart thumped loudly in her chest. Finding Sidney's tombstone, Harper paused, wondering if she was ready for this. It had been almost six months since they were laid to rest, yet, as she stood in the stillness of the morning, it felt like only yesterday she had lost them. Harper averted her eyes from the tombstones, not quite ready to read the inscription carved in the cold stone. Instead, she let her eyes wander, taking in the soft light of dawn as it washed over the graveyard. She moved slowly, tracing the edges of nearby tombstones with gloved fingers, an attempt to connect, perhaps, with those who had likewise experienced incalculable loss.

Pausing at the foot of Sidney's grave, Harper composed herself before speaking.

"Well," she said, her words shattering the stillness of the morning. "Here I am. I wish I could say I had the courage to come here on my own, but the truth is Cameron talked me into it." She took a deep breath and looked down at the snow beneath her feet. "I wasn't sure if I was ready, but now that I'm here ..." She trailed off, her lip quivering. "I just miss you so much." Her words echoed in the emptiness of the cemetery, filling the space with profound grief. "You were more than my best friend," she choked out. "You were my family, and I don't quite know how to go on without you."

"One day at a time," a familiar voice said.

Harper looked at the bench under the oak tree where a familiar figure sat. "Sidney?"

"What? Haven't you seen a ghost before?"

Shaking her head in disbelief, Harper replied, "No."

"Remember when you believed that if the love between two people was strong enough, there was nothing that could keep them apart?"

Harper nodded, tears welling up in her eyes.

"I guess you were right. This place is peaceful, isn't it?" Sidney asked, taking in their surroundings before turning back to Harper.

"Yes, it is."

"Come, sit." Sidney patted the spot next to her on the bench.

Harper hesitated before slowly sitting down on the edge of the bench.

"I won't bite," Sidney reassured as she reached out to take Harper's hand.

The touch of Sidney's skin against hers sent chills down Harper's spine. "It's really you?"

Sidney smiled.

"But, how—?"

"I may be gone, but I still have a few surprises up my sleeve." Her grin shimmered in the morning light.

Harper shook her head. "I've been lost without you," Harper confessed as icy tears streamed down her cheeks. "It's all I can do to make it through the day."

"I know," said Sidney. "I've been watching." She looked up at the sky. "Tell me, how's Abigail?"

"She's doing better than any of us, believe it or not."

"Children are amazing, aren't they? Hey, Harp, do you know what I miss the most? Playing in the creek on those lazy summer afternoons, catching tadpoles and crawdads. What I wouldn't give to have just one of those days back."

"Me too," said Harper, wishing she could turn back the hands of time.

"Hey, do you remember the last time we were down there?" She nodded toward the creek.

"Yeah, I do," Harper responded, the memory of that day still fresh in her mind. "That's the day I lost the necklace you gave me. I spent weeks looking for it, but it never turned up."

In the silence that followed, Sidney reached into her pocket and pulled out a small, tarnished silver necklace with an infinity symbol pendant. Its once bright sheen had faded over time, but the unmistakable design still held its charm. Harper was stunned as she stared at the piece of jewelry that held so many memories.

"Is that ...?" she breathed, unable to form any other words. "Where did you find it?"

"In the most unexpected of places," Sidney said, her voice tainted by a hint of amusement.

As soon as the silver touched Harper's hand, a fresh wave of tears streamed down her face.

"When Abigail gets older, I'd like you to give it to her. Would you do that for me?"

Harper nodded, swallowing the lump in her throat. "It would be my honor." She composed herself before going on. "I wish we had it all to do over again, every bit of it. I wouldn't take even a second for granted."

"I know what you mean," said Sidney. "But we can't go back, can we? All you can do now is try to live each moment like it's your last, because one day, when you least expect it—it will be."

Harper swallowed hard, her throat tight with the weight of Sidney's words. "You're right. I need to live. For you and Jason, for Cameron ... For Abby."

Sidney nodded. "And for yourself, Harper. Don't forget yourself."

Harper's gaze traveled toward the snow-laden trees surrounding the cemetery, their bare branches stretching out into the advancing dawn sky. The soft morning light kissed the ice-coated leaves, setting them ablaze with a radiant shimmer.

"I don't know if I can do it without you," Harper admitted.

"But you're not without me," Sidney reassured her with a soft smile. "I'm here in everything: in the sunrise and sunset, in Abby's laughter, and in your heart."

A smile tugged at Harper's lips as she took in Sidney's words. A comforting warmth encompassed her, just as Sidney's presence always had. In that moment, it felt as though a small piece of her shattered heart had found its way back home.

"I don't know how to say goodbye to you, Sid," Harper confessed.

"You don't have to," Sidney replied tenderly. "Just because I am no longer physically with you doesn't mean I'm gone. A piece of me will always be with you, just like a piece of you will always be with me. Now," she said as she rose to her feet, "I should go, or else Jason will think I've forgotten about him."

"Wait," Harper said as she jumped to her feet. "Will I ever see you again?"

Sidney paused, looking back at Harper with a sorrowful smile. "I wish I could promise that," she said, her voice full of regret. "But I can't. Just know that wherever you are, I will be with you. Goodbye, Harper," Sidney said, her eyes brimming with tears. She extended her arms and pulled Harper into a tight hug, squeezing the breath out of her one last time.

When they parted, Sidney turned and walked away toward the woods. As she disappeared into the fog, Harper stood motionless, her heart heavy yet somehow at peace. She watched until Sidney's silhouette had faded completely into the swirling white haze until all that was left was the solitary echo of her words and the crunch of her departing footprints in the snow.

When Harper returned home, Cameron was standing in the kitchen, cooking breakfast.

"Did you have a nice walk?" he asked, looking up as she entered.

Harper gave a small nod, her hand clutching the necklace Sidney had given her. "Yes," she said as she put on the necklace

Sidney had given her. "You were right—it was just what I needed."

EPILOGUE

Six months later

Harper lovingly gazes at the photograph from her wedding, tracing the lines of her dress and the gentle smile on Cameron's face. Memories flood back, each one vivid and alive—the flutter in her stomach as she walked down the aisle, the joyous tears that fell as they exchanged vows, the feeling of pure happiness as they stood beside Sidney and Jason beneath the fragrant floral arbor. A bittersweet sense of joy washes over her before reality sets back in.

Suddenly, laughter drifts down from upstairs, breaking through Harper's thoughts. She tucks away the photograph and ascends the stairs. Outside the bedroom door, she pauses to listen to Cameron and Abigail's animated voices as they lose themselves in a story, momentarily forgetting about everything that has happened since that fateful day. Seeing the carefree smile on Abigail's face stirs emotions inside Harper that she still hasn't fully come to terms with. Confronting them means accepting a sense of finality, of moving on, and she's not sure if she's capable of that just yet. Or if she will ever be.

Taking a deep breath to steady herself, Harper pushes open the bedroom door. The warmth of Abigail's embrace instantly soothes her troubled heart, and for a fleeting moment, it feels as if everything is okay. Cameron looks on with a heavy heart, knowing all too well what Harper has been through since the accident. He has been by her side, offering support while also trying to navigate his own grief.

Harper gently tucks Abigail into bed and gives her a warm smile. "Time for bed," she says softly.

Abigail's face falls into disappointment. "Already? But Daddy was just getting to the good part," she pouts.

Harper exchanges a knowing glance with Cameron, before addressing Abigail. "All right, five more minutes, but then it's lights out. You start preschool tomorrow." With one final look at Cameron, Harper rises and leaves the room.

Once Abigail is settled in, Cameron joins Harper in their bedroom.

"How is she?" Harper asks as she takes off her earrings.

Cameron hesitates before answering. "I think she's okay," he says slowly. "This transition has been difficult on everyone, but she seems to be taking it in stride. Kids." He shakes his head. "They're resilient, aren't they?" He pauses before going on. "So how are you doing? I saw you had the wedding album out earlier."

Harper lets out a long and exhausted sigh before answering him. "Honestly, I don't know. I want more than anything to be okay, but ... I don't know that I'll ever be okay again." She reaches up and wipes away a single tear that has escaped her eye. "How do you do it?" she asks, looking up at Cameron, searching his eyes for an answer. "How do you move on? How is life ever the same again?"

Cameron shakes his head slowly. "It will never be the same again," he replies truthfully. "It'll just be a new normal. But you've done it before, and so have I. And we can do it again— together." He turns to face her fully now. "We must do it, for

Abigail." He then looks down at Harper's baby bump lovingly. "And for this little miracle."

Reflexively, Harper places a hand on her stomach and nods in agreement. "You're right. I must be strong."

"That's my girl." Cameron smiles and leans in to kiss her forehead tenderly. "And when you can't be strong, just lean on me, and I'll be strong for all of us. So, have you thought any more about baby names?" he asks, shifting the conversation.

Harper's face softens at the mention of their baby. "Yes, I have. If it's a boy, I was thinking Trevor."

A bittersweet smile spreads across Cameron's face. "Trevor—that's a good choice," he says softly. "And if it's a girl?"

Harper takes a deep breath, mustering up every ounce of courage she has. "Sidney."

ACKNOWLEDGEMENTS

As always, I would like to thank the individuals who played key roles in shaping this story into what it is today.

To my agent, Katie Monson, thank you for your continued support. To Meredith Wild, Solange Jazayeri, and the crazy talented team at Page & Vine, it has been an absolute pleasure working with you on this book.

A special shoutout to my beta readers, Shania, Chloeey, Kristy, Kim, Evelyn, Miriam, Taylor, Brooke, and Vanessa, for their time in scrutinizing this manuscript and helping make it the best it can be.

I must also thank my wife, Josette, for her patience and understanding as I immersed myself in the world of Harper and Cameron. None of this would be possible without your love and support.

And lastly, to my readers, your unwavering support is what keeps me writing. You're the best!

ABOUT THE AUTHOR

Buck Turner is the bestselling author of seven novels, including *The Long Road Back to You, I'll Wait, The Hearts We Leave Behind,* and *Evergreen.* A former IT professional turned writer, he lives with his family in Northern Kentucky.

Keep reading for a preview of:

THE
KEEPER
OF
STARS

A NOVEL

BUCK TURNER

PROLOGUE

*You don't find love. It finds you. It's got a little bit to do with
destiny, fate, and what's written in the stars.*
—Anais Nin

May 2020

Sims Chapel, TN

They say our lives are written in the stars, that our fate is
predetermined. But after the life I've lived, I believe that we are
the authors of our own destiny, endowed by the Almighty with
the power to choose our own paths, and, when necessary, to
rewrite the stars.

Tonight, I sit alone under a chilly Tennessee sky. My only
company, aside from a crackling fire and a glass of Jack Daniels,
is a chorus of crickets and bullfrogs. It is a tune I know well.
From the comfort of my rocking chair, I lean back and gaze
deep into the heavens. Above me, the stars stretch to infinity
like lighthouses on a thousand distant shores, waiting to guide
my thoughts across the velvet sea.

But before they set sail, the sound of the telephone ringing
brings me back to earth, so I push myself out of the rocker and
shuffle into the house.

"Hello."

"Hey, it's me. It's done."

"Everything? Are you sure?"

"The moving truck is on its way to the storage facility, the door is locked, and the alarm is set. Sherrie will be by in the morning to stick the sign in the yard, so there's nothing left to do now but wait."

Between the alcohol and the notion that the house that had known sixty years of love and laughter now sits empty, it takes me a moment to process.

"I can't thank you enough, sweetheart. I don't know what I would do without you."

"You're welcome, Daddy. I only wish I could do more. Speaking of that, I know you said you didn't want any company tomorrow, but I wish you'd reconsider. I could leave first thing in the morning and be at your place by noon. That way we could go together."

"Who would run the store?"

"Annalise can manage. She practically runs the place on her own as it is."

"I appreciate the offer, Caroline, but you've more than held up your end of the bargain. The last mile is my cross to bear."

"Well," she says, sighing heavily into the phone, "if you change your mind, you know how to reach me. I don't mind dropping everything and leaving at a moment's notice."

"I know, and thank you. Oh, before I forget, did you find your mother's memory box?"

"No, I'm afraid not, and I searched every inch of the house. Twice in fact. The only thing I can figure is she must have moved it without telling you."

"You're probably right," I say, fearing it is lost forever. "I'll check again in the morning before I head out."

"Just promise me you'll be careful. I don't know what I'd do if I lost you too."

"I will. But try not to worry. I've been making this trip since before you were a twinkle in your mother's eye."

"Yes, but not like this—this will be different."

I consider that, thinking that tomorrow will be one of the toughest days of my life.

"Well, I should go," she says a moment later. "I've been at it all day, and I'm exhausted."

"All right, darlin'. Tell Don I said hello, will you? Annalise too."

"Sure thing, Daddy. I love you."

"I love you too, sweetheart."

I mosey outside, add a log to the fire, and settle in for the long night ahead. "Now where was I?" At the bottom of my glass, it all comes back to me. Leaning back in the rocker, I catch the glimmer of the North Star as the tail of a comet's light streaks across the sky.

CHAPTER 1

GULLY WASHER

May 1950

"Jack, if you get us killed, so help me God..."

The storm that had been building in the western sky rolled east, and a column of low, swirling clouds swept up the valley, blotting out the sun. By the looks of things, this was going to be a gully washer, which meant Jack Bennett had one shot at getting the motor to turn over. Otherwise he and his passenger would have to ride out the storm on Rock Island.

With the last bolt tightened, Jack turned and shouted into the wind. "All right, George, here goes nothing." Bracing himself, Jack pressed one hand firmly against the engine, grabbed the pull cord with the other, and yanked with all his might.

The engine spat and sputtered until finally, to Jack's delight, the steel beast gurgled to life. From the bow, George Duncan put his palms together and raised his eyes to the heavens.

Jack grinned. But with a mile of open water between them and the dock, they weren't out of the woods yet.

***

A little while later, Jack and George huddled in the weathered shack at the end of the dock as rain fell in wind-driven sheets around them. Thunder echoed over the vast expanse, and like starlight pulsing through the graphite sky, lightning twisted and forked, bridging the gap between the heavens and the earth. It was as awesome a display of Mother Nature's power as either of them had ever witnessed.

They were an unlikely pair, George and Jack. George Duncan was a seventy-five-year-old Black man with a reputation for drinking too much. Bright-eyed, bushy-tailed, and unblemished, eighteen-year-old Jack Bennett was the antithesis of George. But despite their differences, the one thing they shared was their love for the water.

As the dilapidated shack swayed and creaked around them, Jack took in a couple of deep breaths. He smelled rain, gasoline, and the sweet aroma of chewing tobacco, then turned and stared out the window. "God must be angry today."

"I don't know nothin' about that." George's weathered body lumbered to the icebox, plucked two beers from the top shelf, and tossed one to Jack. "But if we'd waited five more minutes, we could have asked him ourselves."

Jack smiled amusedly and opened his beer. "I ain't gonna let nothing happen to you, George. Besides, you keep forgetting I'm the best damn mechanic around. No one knows boats like me—or how to fix them."

"Speakin' of that, you should think about making a livin' out of it."

"What, boats?"

George wagged his head back and forth. "Bein' a mechanic. I mean, you can fix just about anything, and since there's no shortage of things breakin', you'd never run out of work."

Jack entertained the idea while he nursed his beer. "Maybe you're right," he finally said. "I may look into that. Thanks, George."

"Don't mention it." George gulped his drink and drew a hand across his mouth. "I'm sure glad to get outta that hot sun...and away from the storm. Now look at us." A smile worked across his wrinkled face. "We got a roof over our heads and somethin' cold to drink. A man don't need much more'n that." When he'd finished, he nodded toward the icebox. "There's more beer in the chest if you get a hankerin'."

"Thank you kindly," said Jack. "But you know I only drink one. I wouldn't want to get you into any kind of trouble, not on account of me."

George leaned back and let out a laugh that filled the small room. "The way I see it, if you're old enough to fight, you're old enough to have a beer. It's one of them rites of passage I heard the preacher talk about when I was younger. B'sides, there ain't nothin' wrong with it so long as you don't go burnin' up the roads. The water, on the other hand." He nodded toward the lake. "Why, you could go off course for pert' near an hour and not run into nothing."

While George fetched another beer from the chest, Jack pulled out his wallet and counted the bills. *Thirty-five plus the four sixty-five I have at home makes...* He did the math in his head. Five hundred big ones. *Not bad.*

"Whatcha gonna do with all that cash?"

"I reckon I'll save it."

"For what?"

"Same thing as the last time you asked me."

"You mean that house on the hill?" Before Jack could respond, George shook his head in disgust. "Don't be a damn fool, boy. Like I told you before, only rich folks live on the hill. Folks like you and me—real folks—we ain't got no chance at a life like that. It ain't in the stars. We're lucky to scrape by down here at the water's edge. Which, if you wanna know the truth, ain't a bad deal."

George leaned in his chair and belched. Then Jack watched as a smile spread across his face.

"That's what you keep telling me. But even rich folks gotta start somewhere." Jack put away his money and stared out at the dark water, disinclined to accept the fate George had predicted for him.

"Think what you want, but someday you'll see what old George is talkin' about." George finished his second beer. After crushing the can and tossing it in the corner, he said, "Hey, listen. I appreciate you decidin' to stay on with me this summer. Honestly, I don't think I could run things without you. Not anymore."

Jack wondered if it was George or the alcohol doing the talking. Probably a little of both, he concluded as the man started on his third beer. "Aww, come on, George. That ain't no way to talk. You still got a few years left in you." He watched as George stared sullenly at the rain. "But in any case, I'm glad to do it and thankful for the work. Besides, it beats the hell out of working at the mill. I was talking to Ray Tucker the other day, and he said with all the windows they have in that place, it's like an oven in the summer. And in the winter you nearly freeze to death. That's no life I want. No, sir." Jack shook his head and glanced outside as the rain tapered off. "At least here I get to be on the water, and like you said, that ain't bad."

"Amen!" George slapped the table with an open palm. "I'll drink to that."

By the time Jack's house came into view, the storm had pushed east into the mountains, but evidence of its passage remained. The hike from the dock to his house, which was over a mile, took Jack along the lakeshore, through a dense stretch of woods, over a creek, and across a field of heather so thick he had to cut a path with his machete.

When Jack finally reached the porch, it was nearly suppertime. After slipping out of his damp clothes, he set them on the rail to dry before pushing open the front door.

"That you, JB?"

"It's me, Mama," Jack answered wearily. He shuffled into the bathroom, washed his hands and face, and changed clothes before coming to supper.

"How was work today? You didn't get caught out in that squall, did ya? Donna Rae said Deep Springs Road is a mess."

"The woods too," said Jack. "On the bright side, there's a couple of trees down at the edge of the yard I can cut up and use for firewood. And to answer your question, me and George made it back just in time."

She snapped him a look, her steely blue eyes tightening at the corners. "You didn't pull that engine-trouble trick on old George again, did you?"

The fact that she remembered shocked Jack. "What if I did? You gonna tell old George on me? I was only having a little fun." He rocked back in the chair, balancing on two legs. "Besides, I got us back with five whole minutes to spare."

Helen Bennett narrowed her eyes at him. "Jack Edward Bennett. I thought I taught you better'n that. And put that chair on all fours. If God had intended it to have two legs, he'd have made it that way." She shook her head in disgust. "You got too much of your daddy in you. That's your problem. If you ain't careful, one of these days you're gonna fool around and give old George a heart attack. How would you feel then?"

"I'm sorry." He set the chair right. "It won't happen again. Promise."

"Well, good." Her tone softened. "After all, George ain't as young as he used to be. I reckon none of us are." She checked the biscuits. "You hungry?"

"Starving."

When the biscuits were golden brown on top, Helen took them out of the oven, covered them with a towel, and set them on the table to cool. Next, she brought over the jar of honey and a plate of fried bologna, put it beside the biscuits, and finally collapsed into her chair. "You wanna say grace or should I?"

"You go ahead," said Jack. "You're so much better at it than I am."

Continue reading in
The Keeper of Stars
by Buck Turner

ALSO BY BUCK TURNER